Following Roscoe

By Milt Anderson

For Pat,
Good luck on your book,

Milt Anderson

This book is a work of fiction. Any resemblance to actual events or persons, living or dead, is entirely coincidental.

"Following Roscoe," by Milt Anderson. ISBN 978-1-62137-261-5 (Softcover), 978-1-62137-262-2 (Ebook).

Published 2013 by Virtualbookworm.com Publishing Inc., P.O. Box 9949, College Station, TX 77842, US. ©2013, Milt Anderson. All rights reserved. No part of this publication may be reproduced, stored in a retrieval system, or transmitted in any form or by any means, electronic, mechanical, recording or otherwise, without the prior written permission of Milt Anderson.

Manufactured in the United States of America.

Acknowledgements

First and foremost, I must thank my wife for her love and support throughout this adventure. Thank you to Lee Allen Howard for a very helpful edit. A special thanks to Dr.'s Lee McClain, Albert Wendland and Mike Arnzen for making the *Master of Arts in Writing Popular Fiction* program at Seton Hill University possible.

Chapter 1

Uncle Roscoe is a hypochondriac when he's not horny. His libido seems to dominate his existence, and that includes the stress disorder he developed later in life after a stint in Vietnam, a government job he won't talk about, and marriages to three curvaceous, buxom bimbos who collected alimony until he was penniless. He's a proud and stubborn old man who wouldn't think of taking a handout from anyone—except me. I'm August Gustafson, Augie to most people and, by a cruel quirk of fate, the only family member available who's young enough to take care of Roscoe. Sometimes genealogy comes back to bite you in the ass.

Nine months ago, after Roscoe's Social Security kicked in, he moved back to Pennsylvania and into the duplex I bought as an investment. The units are side by side and have identical floor plans. Roscoe lives in the right half, I live in the left. I had the wall between the two kitchens knocked out to keep our lives bearable, except for meals.

Roscoe slogged into the kitchen dragging last night behind him as he had often done the last nine months, leaving me to prepare breakfast. Streaks of early morning sunlight shone through the mini blinds, highlighting his rumpled black-and-gold Pittsburgh Steelers pajamas. He eased himself into a chair at the maple table under the thick pine beam that took the place of a bearing wall between our two apartments. His face advertised *Oh shit, another hangover* as he looked up at me. He sipped java from his Steelers mug. His thick, unkempt hair matched his furry grizzly bear paw slippers.

Furry grizzly bear paw slippers? "Where'd you get those things?" I pointed to the hairy tramps.

"On the Internet. Came in yesterday's mail. Like 'em?"

I didn't want to dampen his apparent good spirits. "Yeah, cool."

Roscoe set the mug on the table next to a bowl of puffed rice and then rolled up his right sleeve, exposing a lean, sinewy forearm.

He pointed to the tip of his elbow. "I think I have a bone splinter. It hurts and it's swelled up."

Good-bye good spirits. "Could be from hoisting those twelve-ounce Iron City beers," I said, examining his elbow. "And that's not a swelling, it's a huge callus from leaning on the bar at Murph's."

"I don't think so. It really hurts. Maybe it's cancer."

"Maybe you bumped it. Perhaps on the bar?"

"I would have known if I bumped it, don't you think? I just don't walk around bumping into things."

"You probably didn't realize it," I said, turning a knowing eye. "You weren't feeling any pain last night, were you?"

"We've had this discussion before. I'm just a social drinker. I—"

A knock on the door interrupted Uncle Roscoe's feeble excuse. Emma Lou Rawlins' round face appeared in the exterior door's window. Emma is my office manager at my latest endeavor, a maid service called Desperate Domestics. She opened the door and stepped into the kitchen with Adidas Big Mo 2G sneakers. Her pear-shaped two hundred and fifty pounds of five foot four snugged through the doorway. She wore a blue print kimono jacket that flared to a wide waist and covered blue stretch Lycra Denims. A gold necklace held a green alexandrite stone against her dark brown skin.

Uncle Roscoe yanked his pajama sleeve back down to his wrist and jumped to his feet, the symptoms of his cancerous bone splinter having miraculously disappeared.

"Emma Lou," he said through a wide smile. "How you doin', sweet cheeks? It must be Monday again. After you clean Augie's apartment, how about you come over to my pad? It needs a little sprucing up."

Uncle Roscoe is an equal opportunity deviant. He likes big women, slender, tall, short, pretty and not so pretty women, and women of all colors and religious affiliations. The only exception... an older woman.

"Not in your dreams, you old fool. You been drinking again?"

"Just a little. It's your fault, you know. When you spurn me, I drink to forget."

"Good," she said. "I'm glad you forgot."

Uncle Roscoe looked like he felt upstaged, and I knew he might say something on the far side of uncouth. I thought I'd interrupt to break the tension. "Would you like something to eat, Emma?"

Emma Lou shook her head.

"Here, have some puffed rice," Roscoe said, shoving the bowl toward the edge of the table. "It's good titty food. Puffs 'em up."

Emma spun on him, her mouth open in shock.

Oh shit, this is going to be ugly.

"You know, like Aunt Jemima's boobs."

When Emma's eyes narrowed, I jumped between them. I feared for Uncle Roscoe's well-being.

Emma reached past me and pointed a threatening finger at Uncle Roscoe. "You watch what you say out that beer-hole. You could get seriously hurt."

"Pahleeeze," Roscoe said, dragging out the word. "Hurt me. I can't wait."

Months dealing with Roscoe's behavior had proved fruitless. Physical violence only excited him.

Emma tried another approach. She stepped backward, and took a few deep breaths to calm herself while slowly rubbing the alexandrite stone on her necklace. She looked into Roscoe's eyes as if to say, *Don't mess with me, white man.*

"What?" Roscoe asked. "Are you putting the juju on me?"

Before a physical confrontation erupted between Roscoe and Emma, the doggy door opened and fifty-five pounds of alpha canine attitude shuffled into the kitchen. Pissmore, my English Bulldog, strode up to Emma and looked at her with dark eyes. Emma bent over and petted him on his massive, wrinkled head.

"Aren't you handsome. You remind me of my third husband, Reggie."

"How many husbands did you wear out, Emma? Sexually, I mean."

Before Emma could reply or make physical contact with Uncle Roscoe, Pissmore charged Roscoe and attacked the grizzly paw slipper on his right foot. The dog shook it like a washing machine agitator on spin cycle, ripping it to shreds. Trying to escape the canine's wrath, Roscoe back-peddled, kicking at the table and Pissmore, but the mighty mutt snatched the other slipper from Roscoe's foot. The dog violently shook the grizzly paw like a wild animal, an opossum perhaps, and threw it up in the air. It landed in the bowl of puffed rice, its talons hanging over the edge. I grabbed Pissmore by his spiked collar and checked Roscoe for any damage. Finding none, I led Pissmore to the back door.

"Come, little buddy. Time to go out." Pissmore's short, strong legs easily carried his massive head and body as he lumbered through the outside doggy-door.

Now was the time to separate the combatants for the day. I walked over to the door to my apartment and held it open. "I'll see you later, Emma. Probably at the office."

"Golf game or the races?" she whispered as she kept a threatening eye on Roscoe.

"Tee time at eleven," I replied.

Chapter 2

Roscoe was standing at the oven scratching his head, either wondering where to start with the mess in the kitchen or figuring how to entice Emma out of my apartment. I left through the back door, topped off Pissmore's water dish from the garden hose and headed for the garage. I glanced over my right shoulder at Aldine Vanderslice's kitchen window, the window that framed her large, bright blue eyes and full cherry red lips every morning. Only her almost silver hair gave a clue to her sixty-three years. And she had a body to die for as evidenced by her late husband's expiration while working off the effects of Viagra during an episode of *As The World Turns*. For the past six months Aldine Vanderslice had turned her attention toward Uncle Roscoe, wanting a slice for herself. But her advances had proved fruitless. Five months' age difference might as well have been a thousand as far as Roscoe was concerned—his inflated ego couldn't handle being with an older woman.

Pissmore stood at the waist-high white picket fence looking through the slats at Emma's dark green Ford E-350 cargo van parked at the curb. My van was identical to Emma's except for the company logos; hers were painted on the panels, mine were magnetic. I peeled off the logos and threw them in the cargo area next to my golf clubs. I backed out of the one-stall garage, drove through Monview on Pike Street, then Stanton which led to Route 70. Fifteen miles later, I took the Russeltown exit to Route 31. Five miles more I arrived at the Green Willows Golf Course. I pulled into the lot near the building that housed the pro shop and the Blue Dog Tavern. I parked near attorney Bernie Ostapowicz's black E-350 Mercedes sedan. Mike Latchem's Volkswagen sat in the shade under an elm tree. A white logo advertising his podiatrist's business stood out from the royal blue door. Frank Pallone's red Chrysler 300 was nowhere in sight.

I limped toward the tavern. My left knee felt stiff and sore, probably because the kitchen table had slid into it during Pissmore's attack on Roscoe's furry bear paws. Above the door to the bar hung a large wooden plaque with a dog carved into it. The dog resembled Pissmore, only blue. A blast of air conditioning and the smell of beer and bacon grease hit me as I tottered in. Bernie and Mike sat at a table near the counter, a fruit salad in front of Bernie, a stack of flap-jacks in front of Mike. I pulled out a chair and sat next to Mike.

Connie, the waitress who usually waits on our table, glided up. She had a sexy walk, one that invited your eyes to explore her curvaceous body and your mind to conjure up lecherous thoughts. I've watched her walk to and from our table for years and still find the view enjoyable. She dropped the receipt pad on the table and bent over to write on it.

"What'll you have, handsome?" She smiled, showing perfect, sparkling teeth.

I felt my stomach quiver and heard the accompanying growling sounds due to skipping breakfast. I couldn't help but notice her cleavage when she bent over, and the quivering sensation headed south.

"I'll have a ham and cheese sandwich and an Iron City Light." And one hour alone with you in the trees in back of number three green.

I watched her hips sway as she sauntered away. The sensation started to grow bark and I noticed the pain in my knee had disappeared. Oh shit! I wondered if I had some of Uncle Roscoe's genes. I took a few deep breaths to compose myself. I put some weight on my leg, stressing the knee. It hurt again. Hallelujah! I was safe from Roscoe's weird condition.

"Where's Frank?" I asked.

"Not here yet," Mike mumbled through half-chewed pancakes.

"But he'll be here soon," Bernie said. "He never misses a golf date."

"Must be a woman," Mike said. "That's the only thing I can think of that would keep him away from a round of golf."

"I don't think so," Bernie said. "Frank always makes time in his busy schedule for recreation."

"That's recreation?" Mike asked. "I need some of *that* recreation."

I wondered if Frank had carved out some time for Connie. If he had, I envied him. I struggled to bring my mind back to the present.

Thirty minutes later, after my sandwich, two beers, and making two calls to Frank's office, we decided to tee off. Frank would have to catch up. I was concerned about him. When I talked to him Thursday, he said he had a hurry-up job for me and it sounded important.

After eighteen holes of counting my scores on both hands, I paid off six skins to Mike and Bernie. Frank still had not shown up.

"Try the Union Grille," Bernie offered as they headed back to the Blue Dog. "Maybe he had a deposition. Private dick's get called at the last minute sometimes."

After buying the winners their celebratory beers, I headed west on 70 toward Washington, the county seat of Washington County. The Union Grille is noted for good food, its ambiance, and the number of attorneys that can cram into the bar at lunch time. I climbed onto a stool near the center of the bar between a short, stocky man wearing a four-hundred dollar suit and a beefier man in a dark green uniform with a name tag that read "Persico." I ordered a Diet Coke through wafting cigarette smoke and scanned the bar. Frank was not in view, only pensive, concerned, and doubtful faces presumably caused by litigation. As I strolled to the restroom I checked out all the available seating, including the back room. The restroom was empty. No Frank.

I decided to head back to Monview and call Frank from my office. Desperate Domestics is housed in a two-stall garage on Knox Avenue. I entered through the left door, the sharp smell of polishes, waxes and cleaning agents attacking my sinuses.

Emma sat at a large desk in front of four file cabinets. Facing Emma, on the opposite wall, hung a 32-inch TV with Jerry Springer's face plastered on it.

"*Jerry, Jerry, Jerry!*" the audience members chanted until Jerry finally calmed them down and introduced his next guest, a bi-sexual Puerto Rican midget.

"I didn't know you watched this program, Emma."

"Yeah, once in a while. Today they're bringin' back this ho who slept with her mother's boyfriend."

"Sounds like a typical *Jerry* show."

"Her mother's boyfriend is confined to a wheelchair."

"What!"

"Yep. And when they were goin' to it, this ho's leg somehow went under the armrest, through the wheel spokes, and got stuck. She couldn't get out."

"I'll bet that was embarrassing when the mother had to pry her out of that situation."

"No sirreee, unh-uh. It was embarrassing when the mother called the fire department and six members of Squad Nineteen showed up. Might as well been the whole world—two of the firemen had digital cameras. They had to use cutters, winches, pulleys and everything. All the while the digital shutters were snappin' away. One fireman was lighting a cutting torch when they finally liberated the linked lovers."

"That's the ultimate embarrassment," I said. "By the way, how do you have time for this kinky stuff?"

"Time? You're talkin' about time? You're late. What'd you have, a playoff or somethin'?"

"We waited for Frank. He didn't show up."

"What's that, a two stroke penalty? By the way, what's up with all these strokes? You guys stroking each other. Now that sounds kinky to me."

Emma always seemed to ask a question that couldn't or shouldn't be answered. "Everything kosher?" I asked. Team leaders report in by computer or in person at the end of the day. They tell Emma whom they provided service for and how many hours they worked. They also report any problems they had or equipment they may need for an upcoming job. Emma takes care of the finances and paperwork. In short, she runs the business.

"Stella the Polish princess hasn't called in yet," Emma said, with a bit of attitude.

"She'll call," I said, grabbing the phone on Emma's desk. I punched in Frank's office number. "She's dependable, just a little late."

"A little late! She's always a little late. I got a dinner engagement at six-thirty. I gotta get home and get myself together."

Frank's phone rang three times. "Who are you having dinner with, Roscoe?"

Emma narrowed her eyes. "I don't associate with preverts." Then with a wry smile she said, "Not in public, anyway. I'm dining with Felton tonight."

After three more rings and the pre-recorded message, I hung up and called Frank's home number to another pre-recorded message.

"How was Roscoe anyway? Did he give you any trouble?"

"He sang his usual repertoire of love songs and tapped on the door. I told him if he didn't stop I'd castrate him."

"What did he say to that?"

"He said he had dyspepsia. I told him I didn't know what that was and I didn't care. I know his tricks. When I left by the front door, I could still hear him muttering 'bout something."

It's the same routine every Monday when Emma comes to clean my apartment, and variations of the same story afterward. I checked the mail, told Emma I'd see her tomorrow, and headed out the door.

Chapter 3

My stomach quivered, as it had earlier, with the accompanying growling sounds. I checked my watch. Four o'clock, time to head for home. Twenty minutes later, the hilly skyline of the city limits came into view.

The founding fathers named the town Monview because of the scenic view of the Monongahela River, which snakes its way from West Virginia in the south to Pittsburgh in the north where it joins the Allegheny and Ohio rivers, forming a confluence.

Steel mills once had cluttered the banks along the river from Pittsburgh to Allenport in the south. River barges hauled coal, coke and other raw materials for steel-making, but in the eighties the industry had fallen into depression. Presently, only pleasure boats created wakes in the placid water.

I swung onto the driveway and pressed the garage door opener. The sound alerted Pissmore, who lumbered through the grassy backyard to greet me. I parked the van, clicked the closer and exited through the back door to greet the slobber-mouthed canine. After a few pats on his wrinkled head, Pissmore high-tailed it for the kitchen, squeezing through the doggy-door.

When I walked in, Pissmore was hovering over his ceramic food bowl, waiting for his supper. I stirred up his favorite mixture of Beneful dry dog food and Mighty Dog Natural Balance reduced-calorie canned food.

Uncle Roscoe stood at the stove, stirring spaghetti sauce. He had traded his Steeler's pajamas for a number 66 Mario Lemieux Penguins jersey and a University of Pittsburgh football cap. A Terrible Towel was draped over his belt, serving as an apron. His facial expression read: *You're late. I've been standing over a hot stove for hours. Can't you be on time? It only takes a minute to call. Yada, yada, yada.*

I thought I'd return the disdain and stir Roscoe's pot a little. "Emma said you don't sing very well."

"What does she know?" Roscoe pulled a mound of spaghetti from a strainer. "Look at me, I'm a Greek god. She doesn't know a good thing when she sees it. I threw her a touchdown pass and she dropped the ball."

"How soon to supper?" I needed to change the subject or suffer through Roscoe's enormous list of sexual-egocentric descriptions that I'd heard too many times.

"Five minutes."

I went into my apartment and tapped in Frank's home number to the same pre-recorded message I'd heard earlier. Maybe he's been busy. Maybe he didn't have time to call. He'll probably be at the club tonight. I washed up, changed into black slacks, a blue short-sleeved polo shirt, and a pair of bourbon-colored Rockport Tuamotu slip-ons.

I sauntered into the steam-filled kitchen. The aroma of garlic, oregano, and pasta sauce smelled inviting. Roscoe was dishing out the goodies as I sat down.

"Have a seat, your highness," he said. "You come in, sit down and expect dinner to be waiting. Right?"

I didn't want Roscoe's agenda to control the evening, so I ignored his question. "I'm worried about Frank. He didn't show up at the course today, and I can't reach him by phone."

"Maybe a cheating husband caught Frank spying on him and pulled him through the keyhole."

Following Roscoe

"Come on, Roscoe, this is important. Something must be wrong."

"Okay, maybe a cheating wife—"

"Cut the shit! I'm worried."

Sensing my concern, Roscoe said, "Maybe he's been in court. Or on a case."

That's better. I didn't need Roscoe's crappy retorts. "He could be on a case, but... he would have called. He said he had some hurry-up work for me. It sounded important."

"He'll get back to you sooner or later." Roscoe sounded unusually optimistic.

"If he does, call me on my cell. I'll be at the club."

I gulped the rest of my food and took a packet of Alka-Seltzer with me—just in case.

The reek of alcohol and tobacco smoke assaulted my sinuses as I entered the building that is now known as "The Club." The place was built in the late forties by The Benevolent and Protective Order of Elks. The membership's lack of support caused it to close in the fifties when the Veterans of Foreign Wars took over the club. A faded mural depicting airborne troops landing in battle covered the wall over the table shuffleboard at the far right side of the room. The building had been sold in the mid-seventies to the Slovak Club. Two years ago a number of local investors, including Frank Pallone, had bought the place as an investment. A waist-high flagstone room divider supported a wooden trellis that stretched to the ceiling and served as a buffer between the dining area and the bar.

I strode into the bar. Moldy the bartender was bent over the sink, cleaning glasses. Nicotine-stained and crooked teeth didn't detract from his infectious smile. Women of all ages, colors, sizes, and shapes loved him. Children, dogs and even evil cats loved him. The only person who didn't was paranoid Perry Sanders, who sat at the far end of the bar with his wife, Grace. No one knew what lurked in Perry's twisted mind, but it wasn't trust. He trusted no one except his wife, a shampoo lady at a local salon. She didn't help matters by bringing home malicious rumors that fed his addiction.

Moldy noticed me, dried his hands, and grabbed an I.C. Light. He popped the lid and set the bottle in front of me. "What's up, brother?"

"Samo, samo," I said. "What's happenin' around here?"

Moldy jerked his thumb toward a couple seated at the bar under the TV. "Professor Doris Jean just instructed Archie that the past tense of the verb *to see* is *saw* and not *seen*."

Archie "Bunker" Brown's wife Doris Jean teaches English at the local junior high school and corrects Archie's "Bunkerisms" in public.

"Everyone in the burg seems to agree with Archie," I said. "Doesn't say much for her teaching skills."

"For sure," Moldy said. "And paranoid Perry is off on a new trip. He thinks mailmen turn in the names of gun magazine subscribers to the government so they can take away their weapons."

"Really?"

"Yep. He says mailmen are *big brother* employees. He even questioned the club's mailman, 'Junk-mail Joe' Hawthorn about it."

"Nothing unusual then." In a serious tone I said, "I've been looking for Frank. Have you seen him?"

"Couple days ago... Friday, I think. Does he have some work for you?"

"Yeah, he said he's got a hurry-up job for me."

"Hurry-up job. Sounds intriguing," Moldy said.

"It does. Frank said he would fill me in today after golf. But he didn't show up."

I explained the checking I did earlier and the unanswered phone calls.

"That's not Frank. And he doesn't miss golf. Something large must be in the works. You check his house?"

"That's my next stop. Maybe he'll be home when I get there."

Grace Sanders caught Moldy's attention with a raised index finger. "I'll have another," she said, and lifted her empty glass.

Moldy grabbed a bottle of Captain Morgan and headed in her direction.

I noticed Tommy "Two Shots" Tuttle off to my right. Okay, I saw his wife, Reba, first. She's drop dead gorgeous and I wondered why I hadn't noticed her earlier. She had auburn hair, large blue eyes, full sensuous lips, and a body that begged your attention, but Tommy Tuttle never seemed to notice. He would rather drink beer. And when he did, he drank a lot of it. He could drink beer for hours on end and wouldn't get drunk. But when he had more than two shots of whiskey with the beer, his head would end up on the bar. That's where it now rested—in a mixture of beer, whiskey and cigarette ashes.

"I have to grab some more rum," Moldy said and headed for the stockroom.

I sat nursing my beer, wondering what Reba thought when Tommy collapsed on the bar. It didn't seem to bother her. She just stared at the TV like a zombie, apparently bored to death. She had to know she was beautiful. I wondered what it would be like to sleep with her. Just one time. But I'm not in her league—or her universe for that matter. She's got what she wants: a beautiful home, clothes, jewelry, and stature in the community.

And then I looked at Tommy, his face smooshed on the bar. He had money, prestige, and a number of plumbing supply stores. But tonight he wouldn't be laying any pipe. It made no sense.

Well that helped, I thought. Wealth and stature aren't everything... maybe a little more money wouldn't hurt.

Moldy strutted back with two bottles of Captain Morgan and slid them onto a shelf under the bar. "Have another?" he said, pointing to my beer.

"No thanks, I've got some checking up to do."

I downed my beer and slid off the barstool. I glanced down the bar toward Reba. She smiled and winked at me.

Why did she smile when she knew I was leaving? She's just another egocentric tease. I'll leave casually and pretend her flirting didn't bother me.

Chapter 4

I headed west on Parkinson and took 47 to Meadowlark Avenue. A right put me on Balazia Avenue with its view of the water tower that sat atop the hill. A housing plan built a quarter century ago by J. B. Stockard clambered up the thirty-degree slope. Frank's house sat halfway up on the right side of the street.

Before the development, only the tower had interrupted the horizon. Since plastered with graffiti, its underside bore the names of former high school seniors. People covered the hill like ants to watch the Fourth of July fireworks. From that vantage point, they could watch the display from three surrounding cities. That's where I'd spent two holidays with Genie DeFlorio.

We had been going steady for two years and I thought she was the one, until her mother, Delores, deflowered me and Genie found out. That's when our relationship flamed out. Genie concocted a story that I had been in a sexual liaison with Mrs. Olslansky, a spinster Spanish teacher who retired to Florida that May. Any thought of a new relationship with anyone my age was doomed with Genie's press-like coverage of her fabrication to all the available girls at the school, city, the valley, and southwestern Pennsylvania,

But all wasn't lost. Word spread throughout the cougar queendom and a number of relationships developed over the years with the furry felines. The thought of being with an older woman excited me then—and still does. And since then, I've never felt comfortable with a younger woman, the opposite of Roscoe's cravings.

I parked the van in front of Frank's house between two of the Linden trees that lined the empty street. I sidestepped the sticky sap that had fallen, the reason people parked in their garages or driveways, and approached Frank's front door. The orange-buff brick of the house contrasted with the evergreens and yews. The bushes smelled like creosote. My shoulder brushed a magazine sticking out of Frank's mailbox as I opened the screen door to knock. A newspaper dropped to the threshold. I checked the date. It was Saturday's paper. Frank hadn't been home for at least two days—or couldn't come to the phone.

I parted the shrubs under the front window and peered into the living room. Nothing seemed out of place. I went around the house, looking in windows and checking doors but found nothing suspicious. I tried to lift the garage door, but couldn't because it was locked. But I noticed a small crack in the door. I smooshed my face to the door and peeked through the opening. All I needed was the dim night light in the far corner of the bay to see that his red Chrysler 300 was missing.

Then I heard a shriek and a whooshing sound. My nose flattened against the door and the rest of my face followed suit from a blow to the back of my head. I spun around to another swat from a she-devil brandishing a broom.

I managed to duck and juke myself out of harm's way, but only for a second. The large woman scampered after me, her bright flowered shift heaving and swaying as if a pair of pigs were trapped underneath and trying to escape. A babushka pulled over hair curlers surrounded a menacing, bulbous face. Her eyes were narrowed and angry.

"Take that, you pervert!" She raised her broom for another attack.

"Stop, I'm—"

She landed an overhead swat, another technique in her offensive arsenal. Not being a very proud person, I fled. I raced to the van, jumped in and sped away. In the rear view mirror I watched her waddle after me, the pigs still trying to escape.

I headed for home. It took a while for the encounter with the she-devil to diminish. And then my head buzzed with ugly thoughts of what might have happened to Frank. After all, he was a private detective, and his work sometimes created ill feelings.

I decided to enlist the aid of the local constabulary. Fifteen minutes later, after taking a shortcut through Grandview Cemetery and streaking through a few yellow lights, I stood before the desk sergeant at police headquarters. I told him I wanted to file a missing person's report. He pointed a gnarled finger toward the rear of the room and, in a voice that registered surrender at the end of a miserable career, said, "Detective Fahey. Second door to the right."

Fahey turned in her swivel chair as I walked in. Short auburn hair surrounded an alabaster face bejeweled with emerald green eyes and ruby red lips.

"What can I do for you?" Her tone was business-like.

I took a few seconds to capture her beauty before answering. "I'd like to file a missing person's report."

She pulled her computer keyboard close to her and, in a military manner she asked, "Name of the person who went missing?"

I gave her Frank's name and address. She studied my face. Her beautifully formed lips separated to reveal white, glistening teeth. A smirk revealed that she already knew the answer that she was about to ask.

"Are you the pervert that Nellie Niznanski, the neighborhood watch sergeant, chased off Balazia Avenue?"

I touched the strawberry on my forehead and said, "She's stealthy, quick, and packs a mean broom."

My quick wit got a chuckle out of Fahey. She was even more attractive when she stepped out of her business persona.

"Nellie means well," she said. "Sometimes she acts impulsively."

"No harm done." I jerked my head back and forth and rolled my eyes as if suffering a head injury. When I looked back for her approval, she was gazing at her monitor. My feeble attempt at humor had gone unnoticed.

"When did he go missing?" she asked.

I answered.

"Just today?" She seemed perturbed but kept a professional manner.

"Today is when I noticed he was missing. It could have been earlier. I checked his mail and newspapers. Last one was Friday."

"Today, Saturday, it doesn't matter. He can't be considered a missing person at this time."

I couldn't believe what I was hearing. "Why not? He's missing."

"He's an adult male, a responsible person, and able to take care of himself. He's a private investigator, right? He's probably out on a job."

"But we were supposed to have a meeting this morning. He said he had something important for me."

"I'm sorry," she said. "I can't do anything until a reasonable time has passed." She paused. "Unless there are suspicious circumstances surrounding his disappearance." She looked at me for an answer.

"No," I said. "I don't know."

"I've heard of Frank Pallone. He's a consummate professional. I'll keep an ear open, but I'm sure he'll show up." She stood and extended her hand. "Thank you for coming in and showing concern for your friend."

I stared at her in admiration. She had pluck. For a girl in her early thirties she had it together. She seemed more mature than her age and that excited me.

"Thank you," I said. I managed a curt smile and I left with the vision of her face implanted in my memory, thinking maybe there was hope for me in the future with a younger woman.

I didn't want to wake Uncle Roscoe by opening the garage door, so I parked in front of the house. I tiptoed into the living room to a round, mushy-mouth, stumpy-legged pooch wagging the stub of a tail. I plopped down on the couch and Pissmore joined me, his head landing in my lap.

Chapter 5

The discordant sound of a lumberjack cutting a felled tree echoed in the distance, the saw chewing its way through the hardwood, the high-pitched whining when the operator lifted it for another cut. The noise continued for a few minutes until it was interrupted by muffled, sporadic gunshots. Then a foul odor woke me from the dream.

It was 7:00 a.m. I had fallen asleep on the couch after coming in last night. Pissmore lay sprawled across my lap.

"Phew. Bad dog," I said. Pissmore looked up at me with what looked like guilt. English Bulldogs are prone to snoring and flatulence, the latter sometimes causing embarrassing situations. I rubbed my eyes and wafted the odor away. Pissmore followed me into the bathroom where I performed the three S's and then got dressed. Dark blue Docker slacks with a light blue Old Navy crewneck was the uniform of the day.

I headed for the kitchen, dreading to hear Roscoe's latest complaint. Pissmore lumbered after me.

Roscoe stood at the stove, stirring a pot of spaghetti with a large wooden spoon. The left leg of his rumpled Steeler pajamas was cuffed around his calf. Red stains dotted the front of his white robe.

Following Roscoe

Pissmore scrambled across the floor and dashed through the doggy door, the tinkling noise of the ID tag on his dog collar alerting Roscoe to my presence.

"Good mornin'," he said.

"Is it?" I wondered what today's malady would be.

"Nothin', I'm fine," he said. Roscoe looked a little pale and his posture was different. He was hunching.

"Okay, what is it?" I asked. Sometimes a little prodding is all it takes to open the floodgates of verbose medical description.

"IBS," he said. "It's an acronym for—"

"Irresistible bawdy sluts," I said. "A late night at Murph's?"

Roscoe groaned and his face reflected genuine pain. "No," he said. "Irritable bowel syndrome. It's a disorder characterized by cramping and abdominal pain."

"I know what it is."

"Have you ever had it?" Roscoe said, slamming the spoon on the counter.

"No, but—"

"Then you don't know the pain I'm going through, do you?"

I feel the *real* pain from Roscoe's imaginary affliction. Every day. But I can't help him with all the ailments his mind conjures. I can, however, help take his thoughts off his problems by involving him in another activity.

"You're right. I can't feel your pain. I'm sorry."

Roscoe sighed and shrugged his shoulders.

"I could use your help today," I said.

Roscoe wheeled around, his eyes wide with excitement. A smile spread across his face. "Really? With the business? Will I be working with the maids? I could—"

"No. I have more important work for you."

"What could be more important than working with the maids?"

"I need help getting into Frank's office."

"You haven't heard from him yet?"

I told Roscoe about visiting Frank's house and then going to the police station.

"Reasonable amount of time? How much time has to pass before the long arm of the law reaches out to help you?"

"I don't know, she didn't say. Maybe three days."

"Three days! You have to wait three days? People could be in Amsterdam on a sex orgy in less than three days."

This is how Roscoe's logic works. Everything in the universe gravitates toward sex. Are you going to help me?"

"After breakfast, I'll get dressed and meet you out front."

On the way to Frank's office I took Albert's Alley, a shortcut off Brandywine, hoping to save some time. Roscoe seemed agitated at the rough ride over the old, bumpy road.

"This isn't helping my condition," he said. "Are you *trying* to hit all the potholes?" Roscoe had changed into olive-drab camouflage cargo pants and a blue-and-gold Pitt Panther basketball shirt.

"Sorry, I'll slow down." Roscoe cut a couple popcorn farts. It seemed as if he really did have a few physical symptoms he agonized over. "Did you eat anything with mayonnaise or raw meat last night?"

"Nothing unusual."

"What's usual, by the way?"

Roscoe looked at me as if he was being questioned by the Gestapo. "Pizza," he grunted, "Slim Jims."

"What'd you have on the pizza?"

"Pepperoni, anchovies. What the hell?"

"Pepperoni, anchovies and Slim Jims mixed in a caldron with a few quarts of beer, right?"

Roscoe nodded sheepishly. I've seen that look before.

"What else?"

"Pigs feet."
"Pigs feet!"
"They were pickled. And a few hard boiled eggs."
"Holy crap. No wonder you have a stomach ache. You don't have IBS, you have garbage-dump gut. That stuff's been fermenting in your belly all night."
Roscoe rubbed his stomach. "And this ride is agitating the brew."
"This could be explosive," I said. Should I stop and call the fire department? The bio-hazard team?"
"Cut the shit, wise ass. I'll be fine. I'll make it another two blocks."

The Muesler Building sat embedded in the hillside on 17th Street between East Smuckerman below, where we parked, and Danoff Street farther up the hill. We strolled in the lower entrance, next to Jacob's Pharmacy, and treaded upstairs to the three offices on the second floor. Malcolm Goldstein, lawyer and bottom-feeder extraordinaire, had the office at the end of the hall near the Danoff Street entrance. Doctor Hubert Ghass, a proctologist, inhabited the middle office, and Frank's office stood at the top of the stairs.

Three benches sat in the hallway, each opposite an office. Two of them were occupied. A man in a neck brace, his leg nervously twitching to the beat of "where's the money" was apparently waiting to hear the results of a financial settlement. An obese man, sitting on an air-filled donut, looked wistfully at the neck-brace man. I sat down on the bench across from Frank's office and motioned Roscoe to join me.

Roscoe jerked his head toward the big guy. "He's too fat to be sitting on that small donut. He should be sitting on an inner tube."

Chubby glanced at Roscoe with a scowl.

"A Mack Truck inner-tube," Roscoe said.

The comment was a little louder than the last, and Roscoe's smile betrayed his pleasure in having said it. Roscoe took pride in his physicality and thought everyone else should as well. But not everyone had excelled in high school sports, undergone the Army's grueling training programs, or possessed the mindset that he should still be playing sports or tramping through the jungles of South Vietnam. It amazes me that, living a lifestyle that would run down or hospitalize most men his age, Roscoe remained in superb physical condition.

The big man strained to get up, his face red. He started to face us when a nurse opened the door to Doctor Ghass's office. She beckoned him with a crooked finger and said, "Mister Chubboloy, you're next."

Chapter 6

Large black letters spelling *Frank Pallone Private Investigations* stood out against the translucent glass. I had been studying Frank's door and thought a credit card might work to enable our entry. And now the hallway was clear. I nodded at Roscoe and we strolled inconspicuously toward our objective.

I slipped a Visa Classic from my wallet and pushed it between the door and jam, next to the lock. It didn't work, of course. Only on television. Roscoe looked at me as if I were a klutz. That's when Doctor Ghass' office door opened and a man waddled out like a penguin.

"Did you check your wife's bank statement?" Roscoe said.

The man turned and looked at us. Roscoe leered at the penguin man with the expression, *This is none of your business.* Thank goodness for Roscoe's quick thinking as the man turned and hobbled down the hall and left the building.

"Put that card away," Roscoe said, sliding up next to the door.

He pulled a strange-looking tool from a large pocket on his cargo pants. I couldn't see how he operated it, but the lock clicked open in less than five seconds. Roscoe held the door and checked the hallway as I slipped into the room. Roscoe immediately followed me.

"What is that tool?" I asked.

"Never mind. You don't have the *need to know*."

I recognized the phrase as military and again wondered what kind of operations Roscoe had been involved in, but I knew he would never answer my questions.

Frank always kept a neat office. Fastidious was more like it, and it appeared in that condition when I turned on the lights.

"Is that the men's room?" Roscoe pointed to a door located at the right rear of the room.

I nodded. "Don't make too much noise. There's a thin wall between the restroom and the ass doctor's office."

Roscoe quick-stepped across the room into the toilet and closed the door.

Frank's large oak desk sat in front of a wide window at the far wall. Four file cabinets stood sentinel against the left wall. A brown leather couch sat comfortably against the right wall. Above the sofa, a bright multi-colored modernistic painting seemed to jump out at me. I knew it covered a wall safe, and it was slightly ajar. Frank wouldn't have left the framed picture in that condition. Someone else had to have moved it.

How had the intruder gotten in? The door didn't look like it had been jimmied, unless someone had opened it with a tool like Roscoe's. The window overlooking 17th Street was too high for entry and in plain sight of any passersby. I thought I'd check it anyway. I twisted the plastic rod on the mini-blinds and was inspecting the window for any indication of forced entry when I heard a car door close on the street below me. A redhead stood next to a beige Crown Victoria. She was talking on a cell phone. I immediately remembered her auburn hair and her alabaster skin.

"Roscoe!" I whispered. "We have to leave. The cops are here!"

"Just a second."

Detective Fahey closed her phone and started toward the lower entrance on East Smuckerman Street. Soon, she would be coming up the stairs.

"Now," I said, with more volume and urgency.

Roscoe jumped out of the bathroom and quickly closed the door.

We dashed to the door and checked the hallway. Roscoe turned a lever under the knob, locking the door as we left. We strolled to the Danoff Street entrance and stepped out. I stood against the building on one side of the glass door, Roscoe on the other.

"How many cops?" Roscoe asked.

"One. The one I talked to last night."

"The pretty redhead?"

I could sense testosterone take over his being. "Forget her. We've got to get the hell out of here."

"Now don't get all excited and run off," Roscoe said through a seductive smile. "This is our ticket to gather intelligence."

"What?" I then realized that Roscoe was right. It was a perfect opportunity to find out what was going on, and legally, through the help of the police. But why was Fahey here? Did she have some information about Frank? I edged up to the door and peeked into the hallway. She was using a key. "She's in Frank's office. Let's go," I said, and reached for the door handle.

"Wait a minute or two. Timing's bad. Too much of a coincidence if we show up now."

I waited for what seemed to be half an hour, but it was only three minutes. Roscoe nodded and we entered the building and ambled down the hallway to Frank's office. The door was open.

Detective Fahey sat at Frank's desk, looking under a raised desk pad.

"I thought you had to wait until a reasonable time had passed," I said. "Is anything wrong? Do you have information about Frank?"

"Hold on there, Andretti," she said, interrupting my barrage. "What are you doing here?"

Roscoe stepped forward. "I'm Roscoe Kronek," he said, "and the question is, what are you doing here?"

Fahey's eyes widened and her jaw dropped.

I moved in front of Roscoe. "Roscoe's my uncle. We're concerned about Frank."

The detective's eyes narrowed as she studied Roscoe. "What did you expect to find here?" She kept an eye on my uncle.

I spoke up before Roscoe dug a hole he couldn't climb out of. "I thought Frank might show up for work today."

Fahey's face turned into a question mark.

"Maybe he went on a *toot* and sobered up in time for work," I said.

She pulled out a small notepad and grabbed a pencil. "Was Frank Pallone known for going out on so-called 'toots'?"

"Well... not really toots," I answered, grasping for the right words when Roscoe interrupted.

"He liked women. A lot, I'm told. He might have been on an extended romantic weekend. Maybe at the Woodlands. Have you ever been there?"

Fahey started writing on her notepad. "So you think he was on an extended romantic tryst but would show up for work. Is that correct?"

"Could be," I said.

She slammed her pencil on the desk. "Then why try to file a missing person's report? What's going on here?"

I told her that I occasionally worked for Frank and that he hadn't shown up for what *he* called an important meeting.

"He didn't give any indication about the subject matter for the meeting?" she asked.

"No. Nothing. And why are you here?" I asked the lieutenant, Roscoe's question still fresh in my mind. "You said you couldn't file a report on a responsible person until a reasonable time period had elapsed."

"I was in the neighborhood and thought I'd make a quick check."

Following Roscoe

Roscoe spoke up. "The city's finest going an extra yard? Some people in this community might find that a little unusual."

Fahey smiled one of those *I'm not going to let what you said bother me* smirks and said, "Norman Jacobs is a very good friend of my mother's, and when I stepped in to pick up a prescription for her, I remembered the address you gave me for Frank's office. I told Norman about your concern. One thing led to another, and he gave me the key to Frank's office."

"He's the landlord?" Roscoe asked.

"Yes."

"But how...?" I started to ask Fahey how she came straight from her car to Frank's office with the key. She couldn't have gotten it from the pharmacist. And besides, she would know that I was watching her. "Never mind," I said.

"Did you find anything of interest here?" Roscoe asked Fahey.

"Not yet. I'm still checking." She stood up and marched toward the restroom.

"Well then, we've got to be going." Roscoe looked alarmed. "Let's go, nephew."

Before we made it out of the office, Fahey screamed, "Oh my God!" She slammed the bathroom door.

"What's the matter," Roscoe asked.

"That *smell*," she answered, gagging. "It's terrible. It's worse than a stinker."

"A stinker?" I asked.

Fahey interrupted with choking and gagging. We just stood there and watched her. A faint smile crossed Roscoe's lips.

When Fahey's coughing subsided, she managed, "In police terms, a stinker is—"

"A decomposing body," Roscoe said, "usually in a very ripe stage."

"How did you know that?" Fahey asked. Roscoe shrugged his shoulders.

"Is there a body in there?" I asked, keeping the lie alive.

"No. No body," she said, rubbing tears from her eyes. "Just the stench from a recent deposit."

"So Frank was just here," Roscoe said.

Fahey looked puzzled. "Yeah... yeah, had to be him. Looks like your missing person showed up for a bowel movement."

"Let's go, Roscoe," I said. "Looks like Frank is alive and well."

Fahey gathered her purse and followed us out of Frank's office. She stood at the top of the stairs and watched us leave the building.

Chapter 7

We climbed into the van. I slid into the driver's seat, Roscoe took shotgun.

"Is she still watching?" I asked.

Roscoe turned in his seat and looked out his door window. "Yep, like a hawk."

"What's her preoccupation with us?"

"She's worried about us," Roscoe said. "She knows we know."

I pulled out of the parking space. "That she had a key to his office?"

"For starters, yes."

"Do you think she had anything to do with his disappearance?"

Roscoe smiled. "No, she's concerned about him. She knows him."

"Knows him? You mean *really* knows him?"

"Yeah. More than a professional cop, private eye relationship. What's that lawyer's name you golf with?"

"Bernie Ostapowicz."

"Bernie... the attorney. Give him a call. Maybe he knows of a connection between Fahey and the dick."

"I'll call this afternoon."

"Also, ask him if Frank had any enemies or threatening calls."

I studied Roscoe's solemn expression. "Why?"

Roscoe pulled out his handkerchief. There was a reddish smear on it.

I jammed on the brakes and slid the van to the curb. "Is that blood? Where did you get that?"

"I believe it is, yes. And it was on the inside door frame of Frank's office."

"Why didn't you show it to Fahey? The blood would prove that there are suspicious circumstances and the police would open an investigation."

"First of all, the blood I wiped from the door frame was also on the back of your shirt," Roscoe said, tugging on my right shirt sleeve at the shoulder, "and I don't want breaking and entering on my rap sheet. And second, the police are already involved. Right?"

Roscoe meant Fahey. I couldn't argue with his reasoning. My head swam with gruesome possibilities, the least of which would have been a fight with a client.

"We have to find Frank," I said. "This is getting scary."

"I wonder if Fahey found anything in his office."

"I don't think so. She would have left if she found something. She's still searching."

"What are you doing about three o'clock in the morning?" Roscoe asked.

A cold shiver swept over me. Working with Roscoe could land me in the gray bar saloon for a lengthy sentence. "Aw, gee. Do I have to?"

"I'll need your help, Augie. I can't do this alone. Do you want to find your friend?"

"It's just... nerve-wracking, that's all. There's a lot to be done."

"I've got a lot to do myself. I met this Georgeanne chick today. Got a date with her later. I'll be back in time for the three o'clock caper."

Following Roscoe

"Pull over here," Roscoe said, pointing to the intersection of 21st and Columbia.

"What are you going to do?"

Roscoe motioned for me to stop in front of Ed's Electronics Store.

"Never mind what I'm doing. And Ed will drive me home." Roscoe slipped out of the van. "I'll see you later, Nephew."

I headed for the office wondering about Roscoe and his other preoccupation—besides women and sex—with electronics. I've seen packages in his mailbox from electronics specialty companies, and now he's on a first name basis with Ed, the store owner.

Emma was tapping information into the computer when I arrived.

"Where you been?" she said through gritted teeth.

"Why? What's wrong?"

"Everything. Everything's wrong. You wouldn't know. You're galavantin' all over. Golfing, betting, climbing trees, spying on people. I gotta take care of business, if you call it a business. What kind of business is in a garage?"

"Date with Felton go bad?"

"Bad ain't the half of it. Sumna bitch will never see this fine-looking, full-figured woman again."

"Want to talk about it?"

"No. Hell no. I'll never mention that cheap-ass, girly butt-looking, self-centered, frog-faced man again. And, to top it off, when I wasn't looking, that mutha-fucka stole one of my pork chops."

"You didn't hurt him, did you?"

"Not right away. I should've hit him upside his head. But I waited until after we made out and kicked him out the truck. Without his pants."

"After you made out? And you left him—like that?"

"Naw. I threw his Gabriel Brothers pants out the window a block away. I parked his truck at the taxi stand four blocks away."

I felt relieved, but I knew some day Emma's name would be well known by the judicial system or worse, and business would come to a screeching halt. I had to get her out of her bad mood. I would have taken her to lunch, but the empty McDonald's bag and Kentucky Fried Chicken box on her desk put a stop to that idea.

She had previously mentioned detective work and I thought it might be a good idea to have her tag along on an interview. I told her about what happened this morning. I noticed her concern.

"Why don't you lock up and come with me. I have to question a doctor at Frank's office building."

"Hell, yes, I'll go. I could use a break. And besides, I'm good at questioning suspicious people."

Chapter 8

I waited for Emma outside her apartment building, a three-story, twelve-family dwelling, for close to twenty minutes while she changed her clothes. She said she had to dress appropriately to get in the mood for questioning suspicious characters. I was beginning to think—no, scratch that—I *knew* I had made a mistake asking her to accompany me when I saw Emma strut out the front door.

She wore a black Tahari suit with a single-button jacket and matching pants, and black Melin oxfords. With the addition of a Stetson Chatham fedora, she looked like a black William Conrad who played Frank Cannon in the popular Seventies P.I. TV show.

"I'm ready now," she said, holding up a small notepad and pencil. "Bring 'em on. I can interpolate with the best of 'em."

Emma's size, coupled with her menacing facial expression, scared me—and I'm on her side.

"I'm glad you didn't bring brass knuckles with you. We're just asking questions, remember?"

"Hunh? Hell with the questions. I'm after answers."

It took twenty minutes to drive to the Muesler Building, which was more than enough time to reason with Emma. I told her we were only asking a few questions to find out if anyone had seen or heard anything about Frank.

I parked on Danoff, the upper street, so Emma wouldn't have to trudge up the steep flight of steps—it might darken her mood. I held open the door to Doctor Ghass's office for her. She studied the writing on the glass.

"What kinda name is Ghass? He's an ass doctor. Ghass. Ass. Why not Butts? Doctor Booty would be trippin'. And Hubert?" Emma said. "I bet kids at grade school did a number on him."

I motioned Emma into the office. The tall, bespectacled receptionist stood wide-eyed, a puzzled look on her face. Her nametag read Lily.

I stepped forward. "Is Doctor Ghass in? I'd like to speak to him for a moment."

The receptionist blinked a few times—probably to bring herself back to reality. "He's not in."

Emma lunged forward and leaned on the counter. "Don't give me that crap," she said, pointing to a schedule on the wall. "This is office hours, right?"

Oh shit, here we go. Emma was on a roll and the receptionist looked like she was ready to lose her urine or pass out.

I maneuvered myself between Emma and Lily. "It's important that I talk to Doctor Ghass. Do you know where I can reach him? When will he be back?"

Lily side-stepped to her right, extending the distance between her and Emma. Perhaps this made her feel safer.

"He's at a Weight-Watcher's meeting." She noticed the strange look on my face. I wondered why a doctor would interrupt his practice to go to a Weight Watcher's meeting. "He goes twice a week for forty minutes each. The meeting started ten minutes ago. It's only a block away."

She scribbled down the directions on a sticky-paper and jabbed it at me, obviously wanting us out of the office and out of her life.

"I'm also looking for Frank Pallone. Have you seen him?"

Lily's eyes squinted as she searched the ceiling for an answer. "I think Thursday was the last day I saw him." Her eyes met mine. "Yes, Thursday."

Not wanting to tire out Emma, we drove one block to a small strip mall of a dozen businesses, one of which was Weight Watchers, that sat between an Indian restaurant and a drycleaners. I again lectured Emma on using discretion. Finding Frank was of the utmost importance. She nodded.

We walked into the meeting room. Fifteen or so people sat on folding chairs in a semi-circle. A woman with red hair, the leader, I guess, sat at a table in the middle of the arc. She looked up from what she was reading.

Before I could speak, Emma blurted, "Is there a Hugh Ghass in here?"

A white-haired old man looked at the backside of the woman seated next to him.

Ohmygod. Emma didn't. When she pronounced the doctor's name, it sounded like *huge ass*. She can quickly find a way to create an embarrassing situation. Clever, but not in good taste. People were looking at each other, maybe to see who had the biggest ass. I almost grinned, but the thought of Frank sobered me.

"Ma'am?" the redhead said. "You're interrupting our meeting."

"I want to know if there is a—"

"Doctor Ghass," I said. "Is Doctor Hubert Ghass here?"

A big man, balding with a flush-red face stood up. The woman next to him looked at his backside. I headed toward the door and motioned for him to follow me. Emma didn't move. She stood there, smiling, seeming to relish her rude homonym.

The doctor followed me outside as Emma watched the Watchers.

"I'm trying to locate Frank Pallone. Have you seen him?"

"He's not in his office?"

"No, and it's important that I find him. When was the last time you saw him?" The ass doctor looked for an answer on the sidewalk. "I really can't say. I'm busy all day. Our office hours are different."

I thanked him for his cooperation and herded Emma out of the building.

"That was quite a performance, Emma. Ad-lib?"

"Naw. Took a few minutes to compose."

The drive back to the office seemed quicker. The concern over Emma's behavior had left, replaced by humorous banter about the Ghass situation.

At her desk, Emma resumed typing on the computer. I picked up the phone and punched in Bernie Ostapowicz's number.

After the third ring, he answered, "Hello."

"Bernie, hear anything new about Frank?"

"No, nothing. I called attorneys in the area and no one has seen him. Do you think he went on an impromptu vacation?"

"No. Remember he was to tell me about an important job he had for me and didn't show up for golf?"

"That's right. What have you dug up?"

I couldn't reveal any information Roscoe and I had obtained illegally, as Bernie was an officer of the Court. "I went to police headquarters and talked to Lieutenant Colleen Fahey. She said the police couldn't intervene at this time because she knew Frank to be a reasonably prudent adult and that there's nothing to indicate any signs of foul play."

"That's true," Bernie said. "In a case like that, police wait for a reasonable amount of time. Of course, if evidence surfaces that the person has been harmed or

Following Roscoe

taken forcibly, they will take action immediately, as they will with all children."

"But after telling me why the police can't intervene, she showed up at Frank's office the following morning and entered with a key."

"That's strange," Bernie said. "I'll check out this lieutenant and see if she has any connection with Frank."

I thanked him and hung up.

I was about to leave when the phone rang. Emma took the call and motioned that it was for me. I accepted the receiver. It was Aldine Vanderslice and she stated she was bringing over Chinese for dinner. She wouldn't take no for an answer.

"Emma, do you like oriental food?"

Pissmore's bark alerted me to look out the kitchen window. Mrs. Vanderslice strode toward the door carrying a stainless steel wok, the dog in hot pursuit. I dropped the damp paper towel I'd used to wipe the table into the waste basket and opened the door. I escorted the mutt and the Mrs. into the scullery. The smell of the food excited Pissmore, and he scampered to his doggy dish.

"Pissmore, people food doesn't agree with you," I said, dumping a heap of dry mix into his bowl.

Mrs. Vanderslice placed the wok on the stove and set the dial to simmer, the same condition I was in as I studied her gorgeous figure. She wore a long, red Chinese silk brocade dress with sleeveless shoulders and Mandarin collar. A muted dragon pattern covered the material. Red silk embroidered shoes matched her dress.

Aldine's blue eyes scanned the kitchen. "Where's Roscoe?"

"He can't come. He had previous plans."

"Your uncle seems to make himself scarce when I'm around. I thought if I made him some supper... you know, the quickest way to a man's heart."

I didn't want to tell her that the quickest way to Roscoe's heart wasn't down his esophagus.

"He really had plans before you called," I said. "Maybe another time."

"Maybe a different culinary experience sometime."

Hooters came to mind. The more I looked at her curvaceous body, the better the idea sounded.

"Mexican food," she said. "Does he like Mexican food?"

"I think he might."

Pissmore stopped eating and darted to the door, wagging his stubby tail.

Emma's face appeared in the door's window, and I waved her in. She wore a blue lightweight bomber jacket over gray distressed cargos. Pissmore snuggled up to Emma, and she responded with a pat on his broad head.

"Good boy," Emma said to the mutt. She looked up at Mrs. Vanderslice, who was stirring the contents of the wok. She glanced at me. "I've heard of take out, but don't you think you went too far?"

Mrs. Vanderslice turned around.

I thought I'd stop Emma's momentum by introducing them to each other. "Emma, this is—"

"I've never seen a silver-haired Chinese person before," Emma said. "And blue eyes? What you got here is an imposter. I'd get a refund."

"Emma, this is Aldine Vanderslice, our neighbor. She's been good enough to bring dinner over."

Emma checked out Aldine's appearance. "Oh yeah, I remember. She's the one got the hots for Roscoe. Nice outfit. Where'd you get it, The Party Store?"

Aldine put her hands on her hips. "Excuse me?"

I envisioned a forthcoming food fight with Chinese on the walls and maybe some blood spatter.

"You'll have to excuse Emma," I said. "She had a rough time of it with a date from hell last night."

Aldine settled down and lowered her hands. "Oh, I'm sorry. What happened?"

Following Roscoe

Emma dropped all the sordid details of last evening's events on the kitchen table.

Aldine's eyes expanded as she listened to Emma's story and through a wide smile said, "You go, girl! That's awesome! You really left him without his pants?"

"Yep." Emma cracked a smile. "What's for dinner, Deener? Is Deener okay? Aldine's too formal. Yuppie-like."

"Okay with me," Aldine said.

The previous thought I had of a bloody cat fight in the kitchen was replaced by a relaxing meal. Emma remarked about the zesty zucchini stir-fry and Aldine explained how she cooked the chicken with chile paste and orange juice. We all shared our savory experiences.

It was a nice dinner—except for the explosion.

An unseen thunderous force swatted me to the floor. Its report reverberated in my skull, scattering my senses. I finally discovered that I lay on my kitchen floor along with shards of glass. Emma and Aldine were trying to stand. Pissmore dove through the doggy-door into my apartment. I heard heavy objects hitting the house and thumping into the yard. I finally stood up. I helped Emma and Aldine to chairs. Aldine had a bewildered look on her face.

I stumbled through the debris to the blasted-out kitchen window. A heap of smoking junk sat at the curb where Emma's van had recently rested. Small burnt pieces of paper slowly drifted to earth through wafting smoke. The steering wheel and rear view mirror had hit the side of the house and fallen near the door step. An upright vacuum and a small floor buffer had landed in the middle of the yard next to a service case that had miraculously stayed intact. If the locked doors on the case had opened, cleaning supplies and products would have landed on half a block area.

"Look at the gorgeous boots," Aldine said, peering out the glassless window. "And that nice black vest."

A pair of dominatrix thigh-high leather boots and a leather halter bustier had landed on the walkway to the garage. A leather bondage belt and studded punishment whip hung conspicuously on the white picket fence.

"What boots? What vest?" Emma said, scrambling to her feet. "Where? Where are they?"

Aldine pointed through the window.

"Oooooo... shit. My personals are all over the place, calling for everyone's attention. I've got to get them together." Emma dashed for the door.

"Are you okay?" I asked Aldine. "You look like you're in shock."

"I really like those boots. Do you think Roscoe would like them on me? I'll have to ask Emma where she got them. And look, Emma got a leather harness for Pissmore. Looks a little big for him, but I think he'll like it."

Yeah, she was in shock all right. I picked up the phone and punched in 911. After I gave them all the pertinent information, they said they would send someone over. I then called Roscoe's cell. It went to voicemail. His answering machine picked up. Of course, he had a date with Georgeanne. I left a message that Emma's van had been blown up and I had no any idea what caused it.

I walked outside to check on the damage. Emma was shooing away bystanders with the studded punishment whip as she gathered up her "personals." The van was totally destroyed—in pieces all over the street and my yard. The right side door, with the graphic, Desperate Domestics, leaned against a fire hydrant.

Just as Emma finished stashing her personal belongings in my garage, the paramedics arrived, sirens blaring. They checked us out and, as they were taking Aldine to the hospital for further observation, the cops arrived.

Chapter 9

Three o'clock came early. The excitement over the bombing and the accompanying sleeplessness didn't help matters any. I wondered if the bombing was related to Frank's disappearance and, if so, how it was connected to me. Roscoe's Lincoln MKZ reeked of alcohol and cheap perfume, so we took the remaining van—minus the magnetic decals—and headed for Frank's office. Maybe we'll find information that will explain our questions.

I briefed Roscoe about the destruction of Emma's van.

"What did the cops say?" Roscoe asked.

"A sergeant interviewed Emma. He was mainly concerned with recent boyfriends and any threatening calls she may have received."

"What about the bomb? Do they know what kind it was?" He sneezed.

"Bless you. Dynamite. He said it was probably three or four sticks, taped together."

"No timer?" He blew his nose into a red handkerchief.

"What's with the red handkerchief and the sneezing?"

"I think I got Aspergillosis. What about the timer?" Roscoe said nothing about the red handkerchief.

"The sergeant found no evidence of a timer. He believes it had a fuse. Three officers canvassed the area. They reported that no one saw anything because everyone was probably sitting down at the dinner table. What's with this asparagus disease thing?"

"Aspergillosis is a type of fungus infection. Ruined my date with Georgeanne. Couldn't get to first base. And who would want to blow up Emma's van? Sorry, Nephew, your van."

"Emma can be abrasive at times, and she likes to make fun of people, but I don't think anyone... wait a minute. She had a problem with a date last night." I explained how Emma had kicked Felton out of his truck and driven off, throwing his pants out the window a few blocks later.

"Awesome," Roscoe said. "She has chutzpah. Did she mention this to the cops?"

"No, she doesn't like to talk to the 'po-po', as she puts it."

"We'll have to have a talk with this Felton fella. Get his address from Emma."

We parked on Danoff, the upper street, half a block away from the Muesler Building. Roscoe was dressed in black: jacket, cargo pants, and watch cap—all with Steeler logos on them. We stole toward the building's entrance. Roscoe slipped on latex gloves and handed a pair to me. He pulled a tool from his pocket and slid toward the door. He shone a penlight on the lock. Roscoe stared at the lock for a couple of seconds and then turned the knob, opening the door.

"What's that, psychokinesis or something you learned working for the government?"

"It's open. Someone jimmied the lock," he said, pulling a .32-caliber automatic from his pocket. "Be careful."

I didn't know Roscoe carried a gun and it disturbed me. But with trepidation, I followed him into the building and down the dark hall. Roscoe stopped at Malcolm Goldstein's door and positioned what appeared to be a stethoscope in his ears. He placed the diaphragm on the door and listened for any movement inside. After fifteen or twenty seconds, he motioned for me to follow him. Roscoe stopped at Doctor Ghass's door and performed the same procedure.

Roscoe listened a lot longer at Frank's door. He shone the penlight on the lock. "This lock's been jimmied also." He turned the knob and slipped into the room.

After checking the office, he motioned me in and locked the door. He pulled a packet of black plastic from his pants pocket and started to unfold it.

"Here," he whispered, "hold this end."

I held the edge of the plastic sheet as Roscoe finished unfolding it. He pulled out a roll of masking tape and began taping the plastic over the door and around its frame.

"I've heard of deep pockets," I said, "but those are ridiculous. You're a walking hardware store."

"Any successful operation depends on good planning," he said.

Roscoe finished taping the glass and then pressed a length of tape across the bottom of the door, sealing off any potential light that would betray our entry. We followed the same procedure in covering the window. Roscoe started sneezing again, this time with an accompanying cough.

"That asparagus thing seems to be getting worse," I said.

"I've changed my diagnosis. I think it's nocardiosis. I have some chest pain and I'm getting a headache."

"Another osis disease? You were in the service; maybe it's Legionnaires' disease?"

Roscoe thought about what I said. "Yeah, it could be."

I turned the lights on. "Now that that's settled, let's find the information we came for."

The room was still neat and tidy, but Roscoe detected that someone had jimmied the locked file cabinets and desk drawers as well. "It looks like someone may have beat us to what we're looking for."

"There's always something left behind that didn't seem important at the time or wasn't easily available."

That's when I remembered the crooked modernistic painting. "The safe," I said, pointing to the framed collection of dissimilar colors. "There's a safe underneath that painting."

"See what I mean, Nephew?"

I pulled the couch away from the wall and removed the painting. The safe was about eighteen inches square. I tried the door. It was locked.

Roscoe reached into his bottomless cargo pocket and pulled out an electronic device with four colored LED lights on it. He fastened it to the door of the safe with what looked like a suction cup. He positioned the stethoscope's listening device next to the safe's combination dial and slowly began rotating the knob. Different combinations of colored lights lit up the LED readout as Roscoe continued, reversing the direction of the dial. All four lights came on at the same time.

Roscoe grabbed the safe's opening lever. "Open sesame," he said, and turned the handle, opening the safe. "Easy as pie, Nephew."

Roscoe handed me an armful of file folders from the safe and motioned for me to lay them on the couch. When I turned around he hefted a stainless 9mm Taurus automatic pistol he had removed from the safe.

"Nice weight," he said. "But it's shiny and reflects light."

"Anything else in there?"

Roscoe pulled out a pair of Yukon Tracker 1 X 24 night vision goggles.

"I didn't think he had those," I said. "I could have used them a few times."

"They're new. Frank must have had a need for them."

Roscoe placed the gun and goggles back in the safe and sat on the opposite end of the couch from me. I handed him one file folder at a time, and he checked

Following Roscoe

them. They mostly held routine papers from Frank's house and business: insurances, deeds, professional certifications, permits. Roscoe reached for the last file.

"This is what we're looking for," Roscoe said. He marched to the desk and turned the tabletop light on. "We'll study this information later."

Roscoe pulled out yet another device from his cargo pants—a small digital camera. He placed one of the pages from the file under the light and captured its image. As Roscoe continued with the pages, I checked the rest of the office. Nothing seemed out of place or unusual. Frank was fastidious. No notes or papers lay on his desk, and the waste can was empty. All meaningless papers had either been shredded or taken out with the trash.

The restroom was spotless as usual, except for the faint odor of Roscoe's deposit seventeen hours earlier. As I stepped out, I noticed a small grease stain on the door, its shape and location indicating it came from the toe of a shoe. Roscoe had just finished photographing the papers from the file, so I asked him to have a look at the mark. He pulled out a cotton swab from his jacket pocket. He swiped a sample of the substance and placed it in a plastic bag.

Roscoe carefully replaced everything in the safe as he'd found it and locked it. He even returned the painting in its original tilted position in case Lieutenant Fahey had noticed this also.

We checked the office carefully, turned out the lights and removed the plastic from the window and door. Roscoe tucked the plastic into his cargo pants, then we locked the door and left. The street was dark and desolate. We hopped in the van and inconspicuously left the scene.

I had been quite nervous during the whole episode, but after a few miles of crisp night air I felt relieved that we might have some information about Frank's disappearance.

"Did we get some good stuff?"

"Don't know yet," Roscoe said. "I'll have to look at the photographs, but it seems promising."

"On your computer? When can we look at them?"

"I'll convert it to hard copy. You can look all you want. Might take some time. Why don't you talk to this Felton guy while I print out the info?"

I'd heard it before. Roscoe's tone meant: *You're not getting into my apartment, nephew. Not now, not never. Stop trying.*

I knew Roscoe had electronics stuff secreted in his apartment. And sexual stuff? Definitely. I had caught the mailman snickering while reading the return labels on Roscoe's packages. And who knows what paraphernalia he'd pulled out of those two locked footlockers when he'd moved into the apartment? But that's Roscoe, and maybe that's what kept him from being in a permanent hypochondriac state. And besides, the electronic stuff was definitely helping so far in obtaining information about Frank's disappearance.

Roscoe said no more on the drive home. He seemed to be thinking. That was good, too. It would keep his mind off imaginary physical problems.

Chapter 10

The following morning's breakfast wasn't one of Roscoe's best, but it was satisfying: ham, eggs over easy, toast and coffee. A breath of morning air lifted a corner of the plastic that covered the blown-out window.

"I'll have to call someone to replace the window." I sauntered over to tape the opening closed.

Roscoe had swept up the shards of glass with a dustpan and dumped them into the garbage can. When he moved to the table with a second cup of coffee, I noticed he was limping, but I had no time for a lengthy explanation. He wore his Steelers PJs, Pittsburgh Penguins black slipper socks—Pissmore had shredded his furry bear paw slippers—and drank his coffee from a matching Penguin Slapshot stein.

"You've got to watch their eyes," Roscoe said. He was instructing me about questioning Felton concerning his possible involvement in the bombing of Emma's van. "If they look down and to the left, they're lying."

"Yeah, yeah, I hear you. Listen to the voice, watch for nervous mannerisms, I get the picture."

"One more thing. This is important. Keep your back to the door. If the suspect makes a move, get the hell out of there."

"Oh great! Now I have to worry about getting the shit kicked out of me."

"That's a possibility," Roscoe said, looking over my physique. "You look more like the *before* picture than the *after* picture in those bodybuilding ads."

Of course he was exaggerating. I'm six feet, 185 pounds and in pretty good shape—but not to Roscoe's standards. But I knew he was pulling my leg. I had already described the altercation Felton had with Emma to Roscoe. If Emma could handle him, I surely could.

"Well, I guess I'm going to find out," I said and gulped down the last of my breakfast. I filled Pissmore's dishes with water and his usual mixture of dog food. "Off to fight the fight, little buddy." He canted his head to one side as if he didn't understand.

I arrived at Desperate Domestics, the two-stall garage I call headquarters, at 9:05 a.m. After fifteen minutes of jawing with Emma about Felton, she gave me his address. Regardless of her criticisms, I think she still had the hots for him.

The air smelled acidic with a touch of Varsol, a cleaning agent used extensively by industry, as I drove through the Wallstead section of town. Small shrubs and clumps of grass erupted through cracks and fissures on concrete floors, floors that once supported a superstructure housing the plant that hundreds of souls once called their workplace. Almost all of the corrugated roof sheeting was gone, blown away over the decades, and the remaining beams that had formed its skeleton were now bent and rusted. Any thought of the steel industry returning to this town, or this state, had evaporated with the hopes and dreams of its workers.

Union Street had also decayed as workers left, looking for work in the south and the west, leaving their homes to the same fate as the mills. I stopped in front of Felton's house. The garage seemed to list at a dangerous angle. A feeling of despair fell over me and I thought about turning around and going home.

I finally got a grip and dragged my ass out of the car. I locked it and trudged up to Felton Felton's front porch, the floor boards squeaking and sagging underfoot.

When I knocked on the door I thought it would fall off what remained of the hinges. When Felton stepped out onto the porch, I understood why Emma called him Felton Frog Face. I agreed with her assessment. He looked like a black frog after coming out of hibernation. He had huge eyes with large, black centers. The sclera was yellowed, road-mapped with red capillaries. The rest of his face was wrinkled black leather covered with a two-day growth of silver stubble.

"What chu want?" Felton said through crooked, nicotine-stained teeth. His eyes tried to focus on me.

I found it hard to believe that Emma had anything to do with this person standing in front of me.

"Freddy Felton?"

"Uh-huh."

"I'm August Gustafson, and I wondered if you have a red truck." Emma said he had a truck, but failed to mention the color. It didn't matter because I had to begin a conversation with Felton, and the dozens of scenarios I had gone over, this is the one I came up with.

Freddy's eyes took me in, head to toe. "I have a truck, why?"

"A box fell out of a truck on Morganza, near Torrence Street. It had valuables in it. Were you in that neighborhood around supper time last night?"

Freddy rubbed his chin. "Morganza Street? What color truck?"

"Red."

Freddy shook his head. "Naw, my truck's black. And how'd you get my name and address?"

I wondered if Freddy was playing dumb. He didn't fall for the valuable box trick. I tried another approach.

"I'm a friend of Emma Lou. She thought maybe it was your truck."

"What kind'a friend? You don't look like nobody's friend... not Emma's anyway. You not from around here, right? What's she see in you, pretty boy?"

"Nothing. No, no it's not like that. She works for me."

Felton studied my face. "That domestic thing? I thought she was the boss."

"She might think so, but I own the business, the equipment, and the van that was blown up yesterday."

"What van? The one Emma drives sometimes?"

"The van I own that she uses for her job."

"What you mean blown up? Is she okay?"

"Someone used dynamite to destroy it, and yes, she's all right."

He seemed confused. "Why would...?" He looked sideways at me. "I don't know nuttin' about it. You don't think..."

"It looks like revenge for your disastrous date."

He looked confused again.

"Didn't go well, did it?"

"Whatdaya mean? It was okay. What'd Emma say?"

"Who paid for the meal?"

"She did. I'm between jobs right now."

"Were there other women there? Young, built and pretty?"

"Oh yeah. Fine lookin' womens. I be checking them out all evening. That piss off Emma? They be checkin' me out, you know what I mean. I check on back."

Emma had said he was self-centered.

"What about the argument?"

"I don't know about that. I had a good time. Especially in the truck, you know? We were goin' hot and heavy under the stars. I saw her eyes roll back two times, you know what I mean? And when I was holdin' her close, you know, after, she went crazy. Sompin 'bout pork chops. Knocked me out my own damn truck."

Now I was confused. "How'd she kick you out of your truck, and how did you have sex in a truck?"

Felton looked at me as if I had asked a stupid question. "The tailgate was down. I slid out when she kicked me."

I swallowed a chuckle. "Oh, in the back." I had asked a stupid question.

"Yeah, in the back, asshole. I have a Chevy El Camino, not an el dumpo trucko. Where else could I put that fat fucker? You ever look at her ass? We're talkin' wide body."

"So I guess you weren't mad enough to blow up her van?"

"Hell no. She good to me. I don't want her mad at me, you know what I mean."

I left Felton's house knowing that Felton hadn't blown up Emma's van.

As I turned the van onto the driveway, I noticed Pissmore sitting by the kitchen door. Anyone who saw him would think he was guarding the house, a big, husky bulldog with a menacing face, ready to pounce. But the truth is, it was 12:15 and he was waiting for his lunch.

The mighty mutt dove through the doggy-door and was waiting at his dish when I walked in. Roscoe was seated at the table fiddling with some papers. A ham and egg sandwich, bowl of potato soup and a Pittsburgh Panther etched print glass filled with iced tea were waiting at my side of the table. Roscoe's dirty dishes soaked in the sink. Pissmore skittered around my feet, stubby tail wagging as I prepared his doggy chow.

"I would've fed him shortly, but I was going over the papers in Frank's safe."

"Thanks, no problem," I said, testing the temperature of the soup. I put the bowl in the microwave and set the timer for thirty seconds.

"What did that Felton fella have to say?"

"He's clueless. I don't think he could set off a bomb without blowing himself up."

"Yeah, I didn't think so."

"You knew it wasn't him the whole time, didn't you?"

"Good training. You didn't waste your time. And besides, it gave me time to look over these papers."

"Any leads?" The microwave timer went off. I brought the steaming bowl to the table and sat down.

Roscoe slid three copies of photographs from a manila folder. "Take a look at these." He dealt them to me one at a time.

I picked one up and looked at it while taking a bite out of the sandwich. I couldn't believe what I was looking at. "Is that a dead pigeon?"

Roscoe looked up from the paper he was reading. "Yep."

"Who took it? And why is the bird's throat cut?"

"You ever hear of a stool pigeon? Whoever left this bloody bird on Frank's doorstep was telling him that whatever he did wasn't appreciated. It's a threat. A bloody threat."

I studied the second picture. "That's Frank's Chrysler 300, and the tires are flat. Not as threatening as the bloody pigeon."

Roscoe motioned. "Check out the third one."

The remaining photo had slid behind my glass of tea where I couldn't see it. I pulled it toward me. "What kind of snake is that?"

"Copperhead. It's poisonous. And before you ask, that's Frank's car. Frank took these photos and left them in his safe. The snapshots tell us that the person responsible for these acts had been following Frank."

"Wow, looks like someone really has it in for Frank," I said. The recent events of the last few days congealed in my mind. "This file was meant for me, wasn't it?"

"Looks that way, Nephew."

"But I don't get involved in anything dangerous. I do surveillances, take statements, routine stuff. This kind of shit is for professionals. Why didn't he call the police?"

Roscoe paused his reading. "I'm not so sure he didn't."

"I don't understand."

"I think Lieutenant Fahey is hiding something. She knows more than we think. I think you should talk to her, feel her out."

"How do I go about it? What do I ask?"

"Ask her if she ever worked on cases that Frank had investigated. Listen to what she says; more questions will come to you. You'll be fine. And after you speak to Fahey, I have another person for you to talk to."

"Who's that?"

"I've rooted through most of these papers and found a few people who have motive to harm Frank."

"Like?"

"Like Karl Himmelman. Talk to him first. He's a rich jeweler that was going through a messy divorce with his wife, Helga. She hired Frank to check her husband's assets. Frank found a ton of hidden money that cost Karl one point two million dollars. Settlement was two weeks ago."

"What do we need to know?"

"We already know he had motive. How about opportunity? Where was he last night when the bombing occurred? Does he own pigeons? Snakes? Is he still pissed off? Anything you can find. And while you're at it, make a sketch of the place, security system, cameras, dogs, whatever we need to know if we decided to look around his place."

"How can I ask these questions? I can't just walk in and rattle them off. He'll clam up."

"Pretend you're doing a survey or that you're from the insurance company, checking on the dwelling. Or from the gas company investigating on a leak. Figure it out."

I left the house feeling the weight of the world on my shoulders. How the hell was I going to march into Himmelmann's house and start asking questions? Pissmore tramped through the grass next to me as I headed toward the garage.

Milt Anderson

"Yoo hoo, Mister Gustafson." Mrs. Vanderslice stood on her back porch. "Do you have a minute?"

I reluctantly stopped. It seemed as if the world just got heavier. I felt my body slump under the pressure. Every time I start something important, I get interrupted. "Yeah sure. By the way, are your ears still ringing?"

"No, they're fine. I wanted to talk to you about dinner. I have a recipe for chicken cacciatore that I think Roscoe will love. I can be over at six p.m."

"I don't know if tonight is good."

"Don't you worry about the kitchen. I know your maid comes on Mondays. I'll clean the kitchen spotless before I leave."

That actually sounded swell. It would keep me from having to clean up after Roscoe.

"All right. That sounds good."

"Okay then. I'll be over at six sharp."

Before I could change my mind, she scampered into her house. The heaviness I felt eased but my life felt complicated. I patted Pissmore before leaving for police headquarters.

Chapter 11

I walked into police headquarters to talk to Lieutenant Fahey about the exploding van and to find out what she knew about Frank's disappearance. In my head, I went over the information I had about Frank, but I was nervous because I couldn't share any information we'd obtained illegally. I had to come up with something fast. That's when I realized that I was looking into the face of the desk sergeant.

"Whaddya need?" he said.

"I'd like to talk to Lieutenant Fahey about the explosion in front of my house."

The sergeant motioned with the same grace as he had two days earlier. "Second door to the right."

He seemed engrossed in what he was reading, so I took a peek over his shoulder as I walked past. It was a girly magazine, the title of which might have been *Titanic Tits*. Humongous boobs seemed to jut from the page as if seen through 3-D glasses. I was so absorbed in the photographs that I stood there, staring—until the sergeant turned around and our eyes locked. That's when I remembered what I had come for. I turned on my heel and quickstepped down the hall to the lieutenant's office.

When the detective turned around, her milky skin, and full, red lips blurred in the background as my mind's eye projected a huge set of boobs from the sergeant's magazine onto Fahey's chest. As the orbs slowly became smaller and covered with a uniform jacket, I noticed she was looking at me ogling her.

"I see you made a stop at Sergeant Paholsky's desk."

Embarrassment seemed to set my cheeks on fire. "I... ah... is there anything new on the bomb explosion?" I took a deep breath. "In front of my house. The van?"

She smiled and turned to open a desk drawer, from which she withdrew a thin manila folder. "Not much to go on. Nobody saw anything." She pulled out a yellow paper. "Nothing unusual about the explosive that was used. It could have been stolen from any construction or mining site."

What could I ask her that would connect Frank's disappearance with a blown up van? I hadn't the faintest idea. Roscoe would know; he had a direction in which to go. He should talk to Fahey.

"Lieutenant Fahey, do you like chicken cacciatore?"

———

I wanted to check on Emma's situation since she didn't have transportation anymore. I took Ontario Street and headed through the east side where I grew up. Driving through the old neighborhood brought back memories: Gettler's Store where I bought penny candy; Riddell's Plumbing where I batted rubber balls against their garage door; the playground where Katcho, Monk, Ludgie, Dicko, Hunky Mike, and Spanky hung out—seems everyone in the burg had a nickname; and the empty lot where the Campbell's once lived. Earl "The Pearl" Degregario, who had lived next door, rubbed the local *family* the wrong way, and two thugs from Steubenville, Ohio, had paid a visit to teach him a lesson. Only problem is, they blew up the Campbell's house by mistake. So much for the Mob's intelligence.

I swung the van into Emma's space and set the parking brake. When I entered Desperate Domestics headquarters, as I like to call the two-stall garage, Emma was on the phone.

"Eight o'clock's fine," she said. "Okay, later."

"Got a date with Felton tonight?"

"Hell no! Not that cheap-ass, pork-chop-stealin' sumnabitch. He's on my *don't bother me* list," she said. Then her face gave way to a smile. "That was Terrelle. He's the man, and he's taking me to a movie tonight. He's not cheap, he got tickets."

"Well, I'm glad. I hope you have a good time. Is everything up to speed here?"

"Yeah, 'cept I need transportation. I had to ask old man Cheatam, who live next door, for a ride. He got menacing eyes. He undressed me twice on the ride here."

"Ouch, you *do* need a vehicle, but we'll have to look for something later. I need to interview Mister Himmelmann first."

"This about Frank's disappearance?"

"Yes. Do you know him?"

"Rich guy. He's a client. Lives on Brentwood Avenue."

"A client!"

"Uh huh, that's what I said. Stella, the Polish princess, is over there right now."

"Perfect."

"I know what you thinkin', and I'm goin' with you."

I told Emma that Roscoe wanted a layout of the place including information about possible cameras, dogs or a security system.

"What? Is he a second story man? I heard about those guys. Where was he before he come with you? Prison?"

I explained to Emma that Roscoe had worked for the government in some capacity, but I didn't know what he did. I didn't tell her that, after the last few days, I believe an acronym might be used for his employer.

"He probably come into houses and take back unpaid taxes or promised benefits. Somethin' like that."

Emma and I pulled off Brentwood Avenue onto the governor's drive that led to Karl Himmelman's twelve-room Tudor. On the way over I told Emma about the settlement Mrs. Harriet Himmelman received and the home she now had in Upper St. Clair, courtesy of Frank Pallone. I parked behind a new black Jaguar XK coupe.

As we approached the front entrance, Emma asked, "You say settlement was two weeks ago?"

"That's right."

"Two weeks plenty long to be missing one point two million bucks. Things would be churning and boiling up by now. I know peoples who would kill for less than a hundred dollars."

"Karl Himmelman has plenty of motive to hurt someone for what he lost."

"He didn't lose it, he hid it from his wife."

"The rich don't think that way."

"Hrumph," Emma snorted. She hit the knocker three times.

Stella Sabolsky, also known as the Polish princess, opened the door.

"Emma, Mister Gustafson, what are you doing here?"

"Quality control check," I said. "Something new we're doing at the company. It will only take a few minutes."

Stella moved aside to let us in. She seemed puzzled.

We stepped into the foyer, a large, windowed room with Boston ferns, philodendrons and jade plants strategically placed for optimum sunlight.

"Where's Mr. Himmelman," I asked.

"He's in the recreation room, doing aerobics."

I pulled Emma aside and told her now would be a perfect time to check out the house.

"Stella, is there a security system?" I asked. She pointed to a closet door on the right side of the foyer. I nodded toward Emma. "Take Stella and do a quality control check on the first floor."

Following Roscoe

I took two steps at a time to the second floor. I pulled out a small writing pad and pencil to make a quick sketch of the upstairs layout. The bedroom at the right end of the hall was decorated in French provincial. Obviously Mrs. Himmelman's room. Two other bedrooms were sterile, probably guest rooms. Nothing in the two bathrooms of any interest. The bedroom at the other end of the hall had to be the money launderer's room. A massive oak bed sat entrenched and centered at the far wall. The naked Three Graces were painted on the massive headboard.

I checked each of the two end tables at bedside, looked behind paintings, in closets and any place I thought a wall safe might be concealed. Nothing. All the windows were wired for security, and I saw no cameras on the second floor. I finished my sketch and headed downstairs to see what Emma was up to.

I heard voices coming from the far end of the house, so I headed down the hall in that direction. A large living room was off to my left. The large palladium windows weren't traditionally suited for Tudor architecture, but they looked beautiful from inside. Green plants and artwork stood out against the white furniture. Had to be Mrs. Himmelman's influence on the decorator. The thump of music emanated from the room to my right, indicating where Mr. Himmelman was doing aerobics.

A large mahogany trestle dining table, with seating for twelve, sat in the middle of the next room to my left. The dark stained box-beam ceiling contrasted with the flowered damask wallpaper. The voices were coming from the kitchen straight ahead. Sunlight reflected off stainless steel appliances, cabinets and counters as I walked into what could have been an army mess hall.

Emma pointed to a rack of cookware. "You don't have to clean all those pots and pans do you?"

"Oh no, just damp mop the floor and take out the garbage."

Emma put her hands on her hips. "He make you take out garbage? That's not in your job description. Ain't that right, Mister G?"

I didn't want to lose a customer over a bag of garbage. I asked Stella, "Do you always take out the garbage?"

"No, just since Mrs. Himmelman left."

"Who takes it out the other six days?" Emma asked.

"The butler-driver."

"Butler-driver? What's that?" Emma asked. "He shine the old man's shoes while he be drivin'? Sound like a penny-pincher to me. Hidin' money and shit. I don't like this mutha, unh-uh."

"Does this driver live on the premises?" I asked Stella.

"Above the garage, out back."

Roscoe might find this information useful. "I'll arrange it so you won't have to take out the garbage anymore, Stella. Did he give you any other extra duties?"

"Sometimes I stop at the store on my way here and pick up groceries or underwear at Gabe's. He likes those light blue thongs."

Emma dropped her hands from her hips and turned her head away from us as if wondering if she had really heard what Stella had said. "Why, you dumb—"

I had to interrupt. "I'll take care of that, Stella. From now on, just perform your regular duties."

"Yeah," Emma said, "we handle mister slave-master. He'll be sorry he took advantage of you."

The three of us started down the hall toward the foyer.

"Let's check out the butler-driver's place," I said.

Emma reached for the door that the music emanated from.

"Don't go in there!" Stella said. "Mister Himmelman doesn't like to be disturbed when he's doing aerobics."

Emma has tunnel vision when her dander is up, and nothing was going to stop her from opening that door.

"Hmmph, doing aerobics," she said, and opened the door.

We all watched Mr. Himmelman rhythmically pelvic-thrusting the backside of a bent over young woman with blond hair. She was partially clothed in a French maid's costume. He wore a necktie and knee-high stockings. It looked like a set of 300-carat almonds dangled in a wrinkled sack between two skinny legs.

"OM my God!" Stella said, and covered her eyes. I stood, frozen.

"You must be Miss Aerobics," Emma said, planting her fists on her hips. "Stella said he was doin' aerobics."

Emma's comment snapped me out of shock. I grabbed her arm and ushered her down the hallway for a hasty escape. As I entered the foyer, I heard the skinny man scream something about unemployment checks.

Chapter 12

Emma needed a vehicle for her personal use and to haul supplies and equipment to job sites. She couldn't ask her neighbor, Mr. Cheatam, for another ride—she said he'd creeped her out the last time. Moldy, the bartender at the club, had once mentioned a place that rented used cars. That's where I was heading with Emma.

"Miss Aerobics, that's funny," I said.

"Yeah, I thought of it all of a sudden. He was doing her, so... I hope I didn't lose business for you."

"As far as I'm concerned, he can have the blond clean his house." I pulled my van into the used car rental lot.

Emma's eyes bugged out. "Ron's Rent-A-Rattletrap! You want me to drive a rattletrap?"

"They're perfectly safe, and besides, it's only until I clear up with the insurance company and get you another van." I parked in front of the office, a shiny aluminum sixteen-foot trailer.

Emma crossed her arms and her face settled into a pout. "I don't know 'bout this shit. I'll be looking good in a *new* conveyance."

A short, thin man who wore the clothes of a larger man, came out of the office to greet us. His face resembled that of a rodent, and he smiled through crooked, nicotine-stained buckteeth. A dark hairpiece barely covered what remained of his thin and graying hair.

"Is that Ron?" Emma asked. "He look like he be trapped. He even have a dead animal on his head."

Emma stayed in the van while I went over to meet Ron. I explained what I wanted, and he led me through a maze of venerable vehicles to a lime green 1995 GMC SLT four-door SUV with four-wheel drive. It was perfect for Emma. It had a rear hatchback for easy loading and unloading of supplies and equipment, and a roof rack for larger items. I followed the squirrelly little man into the trailer-office where I filled out the necessary papers. I submitted my plastic cash card. After we shook hands, Ron plucked a set of keys off a wall board and motioned for me to follow him.

"I'll bring your car over," he said, and scampered off into the hodgepodge of vehicles.

I told Emma, "He's bringing over your *temporary* transportation."

Ron parked the SUV next to us, turned off the engine, and slid out.

"That thing look like a giant lime," Emma said.

"It's a sport utility vehicle," I said. "A GMC."

"What that stand for, Grotesque Mossy-looking Car?"

"It has four-wheel drive too. You can safely drive in mud or snow."

Emma smiled. "It's one of them off-road buggies? Go in mud too?"

"That's right," Ron said, handing the keys to Emma, "and you're the pretty lady that'll be driving it."

"Harumph." Emma snatched the keys from squirrelly-man's hand.

"She's a sassy one, yes-siree, Bob," Ron said as Emma lurched the SUV out of the lot, kicking up gravel.

I shook hands with Ron and headed for home.

Milt Anderson

Pissmore greeted me as usual, his stubby tail wagging probably more from hunger than love. He bounced around my feet until I filled his bowl with his favorite mixture of dog food.

I knocked on the door to Roscoe's apartment three times before he answered.

"Whaddaya want?" He wore a white Pittsburgh Steelers robe and smelled of Old Spice.

"You got a couple of minutes? I have some information."

"I'm getting ready for my date with Georgeanne. And besides, I've got Morton's neuroma."

I didn't want to ask, but I had to get him out of his lair. "Okay, what's Morton's neuroma?"

"It's an inflamed nerve in the foot. And it hurts like hell."

"You've got plenty of time before your date, and besides, that's part of what I want to talk to you about. Come in the kitchen and take a load off your foot."

Roscoe reluctantly hobbled in and sat down at the kitchen table. I told him about the Himmelman experience. He seemed more interested in the butler-driver than anything else.

"Did Emma really say that to the aerobics instructor?" Roscoe asked. "She's got pluck." He looked at me. "What else you got?"

"Do you like chicken cacciatore?"

"I do. But you're not cooking, are you?"

"No, Mrs. Vanderslice is."

"I've got a date with Georgeanne tonight. Can't make it."

"Lieutenant Fahey is coming."

"Really? You talked her into coming for dinner?"

"That's right, the pretty redhead with green eyes."

Roscoe looked disappointed. "I screwed up the first date with Georgeanne because of that Aspergillosis thing I had. I can't miss this date."

Following Roscoe

Shit! I needed to somehow convince him to stay for dinner and show Mrs. Vanderslice that Roscoe isn't for her.

"She must be something. Is she worth it?"

"Absolutely. She's gorgeous. I call her gorgeous Georgeanne."

Things don't look good. He was infatuated with this dame. Why hadn't I seen this chick around? "What's her last name?"

"Watkins, Georgeanne Watkins."

"Watkins? Where does she live?"

"On Locust Avenue."

I couldn't believe what I was hearing. This might be the answer I was looking for. "Near the tennis court?"

"Right next to it. Why?"

Hallelujah, that's what I wanted to hear. And the timing couldn't have been more perfect. I wanted to jump for joy.

"It's a good thing you had that osis disease thing. And you better cancel your date tonight."

"Look here, Nephew...."

I let the hammer fall. "I went to school with George Watkins. He lived on Locust Avenue, next to the tennis court. And I heard—"

Roscoe held his head as if it was going to explode. "Don't tell me. Don't tell me. Don't tell me."

"I won't."

Roscoe picked up his cell phone.

Setting the kitchen table wasn't new to me. I'd managed in the kitchen for most of my life, but tonight was different. Mrs. Vanderslice and Lieutenant Fahey were coming to dinner. Roscoe would undoubtedly make a play for the good-looking and *younger* Coleen Fahey, leaving Aldine Vanderslice crushed and available. If Roscoe couldn't handle being five months younger than

Aldine, I would be glad to take the vacant place in her heart and in her bed.

Roscoe was still in his apartment, probably performing some elaborate primping procedure. I donned a black linen short-sleeved sport shirt and pleated khakis for the occasion.

Mrs. Vanderslice tapped the door with her foot, her arms supporting a tray that held two covered pans. I was taken aback by her appearance. She wore an Evgeni Malkin #71 Pittsburgh Penguins jersey over blue jeans.

"Is that the chicken cacciatore? Is there anything else?" I asked, thinking she might go back home to change her clothes.

"Yes, this is it." She limped across the kitchen on black and white sneakers, favoring her left foot. She placed the pans on the stove.

"I... uh, can I help you?"

Mrs. Vanderslice studied the place settings on the table. "No, everything looks perfect. You said a policewoman is coming?"

That same moment, I saw Lieutenant Fahey walking toward the front door. I dashed out and motioned her to the back-yard gate.

"This is the entrance we use," I called. She headed toward me. "Roscoe and I have separate apartments. The kitchen is a common area."

"I understand. You both like your privacy."

I didn't want to tell her how private Roscoe was. His secrets might reveal a sexual pervert of the highest order or a wacko former CIA agent.

I ushered the lieutenant to the kitchen door. She didn't look anything like a cop. She wore a brown scalloped moleskin top with boot-cut, five-pocket khaki jeans.

Pissmore greeted our guest with gusto. He hopped and danced around Fahey's feet, his stubby tail wagging. I dropped a few doggy treats into his bowl to arrest his enthusiasm.

"Oh, what a handsome English Bull! What's his name?"

"Pissmore." The look on her face begged an answer. "He drinks a lot of water. You have a dog?"

"Boston Terrier. His name's Popeye."

"Appropriate also."

I introduced Lieutenant Fahey to Mrs. Vanderslice.

The lieutenant's eyes slowly swept over Aldine's Pittsburgh Penguins attire. "I love chicken cacciatore. Is it your specialty?"

"Heavens no, I'm not even Italian, but I love to make ethnic dishes."

Uncle Roscoe marched into the kitchen in a camouflage outfit like an invading general. White letters that spelled *Franco's Italian Army* stood out against the hodgepodge of the shirt's greens and browns. Below the words, three stars and a small Italian flag were sewn on his right sleeve. Topping off his costume was an olive drab army helmet liner audaciously positioned askew on his head.

Lieutenant Fahey raised an eyebrow.

Aldine noticed the Lieutenant's bewilderment over Roscoe's outfit. "He's one of the many fans of Franco Harris, who played for the Steelers. They call themselves Franco's Army."

It probably looked to Fahey as if we were the twenty-first century's version of *The Addams Family*.

I waited for Roscoe to take off his helmet and seat himself. I pulled out a chair next to him for the lieutenant. I took my place on the other side of Roscoe. Aldine would have to sit next to me. I watched her carry a serving tray to the table.

"What's wrong with your foot?" Roscoe asked.

Why hadn't I asked her that when she hobbled into the kitchen?

"I think I have Freiberg's Disease," Aldine said. A warm smile spread across her face.

"Let me see your foot." Roscoe bent over and started to remove her sneaker.

What's up with Roscoe? I should be doing that.

"No, I don't think so," he said, massaging the ball of her foot. She winced when he touched an area between her toes. "Ah ha, looks like Morton's neuroma. Wear those ripple-soled shoes the basketball referees wear. It'll go away in a few days."

"Thank you, Roscoe. You're a wealth of information."

Aldine put her shoe back on, washed her hands at the sink and brought over a basket of sliced Italian bread. "Help yourself," she said as she served a portion of chicken cacciatore to Roscoe and then handed it to me to pass.

Roscoe squirmed a little in his chair, but managed to crack a faint smile. I hoped he wasn't smitten, but I couldn't really tell; the hypochondriac test wouldn't work with both women present.

"Colleen, how's the chicken?" I asked, putting the spotlight back on the auburn beauty.

"This is really tasty, Aldine. Did you add anything special to the recipe?"

"I used thyme, portabella mushrooms, and olive oil."

"What kind of olive oil?" Roscoe asked. You wouldn't think he'd be a health nut with all his drinking and carousing, but he watches his food and gulps down vitamins like they're going out of style.

"U.S. Grade A extra-virgin olive oil."

"That's the best," Roscoe said. "It has less than one percent acid."

"And what's more," Aldine said, "olive oil has olecanthal, a natural anti-inflammatory enzyme associated with reduced risk of stroke, heart disease, lung cancer and some forms of dementia."

"Really," Roscoe leaned forward. "Are you a nutritionist?"

Crap, the spotlight had shifted back to Aldine. I dug into a piece of chicken.

Aldine replied. "Not really. I watch what I eat and exercise to maintain excellent health and keep my body in shape."

I couldn't stop my eyes from scanning her body. Yes, your body is an excellent example, and I'd like to work out with you a few times a week.

"What kind of exercise?" Roscoe's gaze took in her figure while he chomped on a chicken leg.

Stifle yourself, Roscoe. You're supposed to be ogling the lieutenant.

"I do isometrics, aerobics, weight-training, yoga and outside activities like hiking and sky-diving."

Rats, this wasn't good. Roscoe lived and breathed airborne.

"Sky-diving? Really?" Roscoe almost choked on a piece of chicken.

"That sounds great," Fahey said. "I'd like to try parachuting some time."

"Why don't you go with Roscoe?" I suggested. "He was with the Eighty-Second Airborne Division. He's a master jumper and has HALO experience."

"What's halo?" Fahey asked.

Aldine spoke up. It's an acronym for High Altitude Low Opening, used primarily by special ops personnel."

Double rats, spotlight back on Aldine as evidenced by Roscoe's awed expression.

"That's too scary for me," Fahey said. "I'd rather go with Aldine, if that's not an imposition. We girls have to stick together."

That's good, I thought, Fahey would be with Mrs. Vanderslice instead of Roscoe. Maybe not so good for me because I wouldn't be with Aldine either... or was it Colleen. I was experiencing mixed feelings about these two women; my desires seemed to have been slightly reversed. I was deep in thought about this sensation when my phone rang.

Chapter 13

The phone interrupted the confusion I was feeling for the two women sitting at my dinner table. I plucked the receiver from its cradle and answered with a casual "Hello."

"I left a note on your door. It's important that you read it." The voice was a man's, but altered electronically.

"Who is this?"

"Read the note. If you don't want to end up like your friend, do what the note says." The line went dead.

"Holy shit!" I stared at the phone as if an answer to what was happening would suddenly appear on the small LCD screen.

"Who was that?" Roscoe sounded concerned.

"Someone just threatened me."

Fahey turned around in her chair. "What do you mean, threatened you?"

"I don't know. A man said to do what the note said or I'd end up like my friend."

"What note?" Roscoe asked.

I walked to the kitchen door and opened it. "He said it was on the door."

"Hold it," Roscoe said. "Use a rubber glove. Don't touch it with your bare hands." Colleen nodded approval.

Following Roscoe

I grabbed one of the disposable gloves I use to clean up Pissmore's surprises he leaves in the yard and pulled it on. I checked the door and its surrounding area, but found nothing. The front door, of course. Everyone uses the front door—except me.

"Who was it? Did you recognize his voice?" Colleen asked.

"No, he sounded like Darth Vader. Electronic thing."

I darted across the kitchen, dashed into my apartment and headed for the front entrance. My heart pounded as I approached the door. What if this nut is outside? What if he used the note to bait me into opening the door? What if he has a knife or a gun?

I hesitated at the door and then decided to peek through the picture window that looked out onto Morganza Street. I lifted an edge of the drapes and peered outside. Nothing out of the ordinary except old man Dravechi sweeping his sidewalk while dressed in his robe and pajamas. He's usually sitting on his porch sunning his bared chest. I checked the small double-hung window facing Torrance Street, but I saw no one. It seems as if everyone in the burg stops what they're doing precisely at dinner time and heads for the table.

I inched open the door, carefully inspecting around its perimeter, checking for wires or traps because this guy likes explosives. Seeing nothing, I checked around the sills and threshold as I opened the door farther. The porch and everything on it seemed to be in order. I took a step onto the porch and peeked around the door to see if a note was tacked to it. There was, but not with a tack.

Aldine held her hand over her mouth in horror, Colleen jumped to her feet and Roscoe motioned for me to bring the note to him. It was covered with blood as was the arrow it was attached to.

Roscoe said to Colleen, "Do you have swabs and evidence bags?"

"No," she said. "Not with me. That sure looks like blood."

"It certainly does." Roscoe got up from the table. "Don't touch anything. I'll be right back." He disappeared into his apartment.

"Oh my God," Aldine said. "Who would do such a thing? What does the note say?"

Fahey and I studied the note. Blood covered most of the writing, making it illegible. Fahey pointed to a spot on the perimeter of the paper.

"That looks like a lacquer of some sort," she said.

"Why would someone put lacquer on a note?" Mrs. Vanderslice asked.

Roscoe had walked into the kitchen with a small package and said, "Because it protects the writing underneath and he wanted Augie to read it."

"Why lacquer?" I asked. "Why not put the note in a plastic bag or cover with transparent packing tape?"

"Fingerprints," Fahey said. "This guy is smart. He doesn't want to be discovered."

"That remains to be seen." Roscoe pulled out a number of swabs and plastic bags from the package. "These idiots always leave behind evidence that will catch up with them. Don't touch the arrow; there may be fingerprints on it. Just take a sample from the edge of the note. Your people will take care of the rest."

Roscoe took a blood sample from the paper with a swab and put it in a plastic bag. He said to Fahey, "Fill out the information and don't forget to seal it."

"Aren't you smart, Roscoe," Aldine said. "You really know what you're doing."

Triple rats. I'm the one in mortal danger, and Roscoe was scoring Aldine points.

While Fahey was busy writing on the evidence bag, Roscoe took another blood sample and bagged it, slipping the specimen into his shirt pocket.

"That arrow's kind of short, isn't it?" Aldine asked.

"It's for a crossbow," Roscoe said. "A powerful hunting bow."

Fahey bagged the arrow with the attached note, picked up the swab specimen and headed for the door. Aldine followed her to the door.

"I'll let you know what forensics finds out," Fahey said, and left.

"Why'd you take another blood sample?" I whispered to Roscoe.

"I want to compare it to the sample we found in Frank's office."

"What are you two guys talking about?" Aldine asked.

"Oh, nothing," I said.

Roscoe asked, "Who do you know that has access to or owns a crossbow?"

"I'm going to find out," I said as I headed for the door. "You two can stay here and figure out who the bad guy is."

Roscoe followed me outside and closed the door behind him, apparently to keep Aldine from hearing what he was about to say. "By the way, I called Norman Jacobs before dinner. He said Lieutenant Fahey was in the pharmacy picking up a prescription for her mother the day we were there. She also borrowed the key to Frank's office from him."

"But she came straight in from her car. I watched her."

"She had to ask her mother a question but left her phone in the car. She went outside to make the call. Is that when you saw her?"

"Yeah. That's when I saw her. She was on the phone."

I'm glad we no longer had to wonder if she was on the wrong side.

Moldy looked like a runner in the starting block, waiting for the gun's report to launch him from paranoid Perry Sanders and his perverted sense of reality. Bullshit was hanging heavy in the air. Perry's wife, Grace, was quietly entertaining Captain Morgan.

"What's up, Mold?" My greeting was as good as the starter's pistol. Moldy could hardly contain his enthusiasm as he strode over to me.

"Perry still on the big brother mailmen conspiracy?"

Moldy smiled as he popped the lid from a bottle of I.C. Light. "No, he's into vitamins now."

"Vitamins?"

"Believe it or not. Grace heard at the beauty salon that vitamins are being sold that are laced with disease-causing agents, and—get this—the American Medical Association is supporting it."

"That's really off the wall," I said and took a pull from the bottle.

"She claims doctors and hospitals are making windfall profits with all the new sicknesses."

"It's amazing what you hear at the beauty salon." I noticed Reba Tuttle at the far end of the bar sitting next to her husband, Tommy. "Where's Archie and Doris Brown?"

"They left early. Doris had a rehearsal for the school play."

Reba knew I checked her out. She'd wait a while, turn her head and smile, but I wouldn't be looking. The hell with her. "What's with Tommy 'Two Shots'? I see an empty shot glass in front of him, and he's still upright."

At that moment, Tommy raised his finger signifying that he wanted another shot. Moldy grabbed a fifth of Jack Daniels and headed in that direction. Moldy's back blocked my view of Tommy, but Reba's face hovered over Moldy's shoulder. A smile and a wink. Shit, she got me again, that teasing bitch. She was starting to piss me off.

"It shouldn't take long for Tommy to do a header on the bar," Moldy said, walking up to me. "When Jack Daniels hits his brain, lights out."

"It's amazing that exactly two shots will put another knot on his forehead."

Moldy said, "Must be something freakish about his metabolism and liquor's effect on it. Maybe Doris can get a science teacher at her school to do a study on Tommy."

Following Roscoe

"They can call it Tommy Tuttle's Timely Tribulation."

"I don't think that will be a best seller."

I heard a thunk. We both turned to see Tommy's face smooshed on the bar. Reba kept watching *General Hospital* on the Soap Opera Channel.

"Nope," I said. "Nobody wants to be in Tommy's shoes. Or my shoes, for that matter."

Moldy leaned forward. "What's up, brother?"

I told him about dinner and the threatening note attached to the arrow.

"Lieutenant Fahey, huh? I know her. She's a doll," Moldy said, smiling. I wasn't. "Sorry, I couldn't help it. I didn't mean to trivialize the threat. Have any idea who it was?"

"No, but the police are checking the blood and the arrow for evidence. Know any bow hunters?"

"Quite a lot, really. Bow hunting is increasing in popularity."

"Shit, that's a bunch of hunters."

"Maybe the cops can tell something about the arrow. Some of those hunting broadheads are expensive. Maybe locate a dealer."

"Not from this arrow. It had a cheap target point on it." I took a big swig of beer in resignation, realizing that the arrow tip would be useless. And then I remembered that Roscoe said the arrow was from a crossbow.

"That narrows it down a bit," Moldy said. "Only man I know uses a crossbow is Harry 'The Hat' Briscoe. He's an odd duck, all right, but I don't see him as somebody who would threaten anyone, especially with a bloody note on an arrow."

"I'm gonna have a talk with him anyway. What's with the tag 'The Hat'?"

"He's always wearing a hat that seems to match what he's involved in. An umbrella hat when it's raining, Steelers hat when he watches football, Pirates hat when he watches—"

"I get the picture. Where does he live?"

Chapter 14

I had turned off route 711 onto legislative route 2017 fifteen minutes ago. The two-lane blacktop road turned to dirt, and the winding, uneven road narrowed. A grove of tall walnut trees covered the slopes of a deep hollow, blocking out the sun. A drowsy feeling hung over the land as if a spell had been put on it by some evil entity. I thought of Washington Irving's *The Legend of Sleepy Hollow* and subconsciously caught myself looking into the forest for a horse... with a headless rider. A few minutes later I exited the shadowy valley and drove up to Harry "The Hat" Briscoe's log house.

    Sunshine highlighted the white chinking between the logs of the two-story home and attached garage. Rhododendrons and azaleas snuggled around the house, and a bridal-wreath hedge circumscribed the perimeter of the lot. A small tractor sat parked in the open door of a green aluminum out building. I eased up the gravel driveway and parked next to a Toyota Land Cruiser. The steps creaked as I mounted the porch. As I reached for the door, it opened.

    When I had driven through the dark and menacing hollow, I had conceived a mental picture of Ichabod Crane, which dissolved when Harry "The Hat" Briscoe appeared. He was a short, chubby man wearing a red-

Following Roscoe

and-brown hunting hat that partially covered his large, bald head. He had enormous eyes, and a little pug nose nestled between round, pudgy cheeks.

"What do you want?" His mouth was elflike. I didn't notice a chin. With the hunting cap, he was a ringer for the cartoon character Elmer Fudd.

"Eh… what's up, doc?" I couldn't help myself. His wide forehead furrowed when he frowned. I composed myself. "Mister Briscoe, Moldy told me about you."

"Moldy! Why didn't you say you knew Moldy?"

"He's a friend of mine."

Harry reached to shake my hand. "He's a vewy vewy good fwiend of mine also."

Holy crap! He sounded like Elmer Fudd too.

"Come on in, take a load off," Harry said, gesturing toward the door.

I entered what might be described as a mountain man's bachelor pad from the 1930s. The dingy room had only two small windows and two oil lamps for illumination. The log walls were roughhewn. The floor appeared to be a mixture of cement and dirt tamped to a hard, uneven surface. The style of furniture could be called handmade logs and tree limbs. Three chairs and a couch were covered with cushions and pillows that looked like they came from a flea market. An elk and two deer heads were mounted over a massive cobblestone fireplace above a railroad tie mantle. Animal heads covered the walls like macabre wallpaper. Bear, more deer, wolves, coyotes—you name it—their final stop was at Harry's stuffing shop.

Looking around the room, I asked, "Who's your decorator, Jeffrey Dahmer?"

"He wasn't a spowtsman. He's just a plain murderer."

"And you're a sportsman and a prolific hunter."

Harry nodded. "Have a seat." He pointed to an uncomfortable looking chair made from tree branches tied together with rawhide straps. He sat in a similar chair.

I sat down. I felt knurls on the wood dig into my back, my ass saved only by a throw pillow.

"Moldy said you're the guy to see about crossbows."

Harry leaned forward on his chair. "What do you want to know?"

"An arrow was shot into my door, and I need to find out who shot it."

"How do you know the awwow came from a cwossbow?"

Elmer was back. Harry seemed to fall out of character on occasion. "My uncle Roscoe said a twenty-two-inch arrow had to come from a crossbow."

"Uncle Woscoe is entirely cowwect. A cwossbow is a powewful weapon. My Quad Four Hundwed shoots an awwow at thwee-hundwed-fowty-five feet a second."

"Know anyone who has a cwossbow? I mean crossbow."

Harry thought for a minute. "Only two around these parts. Seems hunting's become a lazy man's sport. All they do is hike in the woods and sit in a tree stand."

I wondered why a bow hunter couldn't also sit in a tree. My concentration wandered to the tree stump next to me that served as an end table. It held a stuffed rabbit's head, mounted on a can of Giant Eagle carrots.

I pointed to Bugs Bunny. "Did you hunt down this trophy all by yourself?"

"That wabbit was my enemy. He and his whole clan waided my garden. Ate every carrot. I had to get rid of the wabbit wascal. Now he can't eat any more carrots."

"What about those two men that have a crossbow?"

"Ol' Jim Lenio has one, but banged up his leg last week when he fell off his roof. His son stops by from time to time and takes care of his meals and whatnot."

"Who's the other guy?"

"Boyd Hanson. Can't be him either, he's in jail. Got caught selling poached deer meat."

"Nobody else?"

"Nope, that's the only two I know of."

Following Roscoe

"Either ol' Jim's son used his father's crossbow or someone stole Boyd Hanson's."

"Maybe," Harry said. "Could be someone bought one and I don't know about it."

"I didn't think of that. I'll have to check it out."

I stood up and Harry followed suit. I shook his hand.

"Thanks for the information," I said and headed for the door. Harry opened it.

"Be caweful," Harry said in an ominous tone. "Sleepy Hollow is bewitched."

"Sleepy Hollow? That hollow I drove through is called Sleepy Hollow?"

"Yep, been called that since the early fifties when a hunter found Robert Stone and his brother, Flint, gutted and decapitated."

Goose bumps jumped onto my skin. How could this be? I'm an adult male and shouldn't be afraid of fairy tales. And who would name their son *Flint* Stone?

"Did they catch the person who did it?"

"No. Some say a bear did it. Some say..."

"Some say what?"

"Some say it's an evil Indian curse. Bad things seem to happen in that hollow."

My goose bumps got bigger. "Is there another way back to route 711?"

Harry pointed in the opposite direction I had come. "That road will take you twenty extra miles."

"That's too far," I said, and headed for my van.

Harry waved from his porch and smiled, the sunlight glistened off the remaining tooth that wasn't nicotine stained. Must have been a new cap. His right eye also sparkled, like the effects used on a villain in a horror movie. My goose bumps were stretched to the limit, and I felt the hair on my neck stand straight up.

I hopped in the van and drove off, feeling dread around me. The sound of pebbles pinging off the undercarriage intensified as I tramped on the accelerator, wanting to quickly put the hollow in my rear view mirror.

My nervousness grew. I caught myself looking into the deep dark woods. That's when something plowed into the left side of the van with a terrible crunch.

I fought to control the vehicle, but the force of the impact sent the van over an embankment and into a tree. My head bounced off the steering wheel. I thought I heard the sound of a galloping horse, but after shaking the cobwebs from my head, I came to the conclusion that it had to have been a car's faulty muffler. A horse couldn't knock a van off the road.

I got out and checked the damage. It looked like the front end had gotten a wedgie. Steam wafted up; anti-freeze dripped to the ground. A fractured tree limb poked into the radiator.

I tried to call Roscoe on my cell, but there was no reception in the deep hollow. That seemed to be a good excuse to get the hell out of there.

I jogged until I exited the hollow about two miles later. My goose bumps disappeared as I entered the sunlight, gasping. My cell now had three bars. I called Roscoe to come get me.

Chapter 15

I looked at my watch. It had only been seventeen minutes since I called Roscoe, but it felt more like an hour. I sat on a large sun-baked rock. Its warmth was soothing compared to the cool, damp, and dangerous valley I had escaped from. Looking back at the hollow, it seemed like a monstrous throat: deep, dark and deadly.

On the road in the distance, a black speck surrounded by a cloud of yellowish-brown dust came into view. Within a minute the Lincoln MKZ skidded to an abrupt stop in front of me, the accompanying dust sailing past and leaving me in its wake. I was shaking off the debris when the driver's window slowly descended.

"You owe me a car wash," Roscoe said.

"I'll take care of it. What took you so long? I could have been ripped apart by some fiendish animal or the huge beast that knocked me off the road."

"Get in. Let's go check out the damage."

"I'll wait here."

"What's the matter, Nephew, some creature got your drawers in a bunch?"

I really didn't want to go back to the hollow. "You got your gun?"

"I have a few."

I reluctantly slid into the passenger's seat and locked the door. Roscoe created more dust as he sped away, down into Sleepy Hollow. Within minutes we were in the area where I was rammed off the road.

"Over there." I pointed to a crushed section in the brush.

Roscoe got out and bounded down the slope into the thicket. He returned a few minutes later. "Your van will have to be winched out and towed to a repair shop."

"I figured that. What else?"

"That beast that knocked you off the road will have to get a new paint job."

"What?"

"The 'fiendish animal' left red paint on your van."

Of course. A car had hit me. "Red paint? Frank has a red car."

"Chrysler?"

"Yeah, how did you know?"

Roscoe pulled a piece of the Chrysler's insignia from his pocket.

"Holy crap. Do you think that came from Frank's car?"

"Seems logical," Roscoe said. "The person who's responsible for Frank's disappearance probably has his car."

"Maybe that's good. The police won't have much trouble tracking down a red Chrysler with a damaged front end."

"It's likely gone already," Roscoe said. "In a river or a lake by now."

This person was stepping up the threats. This one could have been deadly. I was at a loss for words. I didn't know what to do or think next. I looked at Roscoe for an answer.

Roscoe said, "We need to check Frank's house first. There has to be some clue that we can use. And after that I have another person for you to interview."

"Who?"

"Freddy Moldonado. Frank was responsible for Freddy spending three months in prison for insurance fraud. He got out three weeks ago."

"Did you finish going over all the stuff you photographed in Frank's office?"

"Almost."

On the drive to Frank's house, Roscoe complained about leptospirosis. I heard all I wanted to hear about headaches, jaundice, red eyes, abdominal pain and diarrhea, all of which can be attributed to drinking too much alcohol. We finally arrived at Balazia Avenue and pulled into Frank's driveway at 7:55 p.m.

"Wait here until I wave you in." Roscoe jumped out of the car.

Overwhelmed from hearing all about Roscoe's ailments and self-diagnosis, I had forgotten to warn Roscoe about Mrs. Nisnanski, the neighborhood watch sergeant who lived next door.

Roscoe was a few steps from Frank's door when I rolled down the window to warn him that she might perceive him as another prowler, as she had with me. That's when I noticed the sergeant, with broom at port arms, waddling toward Roscoe. The same two pigs were trying to escape from underneath the same flowered shift she had worn on Monday. Only the babushka appeared to be different. She was closing in on Roscoe and raised the broom for an overhead swat.

Roscoe must have heard her coming because he turned around. He raised his hand in a halting motion and forcefully said, "Whoa, Nellie." She stopped and lowered her broom, thinking Roscoe was an acquaintance of hers. I wouldn't have thought that one of Roscoe's familiar expressions would stop a charging she-devil.

"Do I know you?" she asked.

"I'm a friend of Frank Pallone. I dropped him off a couple of weeks ago and noticed you tidying up your yard.

I was in a hurry and... well, I didn't have time to... I wanted to... ah... ask him for your phone number. He hasn't answered my calls."

Nellie dropped her broom. She looked dumbstruck, flabbergasted.

"I didn't mean to be forward, but—"

"That's okay," Nellie said, reaching into her shift. She pulled out one of her neighborhood watch ID cards. She leaned forward and, with a trembling hand, offered it to Roscoe. "Here, take this."

Roscoe accepted the card and looked at it. "My name's Robert Jefferies, Nellie. I'd like to call you some time. If you're available."

I couldn't believe what I was hearing. Nellie might melt into a large blob right on Frank's lawn if Roscoe kept up the bullshit. Nellie gushed a *golly gee* smile and lowered her head, her cheeks flushed. I slumped down in the passenger seat. I couldn't quash Roscoe's performance by having the pig lady recognize me.

"Oh yes," she gushed. "I'll make sure I'm available."

"That's wonderful. If there's nothing else, I've got to pick up some important papers for a court date. I've been trying to reach him but... Anyway, Frank gave me the key to his house a couple months ago. He said if he wasn't available, I was to pick up the folder and bring it to court. The trial is tomorrow."

"Oh, okay, if that's what Frank said."

"You're doing a good job with the watch thing. You're very vigilant. I'll tell Frank you're taking good care of his property and the neighborhood."

Nellie blushed with pride.

Roscoe waited for Nellie to head for home before pulling his little gadget from his pants pocket. He quickly opened the door and waved to Nellie who had turned around and stopped. She waved to the possibility of a new beginning. Roscoe picked up the newspapers that had spilled onto the porch and pulled the mail from the mailbox.

I waited for Nellie to disappear into her house before scrambling to the front door. I slipped into the empty living room. I heard noises down the hallway and followed them to Frank's den.

Roscoe stood next to Frank's desk, holding a destroyed laptop computer. He tossed a pair of rubber gloves to me. "Put these on."

"Is that leptospirosis thing still with you, or did Nellie's presence turn you on?"

Roscoe glared at me. "Yeah, still have it. Must have been that babushka that turned me off." He pointed to Frank's desktop computer. The motherboard on the computer's tower had been yanked out and broken in half. The hard drive was missing.

"Looks like someone doesn't want Frank to use his computers."

"That's not all." Roscoe gestured for me to follow him. Frank's bedroom was across the hall. "This person also doesn't want Frank in the P.I. business."

Scrawled in what appeared to be blood on the light green wall were the words: *Get another job—or else.*

"This guy gets right to the point."

"But it doesn't make sense," Roscoe said. He pulled a cotton swab from his jacket pocket and took a sample of the dark red splotch.

I looked first to the den and then to the bedroom. "I don't understand."

Roscoe pointed to the stack of mail and newspapers he had placed on Frank's desk. "The last time Frank was seen was on Friday, right?"

"That's right."

"And the newspapers in the door were from Monday, Tuesday and today." "Correct."

"Then the perpetrator had to have left his macabre message on Sunday."

"I don't follow."

"Let me ask you a question. If you had broken in Monday, Tuesday, or today, there would have been papers in the door, right? And when you opened the door they would fall to the ground. So the question is, do you put them inside the house or take time when you leave to put them back between the doors?"

I thought about this for a minute. "I'd probably kick them inside to get them out of my way."

"Why wouldn't you put them back when you leave?"

"I wouldn't take the chance, I wouldn't have time."

"Exactly." Roscoe pointed toward the living room. A folded newspaper was lying next to the door. "Saturday's paper was, in fact, in the house, supporting your theory that the intruder kicked it out of the way. And that's why the intruder came on Sunday."

"Okay, but—"

"But why would this person break in on Sunday when Frank went missing on Friday night?"

"I hadn't thought of that. I see what you mean. It doesn't make sense. The person who abducted Frank wouldn't come back to leave a threatening message... unless there were two separate incidents, with two different people."

"That's right. Perpetrator number one abducts Frank probably from his office where we found blood, and perpetrator number two, unaware of number one's crime, breaks in and tears up his house and leaves a threatening message."

It would take some time to interpret all the information. I asked, "Why couldn't Sunday's intruder have bypassed the front door and come in from another entrance?"

"The front door was jimmied and he left a trail." Roscoe pointed to what appeared to be footprints on the carpet in the living room.

I followed Roscoe into the living room. He knelt down and picked up what looked like sawdust. He gathered some of the flakes and dropped them into a plastic bag.

"Maybe the evidence we picked up will shed some light on Frank's disappearance. Now let's get the hell out of here." Roscoe cracked open the door and peered out.

Following Roscoe

"She's standing in her doorway," he said. "Wait here. I'll create a diversion. When there's an opportunity, sneak out to the car."

I watched Roscoe stride toward Mrs. Niznanski's house. Nellie greeted him as if he had just returned from a long overseas battle campaign. She tried to wrap her arms around him. Roscoe parried her initial advance, but she continued to press on. When the contest escalated and the combatants looked like they were auditioning for *Dancing With the Stars*, I crept out of the house and cautiously tiptoed to the Lincoln and slid into the back seat.

Roscoe finally broke away from Nellie's clutches and sprinted to the car, Nellie in hot pursuit. He jumped in and started the Lincoln in what seemed like the same motion. I wondered how he became so adept at this escape procedure.

Roscoe shifted into reverse and stomped on the gas. The tires squealed, producing a cloud of white smoke. He braked and turned the wheel at the same time, putting us on Balazia Avenue headed in the right direction. Nellie was standing on her lawn, her hands on her hips.

"That was close," I said. "If Nellie would have recognized me, and had given your description to the police, the lieutenant would have hauled us both in for questioning."

"Well, she didn't, Nephew."

"Thank goodness for your smooth talk. I'll feel better after a few beers. Drop me off at the club."

Moldy was bent over the cooler, stocking it with beer when I walked into the bar. Two empty cases sat on the floor. Two full ones waited their turn. Must be a tough night; he usually stocks in the afternoon.

"What's up, Mold?"

Moldy turned around. First surprise then delight crossed his face. "Just a minute," he said. He kicked the empty cases out of his way and closed the cooler doors. He popped off the cap of an I.C. Light and slid it in front of me. "One of those days."

    I lowered my voice. "Paranoid Perry anxious again?"

    "Yeah, he's talking about members of his coven."

    "Coven? What the hell?"

    "Yeah, coven. He joined one a couple weeks ago. Said he wanted to learn their spells and whatever else bullshit he could use to protect him from the *other side*."

    "Sounds reasonable. For him."

    "Then Archie 'Bunker' Brown started. He told Perry that men couldn't be witches. That's when the argument broke out."

    "Did Doris Jean correct Archie?"

    "She did and that enraged Perry."

    "Why? She sided with Perry."

    "That's just it. He figured she was trying to pull a fast one, that she was really against him."

    "Again, sounds reasonable. What did Grace have to say?"

    "Captain Morgan put a restraining order on her mouth."

    I peered around Moldy's shoulder to get a look at Grace. Her head was on the bar next to her drink. And then I looked to see if Tommy "Two Shots" Tuttle was in the same position. To my surprise, he wasn't. In fact, it looked like he was trying to listen to what we were saying. I whispered to Moldy, "No shots today?"

    Moldy held up one finger.

    "Hey, Moldy," Tommy said, raising his empty shot glass.

    Moldy shuffled off with a bottle of Jack Daniels. Tommy's wife, Reba, continued staring at the TV, oblivious to Tommy or the second shot of whiskey that would deny him the rest of the evening. I didn't understand it. If I had a wife that beautiful, even though she was younger than me, I wouldn't put myself into a stupor every night of the week.

Moldy rejoined me after serving Tommy. He asked me if I had any new information on Frank.

I said, "You read about Emma's van in the newspaper and the threatening call with the arrow, right? That was yesterday. Today I was plowed off the road in Sleepy Hollow after leaving Harry 'The Hat' Briscoe's house."

"Someone really has it in for you and Emma. Why Emma?"

"Someone made a mistake. Our vans are identical, and she was parked in front of my house. The dynamite was meant for my van."

THUNK.

Moldy and I looked in the direction of the noise. Two Shot's head was on the bar. Reba's eyes hadn't left the TV screen.

Moldy asked, "What are the police doing?"

"Fahey took the arrow and a blood sample, but I haven't heard anything yet."

"Who would do such a thing? You don't have any enemies. Must be Frank. He should have a ton of people after his ass. Do you have any suspects?"

I couldn't tell him about breaking into Frank's office and finding the file with important papers in his safe, so I made up a story.

"Frank got the goods on Fat Freddy Moldonado for insurance fraud. Freddy got out of prison three weeks ago. I heard through the grapevine that Freddy said he hoped Frank choked to death."

"Fat Freddy, huh? I wouldn't want to mess with him. He must weigh four hundred pounds. If he sat on you, it's lights out. Your eyes would pop out and shoot across the room."

"I hope that won't happen. Do you know where he lives?"

"Off Beck's Run Road. Montraver Plan. It's a big white house. Can't miss it."

Chapter 16

Back in the day when I actually worked for a living, waking up on a Thursday felt like the beast was behind me and I had to tolerate one more day before a celebratory two or three hours at Como's Bar after work.

The same feeling enveloped me this morning, but I decided to release my tensions later tonight at the club instead. What had put me in this mood? A she-devil watch sergeant had attacked me at Frank's house; someone stuck a bloody threatening note to my door with an arrow; somebody in Frank's car rammed me off the road in Sleepy Hollow; and my van was in Wince's garage being repaired, leaving me without transportation. On top of that, I faced the unenviable task of interviewing Fat Freddy Maldonado, who had motive in Frank's disappearance and could be the person at the root of my problems.

I showered and shaved, then dressed in Dockers, a sport shirt and running shoes. I called Emma and asked her to pick me up. When I explained what happened to the van, her only words were: "Nuh ah and uh-huh."

Pissmore greeted me when I entered the kitchen. He ran to his empty doggy dish, his stub of a tail wagging, his stocky body quivering. Roscoe had dressed the mighty mutt in a Pirates doggy sweater. Dressed in a similar sweater, Roscoe sat at the table eating a taco.

"Pirate game tonight?" I asked as I poured Pissmore's favorite mixture into his bowl.

"Yep. Double-header."

"Going to the game?"

"Naw, I think I have an ulcer. It would be agonizing to watch them lose two decisions in the same night." Roscoe dangled his car keys at me. "You can drop me off at Ed's Electronics Store this afternoon."

"Thanks, but Emma is picking me up. I'll rent a temporary ride at Ron's place." I didn't want to tell Roscoe the real name of the business—Ron's Rent-A-Rattletrap—because he would insist I take the Lincoln, and I didn't want to experience Roscoe's wrath if he discovered a scratch after I had driven it.

"Emma's coming? When? Do I have time to change?"

"She's not coming in. She said she'd wait in her car for me, and if you so much as stuck your head out the door, she'd lay rubber."

"She's still in a mood, huh? Tell her that I could calm her down. Put her in Roscoe's love mood and on deck to hit the home run."

As Roscoe mused over the possibility, his lips spread into a smile. But Roscoe would have to calm Emma down to the point of unconsciousness to get close to first base with her.

"What are you doing this morning?" My question seemed to evaporate his reverie.

"I have samples to test," he said.

"Blood samples from the arrow and Frank's bedroom?"

"And the blood and grease from Frank's office and the sawdust from Frank's home."

"I forgot about those. Where do you go for the testing?"

"I'll test them right here." Roscoe pointed to the door of his apartment.

"You have equipment to test all that shit?"

"Digital electronics, microchips, nano-technology. Everything's getting smaller."

In the six months Roscoe had lived with me, it seemed that I discovered something new about him every day, but only the information he let escape—his secrets remain closely held.

"What else do you have behind that door? I've seen packages in plain brown wrappers in the mailobox. The return address read Pornocopia Village, California. I wonder what—"

"Never mind, nephew. All medicinal products... and legal. By the way, you going to see that Fat Freddy guy?"

"After I rent the transportation."

Roscoe must have noticed some trepidation in my answer. "You look nervous. I wouldn't worry too much about Fat Freddy."

"Why not? He has motive to hate Frank, and I hear he's connected."

"He's connected all right. Connected to the dinner table. Take it from me, a guy that fat has to be lazy. And a lazy guy doesn't exert energy cranking a crossbow. He uses a pistol with a two-pound trigger pull." Roscoe looked at me as if I didn't believe him.

"Be careful, though. He may lose his temper and sit on you."

When I thought the interview with Freddy looked brighter, Roscoe said, "Oh, by the way, I came across another person of interest last night when I was going over Frank's papers. Name's Duratz. Gino Duratz."

"What's he all about?"

"Take care of Moldonado first. I'll fill you in later."

Emma pulled into the rental car lot. Before she could put the SUV in park, "Rattletrap" Ron bounded out of his trailer. His pace slowed and his salesman smile turned sour when he recognized the lime green 1995 GMC.

"Is everything all right?" he asked.

Before I could answer, Emma jumped into the conversation. "Look at my face. Do I look happy? Peoples think this heap is a float in the Rose Parade. Big green thing. Look like a humongous lime. And it's old. I don't look good in old."

I interrupted Emma before she worked herself to a state of justifiable homicide. "The GMC's fine. I need a vehicle. Mine's in the shop."

Ron's sour face turned into a nicotine-stained smile. Emma sat in the SUV with crossed arms as Ron paraded me through the muggy eighty-five-degree garden of rattletrap clunkers until I had seen all of them.

"There's nothing here I really like, Ron."

"What do you like? I have some models coming in tomorrow."

"Something newer, maybe a Lincoln. My uncle has a MKZ and I really like it."

"I have a black one coming in at four o'clock. It's three years old."

"Perfect. Hold it for me. I'll be back," I said, extending my arm.

Ron shook my hand with such gusto that his hairpiece turned sideways. I walked back to the lime-green car wondering if I had made a mistake. Going to Fat Freddy's could end up getting complicated. I asked Emma to drive because I needed her company and her support.

"What's he smiling about?" Emma asked as I slid into the passenger seat. "You ain't got no conveyance. And I wouldn't smile like that if I had those buck teeth. He look like a groundhog that smokes too much."

"I can pick up a car tomorrow."

"What kind?"

"An MKZ."

"What the hell's a MKZ, a German military vehicle?"

"No, it's ah... a Lincoln."

"A Lincoln! You're going to drive a Lincoln and I'll be stuck with this parade float?"

"It's only temporary. You'll get your van back."

"And what'll you be driving, a Cadillac?"

"What kind of van would you like? You can pick it out yourself, okay?"

"Now that's more like it," she said, putting the gearshift into drive. "Back to the barn?"

"No, I have to interview someone."

"Awesome. I'm good at interrogation. I can squeeze the truth out of anyone, like crushing a grape. Who is this person that hides the truth?"

"Fat Freddy Moldonado. Frank got the goods on him for defrauding an insurance company. Got out of prison three weeks ago. Is he a client?"

"Nope. How we getting in? We can't do the quality control check like we did at Himmelman's."

The proverbial light bulb went on above my head. "Head to River Street."

"What's down there, besides stinky fish?"

"Wince's Body Shop. My van's there."

"Is it fixed already?"

"No, I want to get the magnetic advertisements for Desperate Domestics."

"And?"

"And put them on this GMC."

Emma looked perplexed.

"We'll knock on Fat Freddy's door and say we'll give him a free estimate on our maid service. And while I'm talking to Freddy and trying to weasel information out of him about Frank, you can browse around and make a sketch of the house."

"That's smart, Mister G. You actually should be running this business." Emma seemed delighted at her impertinence.

Chapter 17

Beck's Run Road ran from Thornbush Point on the Mon River through Monview to Archerville. At Polish Hill we turned into the Montraver Plan, a circle of eighty homes built in the early 1940s on Karl Bergenstedt's farm. Twenty years ago, Fat Freddy Moldonado had bought the original farmhouse from Karl's great grandson. A hodgepodge of weathered, old cedar shingles covered the large sixteen-room house, giving it the appearance of the Addams Family mansion on the sixties TV show. We drove onto a semi-circle of tamped red dog slag in front of the house, a futile attempt at constructing a governor's drive.

    The steps and porch creaked as we approached the front door. I raised my hand to knock as the door slowly creaked open. I expected Lurch to greet us, but an enormous woman filled the doorway. She wore a bright red-and-green flowered shift that looked frightening similar to the one Mrs. Niznanski wore the night she battered me with a broom. She also wore sneakers, but the babushka was absent. Close-cropped, gray hair covered her head. Her eyes were wild and penetrating, her lips blood red.

"May I help you?" Her canine teeth, or cuspids as the dentists refer to them, were so long they overlapped her bottom teeth.

I introduced myself and Emma and explained our offer of a free estimate of maid service. The wide smile on her face indicated we had just made her day.

"Come on in," she said. "My name's Freda. This is a pretty big house. It'll take a lot to clean it."

We stepped into the foyer. A wide staircase on the right rose twelve feet to the second floor. Potted plants of different varieties, mostly dead, dotted the room. The carpet was threadbare.

Emma ran her finger over the surface of a corner table, leaving a shiny trail in the dust. "Uh huh," she said. "This table's oak. Looks like butternut with all this dust on it."

"We had to let our last maid go some time ago."

Emma looked at her finger. "About two years ago?"

"Poor woman. She had a drinking problem," Freda said. "What a terrible hostess I am. Can I offer you a lemonade?"

"No, thank you," I said, not wanting to put anything from this house in my mouth.

Emma said. "Lemonade sounds great."

"I'll be right back." Freda lumbered off to the kitchen.

Emma waited until Freda was out of earshot. "Tell me again we're not gonna do this house. It's a nightmare."

"Hell no. We're not going to be involved with this house. They need more than a maid here."

Emma nodded in agreement. "She could tie mops and brushes to her behind and samba around the place. Hire a gardener for the heavy stuff, shoveling and what not."

Mrs. Moldonato walked into the foyer carrying a *Lord of the Rings* glass. I still have one from a 1991 Burger King promotion. "Here's your lemonade, dearie. Enjoy." She crooked her finger at me and said, "Follow me."

Following Roscoe

As I followed Freda, I turned to watch Emma dump the lemonade into a potted plant. Freda slid open pocket doors to a room off the foyer.

"This is our sitting room." She beamed with pride. "It's quiet and very restful. We spend a lot of time in here."

I agreed with her statement. A leather couch and Barcalounger occupied the left side of the room. A rotating fan stood between the recliner and a huge fireplace that took up most of the far wall. A love seat and divan sat to my right. A large coffee table was situated in front of the couch. The room felt comfortable compared to the hot entrance.

Freda offered me the love seat and she took the couch.

I pulled out a pencil. "While Emma's working up an estimate, I have a few questions I need to ask you. Where is your husband employed?"

"Right now he's between jobs."

"Oh, I'm sorry to hear that. Where did he work last?"

"He drove taxi for Lester's Limousine Service."

"Was he laid off?"

"A medical leave of absence would be more appropriate. He sat so long in that taxi he got really constipated and he gained a lot of weight too. He told Lester he had to take time off and get into an exercise program. Lester agreed."

"Did Freddy get into a program?"

"He'd just got started when Lester turned Freddy into the insurance company for filing a fraudulent claim. And then he fired him."

I was just about to ask Freda if Freddy eliminated his constipation problem when a commode suddenly crashed through the ceiling, fell onto the Barcalounger, and ejected its contents. I've heard the term "when the shit hits the fan," but never in my wildest dreams did I expect to see that phrase enacted. Freda let out a blood-curdling scream and flailed her arms, trying to block the onslaught of the porcelain pot's detritus. I was able to escape being splashed from where I was sitting, but its stench blew over me, and caused me to gasp.

Hearing the commotion and Freddy's screams, Emma ran into the sitting room. She gawked at Freda's appearance and then noticed the john perched on the Barcalounger. The fan sputtered and sparked and finally died in a cloud of white smoke, its blades slowing. The smoke drifted upward.

Emma's eyes followed its ascent to the ceiling. "Oh My God, Oooooh my."

Freda wiped excrement from her face and eyes. She screamed again when she saw the lower half of Freddy's buck naked body hanging from the ceiling, his legs running the marathon, his butt-cheeks chasing after them. Freddy yelled, "I'm stuck. Help me, Freda!"

I stood frozen, a spectator viewing an incredible scene, but there Freddy hung in all his glory. Emma stepped forward to see it all. Although Freddy's gluteus maximus was maxed out, it was his girth that prevented him from falling through the opening.

"That reminds me," Emma said, "I have to pick up a dozen hamburger buns on the way home."

Freddy yelled, "Freda, who's talking? Is someone else there? For the love of God!"

Freda said, "Stop looking at my man. He needs help."

Emma scowled and stepped aside, but still looked up at Freddy. "I don't have a winch on my car, better call 911."

Freddy stopped running the marathon. Emma reached a position directly in front of him. Freda grabbed an afghan from the couch and feverishly wiped the debris from her hair and clothing.

"What's that?" Emma said, pointing up to Freddy's crotch. "I never see a naked white man before... well, not for a couple months anyway."

"What's she doing?" Freddy asked. "What's she looking at? Get her out of here. Get me some help."

Emma squinted. "Looks like a turtle." She took a step closer. "Eeeeek! No, it's a baldheaded mouse. It just winked at me."

"That's it," Freda said. "You'll have to leave. Now!"

Emma started toward the foyer but stopped. She turned and said, "I'd like to stay for act two. See how Freddy gets out this predicament."

When Freda grabbed a poker from the fireplace, we left.

Emma peeled red dog as we left, leaving Freda and Fat Freddy hanging. As we turned onto Beck's Run Road, a fire rescue vehicle veered into the Montraver Plan, its siren blasting at 110 decibels, colored lights flashing.

"I hope they brought a block and tackle," I said. "Removing Freddy is going to take some creative engineering."

"They got pulleys, hatchets, and whatnot. And they got those big raincoats with boots and hats. Best thing, though, is those gas masks. Can't be working in there without a mask. Unh-uh."

"They'll have him out in a jiffy."

"They'll be needin' Jiffy Lube to squeeze Freddy out that hole."

Now that Freddy's constipation problem was resolved, I told Emma we needed to check out Freda's story that Lester had accused Freddy of fraud.

"Why?" Emma asked.

"Because if it's true that Lester initiated his prosecution, Freddy would blame Lester and not Frank."

"Uh-huh, that seem reasonable. Let's go interrogate larcenous Lester. Where to boss?"

"On Lexington. Three hundred block."

Emma made an illegal U-turn. "We'll be there in three shakes."

"By the way, how'd your date with Terrelle go last night?"

"Don't ever mention that asshole's name again. He be the cheapest, stingiest, miserly muthafuka I ever gone out with."

"I guess sex was out of the question," I said. Emma cut a look at me. "You know, like with Felton... in the back of the El Camino."

"Hell no! No truck, no car, bike, scooter. We took a damn bus to the theater."

"That's not so bad, is it? Maybe his car broke down. Maybe—"

"Maybe he's so tight he squeaks when he farts. I had to pay my own damn bus fare."

Emma was getting riled up. The louder she spoke, the faster she drove. "And that's not all. That weasel-shit say he had tickets for the movie. Excuse me, a two-for-one deal. He made me split the price."

"Slow down, Emma, *we'll* get a ticket."

"Ticket, huh? Next time I see that worm, I'm going to punch his ticket."

I gave it a couple of minutes until Emma simmered down and slowed down. "I guess he didn't buy the popcorn either."

"You keep it up, Mister G, and you gonna be in the hospital bed next to Terrelle."

"Okay, I'm sorry. Did you share your popcorn with him?"

"What? Yeah, I did. Couldn't help it."

"You're a special person, Emma. Don't change."

"You're just sayin' that to keep on my good side."

I thought it best not to answer. "There's Lester's lot."

Emma pulled into the lot and parked next to the Grey Fox Bus Depot. Lester controlled the taxi business as well as the transit concession in Monview. A large garage stood next to the depot. Four taxis in various stages of disrepair were parked at the side of the building. Four black Lincoln limousines sat under the shade of a large aluminum carport at the rear of the property.

Emma bounded out of the GMC, ready for action. I slid out and joined her at the depot's door. Emma entered

Following Roscoe

first. I walked into what looked like a retro fifties bus station. Two old oak church pews occupied the center of the room. A newspaper and magazine rack, soda and candy machines, and an ancient pay telephone booth finished the décor. I faced what resembled a bank's counter from the era of the old west. Each of the two teller stations had a barred opening that protected the cashier from robbers. An old, baldheaded man stood at the left teller station. Behind the steel bars he looked like a prisoner on death row, his face reflecting decades of misery and loss, his eyes searching for justice.

Emma sauntered up to the counter. Baldy took in her presence.

"What can I do you for?" he said through a small, nasty mouth.

"You never gonna *do me,* old man. You got some nerve. I should—"

I stepped in front of Emma. "Excuse me, ah, Lester? I'm sorry, I don't know your last name."

Baldy shifted his eyes from Emma to me. "Lester Stankowski. I'll rephrase my question. How can I help you?"

"I'd like to talk to Fred Moldonado. I understand he works here."

"Nope, not anymore. Had to fire the lazy fat-ass."

"Harumph!" Emma shifted her weight into attack pose.

"I'm sorry, lady. I didn't mean to imply that *all* fat people are lazy."

"That's it, you little twerp." Emma pushed me aside. "I'm gonna rip you a new asshole."

I tried to stop her, but she grabbed the metal bars and tried to pull the protective unit out of the teller's opening. Lester's eyes looked like pie pans. He staggered back against the wall. He reached for the phone.

"I'm going to call the police. I'll have you arrested, just like Moldonado, and thrown in jail. Now get her the hell out of here."

"Come on Emma," I said. "Let's leave. We got what we came for."

We jumped into the GMC and headed for the office.

"Couple of more yanks and I'd've pulled that monkey cage off. Then I'd've showed that rodent what full-figured women do to skinny, trash-talkin' little shits like him."

"Relax, Emma. You were excellent. You exposed his character, and that answered the question we were looking for. Freddy Moldonado would want to take out his anger on Lester, not Frank. We can eliminate him as a suspect."

"Who's left? Karl Himmelman? Harry the Hat guy?"

"Harry can be eliminated. He couldn't have pushed me off the road with Frank's car. That person was already waiting for me when I left Harry's house. But yes, Himmelman is a person of interest. Roscoe is still digging up information. He came up with a name this morning, but I can't remember it."

"You hungry?" she asked.

"Yes, why?"

"Cause we're eatin' with the district supervisors today."

Chapter 18

I had almost forgotten about the monthly luncheon meeting with the area supervisors. We meet the third Thursday of every month at Smitty's Restaurant and, being the president, CEO, CFO, COO and owner of Desperate Domestics, I pick up the tab.

Emma acted like she was starving. Normally she drives under the radar, but today she averaged fifteen miles an hour over the speed limit, whizzing through three yellow lights and one red light. The trip from Overhill Drive to the Mon River usually takes me fifteen minutes. Emma made it in ten.

The restaurant sat majestically on River Street, half a block from the Number Three Police Precinct. Located in a refurbished nineteenth-century farmhouse, Smitty's reputation for fine dining and ambiance was well known throughout southwestern Pennsylvania.

Claude, the headwaiter, led us into the main room where Gertrude, Stella and Maria were already seated. Original oak floorboards creaked as we followed him to our favorite table, a round cherrywood Bancroft for six. It sat between a huge stone fireplace and a set of double-hung windows that overlooked the garden patio. After a few minutes of studying the menu, a young waiter, probably a college student from nearby California

University of Pennsylvania, suddenly appeared and took our order. He wore black slacks and a long-sleeved white shirt. The nametag pinned to his shirt pocket read Andrew.

What I call a monthly meeting isn't a meeting at all. It's a chit-chat lunch that keeps me in touch with the business. After all, I spend very little time at Desperate Domestics. Emma runs the enterprise. She's the boss of the area supervisors, who have an average of seven maids under their direction. The least I can do is give Emma and her staff time off to enjoy lunch one day a month.

During the usual banter among the supervisors, Emma collected their weekly checks and stuffed them into her purse. Andrew arrived with a large tray and served Emma first.

Emma's eyes widened over the steak bruschetta, steamed asparagus and mixed greens. "Sure took you long enough," she said, frowning. The frown turned into a smile when she said, "You make it up to me later, okay, honey?"

A hint of pink shone through Andrew's olive skin. He continued to serve the remaining meals, the pink turning to red as Maria and Gertrude tried, with little success, to stifle chuckles. Stella sat stoic. Andrew served my tuna steak wrap last and scurried off.

"Anything new of interest?" I asked.

Gertrude Pastorkovich, supervisor of the southern area, said she had picked up a new customer, Mrs. Ederbrink, a retired teacher. "It'll make up for Mister Granger, who quit when Rosey stole his Skagen Denmark watch."

"Did she take it hard when you fired her?" I asked.

"No. I think she expected it. She didn't like the work."

Stella, the Polish Princess, Sabolski, supervisor of the northern area, stirred her steaming lobster bisque. "Everything's okay now, I didn't get fired. I smoothed everything over with Mister Himmelman." Stella turned her attention to Emma. "I'm sorry, I should have warned you."

"Be easy," Emma said. "I loved it. That scene was off the hinges." Emma described Mister Himmelman *doing* aerobics with the blond aerobics instructor dressed in a French maid's costume.

Gertrude looked horrified. "How embarrassing. What did you do, Emma?"

"I be trippin'. I axed blondie if she be Miss Aerobics."

Gertrude almost choked on a piece of pecan-crusted bistro salmon.

"Any other problems?" I asked.

"Well…" Maria Pallini finished chewing a bite of jumbo lump crabcake. "Gino's butler, Russell, is trying to denigrate my position. He spilled spaghetti sauce on the carpeting and blamed it on me."

"What the hell's denigrate?" Emma asked. "Sounds like he be dissing you."

"Trying to. Maybe he thinks he'll look more important in Mister Duratz's eyes… and I think he's afraid of Mister D."

"Did you say Duratz?" I asked. "Gino Duratz?"

"Yes, that's him."

"Why's he afraid of this man?" Emma asked. "This Mister D don't bother you, does he?"

"No, I think he likes me. But Mister D has a temper. He spent some time in prison recently for beating up a man."

What luck. This must be the guy I was looking for. I excused myself and said I was going to the men's room. I headed out the back door and called Roscoe on my cell.

He answered on the third ring. "Hello, Nephew."

I told him about my discussion with Maria. "Did Duratz recently spend some time up the river for beating someone up?"

"Damn near killed Walter 'Nuggets' DeFiglio. Got tried for attempted murder but was convicted on a lesser charge."

"When was he released?"

"Two months ago."

"He's a client. I think I'll go with Emma and feel him out."

"No!" Roscoe said. "I'll go with you later. Get his address and any information that sounds pertinent."

I hung up and rejoined the others at the table. I said to Maria, "I'd like to see you after lunch."

The walk out to the parking lot seemed longer than the walk in. Maybe the process of digesting lunch slowed me down, but I think it was the emphatic kibosh Roscoe put on my decision to talk to Gino Duratz with Emma. What did Roscoe know about him? Was he dangerous? Maybe he was in the Mob, connected to it somehow, or had friends with questionable reputations. Maybe Roscoe's testosterone level was off the chart and his machismo would drag us into deep distress.

Emma was already in the GMC with the engine running when I slid in. As she drove across River Street to Overhill Drive, I looked past her and caught a glimpse of the third police precinct. I wished the police were officially involved, then neither Roscoe nor myself would be jeopardizing our safety by trying to find out what happened to Frank.

"Head for police headquarters, Emma."

"What, you're bustin' me for that piece of crab cake I pinched off Maria's plate?"

"No, it's important I talk to Lieutenant Fahey."

In the twelve minutes it took to drive to headquarters, Emma said nothing. She pulled into the lot, parked the GMC and turned the engine off. She sat behind the wheel with crossed arms. I opened the passenger door half-way, but Emma didn't budge.

"Aren't you coming?" I asked.

"No. I don't want to conversate with the po-po."

I knew Emma wasn't fond of the MPD, but I thought she might be interested in possibly hearing some good news about Frank. "Okay, I'll be right back." Inside the building, I approached the desk sergeant. He had his head down reading another girly book. He heard my footfalls and recognized me when he looked up. He pointed his trigger finger in the direction of Lieutenant Fahey's office. She was studying a paper when I tapped on the doorframe.

"Come in. I've been expecting you."

"Really? Have you heard something about Frank?"

"No, but we heard from Lester Stankowski. He called earlier about an incident that took place in his station. He said a large, black woman accompanied by a white man threatened him with bodily harm. He gave me the plate number of the car they were driving. I traced it to Ron's Rent-A-Rattletrap car lot. And guess what?"

I shrugged my shoulders and, not knowing what to do, nervously jammed my hands in my pockets. "What?" I asked.

"Why would you rent a rattletrap? Couldn't you find a better place to rent a car?"

She was smiling. I couldn't believe it. She had covered for me. "It wasn't that bad, Colleen."

"I know. I've dealt with Lester many times before. He's a constant complainer. What were you doing there in the first place?"

I didn't want to tell her that Frank had left information for me that Roscoe and I retrieved from his safe, so I revised the facts a little. I explained that Frank had told me that Fat Freddy Moldonado was convicted of defrauding an insurance company and that he was released three weeks ago.

"So? What's that got to do with Lester?"

I told her about Mrs. Moldonado's version of what happened.

"I don't get it. Moldonado worked for Lester, so what?"

"Lester contrived the scenario and accused Freddy of insurance fraud. Freddy's mad at Lester, not Frank. That eliminates Freddy as a suspect in Frank's disappearance."

"I see, so you're playing detective, huh?"
"The police aren't involved, are they?"
"We're working on it. Lab results haven't come back yet. If the blood sample from the arrow tests positive for Frank's DNA, there will be a full scale investigation."
"How did you get Frank's DNA?"
"From his sister. She lives in Tucson, Arizona. Local Police sent us a lock of her hair."
"That's terrific," I said. "I didn't know you got the ball rolling. Thanks."
Fahey leaned back in her chair and smiled. "What are friends for?"
I felt a flush spread across my face. I looked at my watch. "Oh crap, I have to go. Call me if anything comes up."

Emma still had her arms crossed when I climbed into the passenger seat. "Learn anything from the Gestapo-po?" she asked.
I told her that the police were using a lock of Frank's sister's hair to determine if it was Frank's blood on the note and the arrow.
"How they do that?"
"Siblings have almost identical DNA."
Emma nodded. "Like on *CSI Miami*. Is David Caruso gonna do the testing? He fiddles with his glasses too much. And he tilts his head sideways, looks like he broke his neck. I'd rather Delco do the testing. He's hot stuff. I could watch him all night. He could fiddle with me."
I noticed Emma was headed in the wrong direction. "Where are you going?" I asked. "I have to pick up a car at Ron's Rattletrap."
"I have to stop at White's Funeral Home on the way. It opens in two minutes and I want to be one of the first to arrive. The deceased is my shit-ass step-father, Roland, and I want peoples to think that we got along. But we

didn't. He be the scum on a cesspool, the turd that wouldn't flush, the ass boil that wouldn't heal."

"I think I get the picture. But why be the first to arrive? You could pretend to show your respect at any time."

"Yeah, fake a few tears and sobs would work any time, but I want to perform early before Reverend Rashad gets there."

Chapter 19

Two cars sat in the shade of a red maple at the far corner of the parking lot when we arrived. The fracas of a group of young men playing basketball halfway down the block disturbed the otherwise serene environment.

White's Funeral Home was anything but white. Dark green aluminum siding enveloped the bulky two-story house. Chocolate brown covered the windows, gutters and downspouts. A red canvas canopy stretched from the entrance of the dead house to the sidewalk, providing shelter for visitors mourning the passing of a black relative or friend.

Darnell White greeted us as we entered the foyer. He smoothly approached Emma and reached for her hand. "I'm so sorry for your loss," he said in a slow, monotone voice. "Are there any special arrangements you would like to make?"

"Oh, I'd like to do something special all right, but I don't mess with the dead. You talk to my Aunt Ida Mae about that."

"I've already talked to Ida," Darnell said. "She'll be here later, but she said you should pick out the casket."

"She wants me to pick out the casket? What's he layin' in now?"

"Brother Roland is resting in a display model until an appropriate casket is decided on."

"She say she payin'?"

"Yes."

Emma got that twinkle in her eye. "Where are they?"

I followed Emma and Darnell White down a flight of steps into the basement. Caskets of all sizes, shapes and materials were displayed around the perimeter of the room.

"I'll leave you two alone to look over the inventory," Darnell said. "Take your time. If you have any questions, I'll be in my office." He turned on his heel and sauntered up the steps like a zombie. Being in the same building with Darnell, a bunch of caskets, and God knows how many dead bodies, was beginning to give me the creeps.

Emma approached a solid mahogany casket and stared at the price tag. "Nineteen hundred and ninety-five dollars? For a wood casket? That's ridiculous. Roland don't deserve that kind of floss on a box to take a dirt bath in."

Emma checked the prices on solid cherry, poplar, and oak veneer caskets and made discouraging huffing noises as she read each one. She quickly passed the children's and infant's caskets to a set of shelves displaying an array of urns.

"Now that's the ticket," she said, holding a cherrywood urn shaped like Napoleon's hat with a clock embedded in the front. "I can keep track of the time since his expiration, that son of a bitch."

"Did you really hate him that much?"

"You bet, and more." She picked up a decorative brass urn, gray with gold colored flowers. "Looky here. Ninety-five dollars. Do you think we can stuff his miserable body in this jug?"

Emma looked at me for an answer. I looked away. She put the urn down and continued checking the price tags on the caskets.

"I like this one," she said, pointing to a two-tone twenty-gauge, brushed steel model. "It's only eight hundred fifty-nine dollars. Ida Mae will like the price."

"You're sure that's the one?" I wanted confirmation so we could get the hell out of there.

"This is the one."

"Good. Let's pay our respects and head for Ron's Rattletraps."

I scurried up the stairs, Emma trudging after me. I stepped into the hallway that led to the main viewing room. I was surprised at the number of people who had arrived in the short time it took Emma to pick out a casket.

"Oh shit," Emma said, catching up with me. "What are all these peoples doing here? Nobody liked the son of a bitch. How can I talk to these hypocrites and pretend to like him too?"

"Think of the good things about Roland."

"There ain't none. And I'd have to do my best Broadway performance to convince anyone."

"Then think of something nice or funny about the person you're talking to."

"Uh-huh, that might work." Emma headed for the crowd.

The conversation slowed and diminished to a murmur as we walked into the knot of theatrical critics. Emma stopped ten feet from her stepfather and acted as if she was going to make an announcement, but instead turned when a black man tapped her on the shoulder. I closed on Emma and stood behind her.

"Hello, Emma. Glad you could make it," he said.

"Oh, I wouldn't miss it, Booker," Emma said with a touch of attitude. She looked around until she saw me. "Mister G, this is my stepbrother, Booker Jefferson."

Booker and I nodded. He pointed to the two sprays of flowers above the coffin and said, "The purple ones on the right are mine."

Instead of a caustic retort, Emma smiled. She said, "You always did like flowers. That was your first job, wasn't it?"

"That's right. You remembered. Brings back memories."

A young girl, around the age of five, yanked on Booker's pant leg. "Grandma wants you," she said, and pointed to a thin woman in a print dress sitting on a folding chair against the far wall. Large diameter lenses on her glasses magnified a menacing stare.

"Talk to you later," Booker said, and slunk toward the woman. Emma smiled as he blended into the crowd.

"That went well. I thought you didn't get along with Roland's family. How'd you manage?"

"Roland sold Booker's pickup truck when he was overseas in the army. Told him someone stole it. Wasn't insured. When he came home he rode a bicycle to a job interview at Joseph's Nurseries. I just pictured him riding that bike. Thought the whole scene was funny. Thanks, Mister G."

While we were talking to Booker, a line had formed in front of Roland's sister and brother-in-law, who were receiving the guests. We stood in silent respect for a few minutes until Emma leaned to the left.

"Monkey George, is that you? Get out that line. I seen you cut in."

A man with a broad face turned around. I could see where he got his nickname.

"I'm in a hurry, Emma. I gotta doctor's appointment."

"That doctor's gonna have to remove my foot from your behind, you don't get out the line."

George reluctantly moved to the back of the line. I cut a glance at Emma.

"What? He deserved it."

"Remember the plan? Think of something nice or funny."

"Nothing nice or funny about that primate."

A short, squat man had finished paying his respects and was walking past when he spotted Emma.

"I didn't think I'd see you here, Emma."

"Otis, how you doin'?"

"Roland was a good friend and neighbor. I'm sorry for your loss."

"Thank you." Emma's smile turned into a wide grin. "You doin' good?"

"I'm hangin' in there. Melba takes good care of me."

"That's good," Emma said, half laughing. "She's..." Emma started to cough and laugh at the same time. "Excuse me. I have to get some water." As Emma strolled away I could hear her laughter getting louder.

I looked at Otis and shrugged my shoulders. He wandered away. After a few minutes, Emma came back, her eyes wet from the laughing jag.

"What was all that about?"

"I did what you said, Mister G. I couldn't think of anything nice about Otis, but a mental picture of his wife, Melba, popped into my head."

"And that was something nice?"

"No, something funny. When I was a young girl I went out in the backyard to pick some chard. I needed a bucket, so I went to the shed to get one. Before I got there I heard some noises and looked in the window. I saw Otis' wife, Melba, bare naked from the waist down, sitting on Roland and ridin' him like a pony headin' west. That's what I remember, her big black ass going up and down, the dark side of the moon outta control."

"That's some story," I said. I caught a mental glimpse of that moon myself.

Emma giggled. The room's chatter decreased to a few murmurs. Heads turned toward the entrance of the room. A tall man in a black suit stood in the doorway, looking over the crowd through wire-rimmed glasses.

"That's why everybody come," Emma said.

"Excuse me?"

"They come to see Reverend Rashad, not Roland. I feel better 'bout that."

"I don't understand."

"You will."

Chapter 20

Reverend Rashad strode to the casket in a solemn and dignified manner. He stood in silent prayer for a few moments. Darnell White entered the room with a lectern, placed it to the left side of the casket, and introduced the Reverend.

The Reverend placed a Bible and his notes on the stand. He cleared his throat a few times, and while scratching his neck said, "Brothers and sisters, we are gathered together not to mourn brother Roland's passing, but to celebrate his life." He shrugged his shoulders twice and twisted his mouth to one side. "Fuckass, whoremaster."

I couldn't believe what I'd heard. I turned around to see if others were as shocked as I was. A white man stood near the doorway, looking at me. When our eyes met, he turned away, as if he didn't want me to see him. He was about fifty, six foot two and solidly built. Under his salt and pepper hair he had a square face with a two-inch scar above his right eye. I got up and headed in his direction. When I turned the corner into the entrance, he had disappeared. I stepped outside and scanned the area. Nobody was on the sidewalks or in the parking lot. I heard the crunching of gravel and the sound of a car in the alley behind the mortuary. I caught a partial view of a black car between the houses as it sped away. It had to be the guy who's been following me. He's getting clumsy, I thought, using his own car to follow me.

I went back into the funeral home and into the viewing room. Emma had taken a seat next to a table with a candy dish on it.

"You missed some good shit," she said. "Roland was a gardener. The Rev said he spent a lot of time in the 'fucked up garden.' I almost bust out laughing."

"Why is he cussing?"

"He got that Tourette's thing."

Reverend Rashad got my attention. He was flapping his hands like a bird and blinking his eyes as if flying through a dust storm. He said, "Roland was a loving and cheatin' ass... and stinkin' shit husband, shit... father."

I asked Emma, "How can he continue being a minister?"

"Hell, he's a celebrity. He bring lots of money into the church. Membership went up at least five times since he come. The bishop loves him."

"Has the bishop ever heard Rashad's sermons?"

"Hell no. He just look at deposit slips."

"Is Rashad about finished?"

"Yeah, he's settling down now. High point when he grabbed his crotch and started sniffing like he smell something bad. He said a few MFs and a lot of dirty whores in between."

I turned my attention back to the Reverend, who said, "His favorite expression was... horny slut... never start what you can't... fuck... finish."

"That's right," Emma said, "Roland never started anything."

"Can we go?" I asked Emma. "Looks like he's finished."

"Yeah, I had enough entertainment for one day."

"By the way, do you know what Gino Duratz looks like?"

Emma shook her head.

Following Roscoe

We got up and started to leave the room. As we reached the door, I heard the Reverend say, "He's beyond the... shit, fucking shit... sunset."

The quickest route to Ron's Rent-A-Rattletrap from White's Mortuary was through Buena Vista, a section of the city with spacious lots and large homes built in the thirties by wealthy industrialists, mill executives and store owners. The streets and parks were tree-lined, giving the area a forest-like appearance.

"Look at that old church," Emma said. "What kind is it?"

I looked at the marquee, but couldn't read the denomination. "I don't know, but I'm sure the parishioners don't have an entertaining minister like Reverend Rashad."

"Hoo ha," Emma yapped. "Those folks don't know what they're missin'. Rashad be slammin', that for sure."

"I still can't believe he called the deceased a cheatin'-ass husband."

"I've heard worse at funerals. And at one wedding I went to, the bride jetted out of the service—and the marriage—during one of the Rev's performances. Rashad can sometimes stir up heated emotions."

Ron was standing at the door to his trailer office when we arrived. He held a set of keys between his thumb and forefinger and shook them at us when I opened the door of the GMC.

"Watch out, that's the signal," Emma said. "He's callin' all the other rodents wit those keys."

I didn't want to answer. "When you see me start the Lincoln, you can head back to the office."

"Them rodents like jingling sounds," Emma said, sliding out of the SUV. "I better stay awhile. You might need protection."

"I'll be fine Emma. You can—"

"And I want to check out squirrelly man's rides. I think I see a red Cadillac back by the fence."

Emma scurried off as Ron approached, his baggy, wrinkled trousers flapping around his skinny legs.

"Right on time, Mister Gustafson." Ron said. "Here are the keys."

As I reached for the keys, I noticed a rat dive under the skirting of the trailer.

Ron motioned toward the office. "If you'll just step inside, I have a few papers for you to sign."

"Ah… can you bring them out? I want to look over your inventory."

"Certainly. I'll be right back."

As I watched Ron step into the rodent cage, Emma plodded toward me with a smile. I wondered if she was happy about a car she had seen or the rat diving a reverse pike under the trailer.

"I really like that red car," she said, pointing to the Cadillac. "Why not trade the green machine for that fine lookin' conveyance?"

"Maria needs a carpet shampooer delivered. You wouldn't want to haul it in a Cadillac, would you?" Emma looked down. "And besides, it wouldn't fit in the trunk. We'll pick up something else soon."

"Well… maybe in two days then. I can't take that shampooer until tomorrow. And then—"

"Why not today?" I asked.

"Because it's broke. Mister Granger ran over it when Rosie left it in the driveway."

Another irresponsible employee. The people at the employment office must get their job candidates from the Darwin Awards list and send them to me.

"I'm glad Gertrude found a new customer before she fired Rosie."

Ron marched into the lot like a conquering general. "Let me see… Emma, right? Did you find anything?"

"Harumph!" Emma spun on her heel and trudged off to the green GMC.

Ron watched her storm off. He looked confused.

"Don't mind her. Are those the papers?" I asked.
"Yes."

I signed the forms and slid into the Lincoln. As I drove away, I looked back at Ron in the rear view mirror. He still looked confused.

Chapter 21

"Look out the window," I told Roscoe. "Check it out."

Roscoe sat at the kitchen table, a number of papers spread out in front of him. He wore a black number 17 Pedro Alvaraz Pittsburgh Pirates t-shirt.

"What's going on, fireworks? Couldn't be. That was last month. Besides, they don't show up very well this time of day."

"Funny. No, the car, Roscoe. I'm driving a Lincoln MKZ, just like yours."

Pissmore ran to the doggy door and poked his head through the opening.

Roscoe halfway stood up and pretended to look out the window. "Congratulations," he said, and sat down.

"You don't look very excited. I finally get a nice ride and you can't find the energy to stand up and look at it."

"If it's just like mine, I've already seen it."

Pissmore lumbered to his doggy dish and looked at me with hungry eyes.

I pointed to the papers on the table. "Are those the blood test results?"

"Yes, and they confirm my earlier conclusion."

"What conclusion?"

Roscoe gathered the papers and held one up. "This sample is from Frank's office. It's his blood. I compared it to a hair sample I took from Frank's house when we snuck in." He held up another paper. "This sample is from the arrow and the note. It's also Frank's blood." Roscoe slid another paper toward me. "This sample is from Frank's bedroom wall. It is not Frank's blood. In fact, it's cow's blood."

"Cow's blood! Who the hell would use cow's blood? Not the killer. That supports your theory that two people were working independently of each other."

"That's what it looks like, Nephew."

I fed Pissmore and turned back to Roscoe. "What about the grease and sawdust?"

"The grease is a multipurpose lithium grease sold in any hardware store. Can't be traced. Sawdust is sawdust. But this sawdust contained bovine fecal matter."

"As in cowshit?"

"As in cowshit."

"So we have a greasy cattle rancher that splattered Frank's bedroom with cow's blood and a murderous archer who likes to write threatening notes."

"That about sums it up."

"That rules out Fat Freddy Moldonado. He's as big as a cow, but a cowboy? No way. And besides, Freddy has a beef with Lester, not Frank."

"That's right, Augie. Freddy's not our guy."

"What about Himmelman?"

"He's not involved, either."

I was surprised at his answer. "How do you know that?"

"I had the place surveilled."

"Surveilled? By whom?"

"Electronics. I planted listening devices in key areas of his house. That's why I had you draw up a floor-plan and check the house for alarms."

"And you heard him talking. Private conversations?"

"That's right, even his butler. They're clean. Well... with Frank's disappearance anyway."

"That leaves Gino Duratz and the guy at the funeral home."

"What guy at what funeral home? This news isn't good for my ulcer."

I explained that Emma and I had put in an appearance at White's Funeral Home to pay her respects to her stepfather. Of course, I described Rashad's rant.

Roscoe said, "Okay, so you have a profane preacher, an irreverent Rashad. I want to hear about this *guy* you mentioned."

"He was watching me," I said. I described him and how he had disappeared from the funeral home when I tried to confront him. "He made his getaway through the back alley. I could only make out that it was a black car."

"You think he's the one that's been following you and watching your every move? If so, this is the guy we're looking for," Roscoe said. "He blew up Emma's van thinking it was yours, stuck the threatening note to your door with an arrow, and pushed your van off the road with Frank's car."

"What's next?" I asked. "He might be waiting outside for me."

"He'll be avoiding you for a while."

"How can you be sure?"

"Short-term memory. He's relying that you'll forget what he looks like in a few days."

"So you think I'm safe for a few days?"

"Maybe. Or maybe not." Roscoe gathered the test results and put them in a manila folder.

"How about you rustle me up my last supper, then?" I headed for my apartment. "I'm going to wash up."

Roscoe called, "Dinner will be served in ten minutes, your highness."

When I returned, Roscoe sat at the table, looking at his watch. "Ten minutes," I said.

"How long did I take?"

"Nine."

"I see you made your specialty again." I pointed to the grilled cheese sandwiches and tomato soup.

"I'm going to Foodland tomorrow."

"What kind of grub are you going to pick up?"

"Maybe some chicken. We're out of veggies and pasta."

"That's odd. You're a meat and potatoes guy."

"True, but I heard that the oriental chicken and cacciatore Aldine cooked was delicious."

Aldine? He called Mrs. Vanderslice Aldine? "Whoa Nellie, hold the phone. I thought you were repulsed by older women?"

Roscoe looked at me defiantly. "I am. I just... well she's a good... I like her cooking. What's wrong with that?" He took a huge bite out of his sandwich.

"But *Aldine*? I didn't know you were on a first name basis with Mrs. Vanderslice."

"I noticed you called Lieutenant Fahey *Colleen* at dinner yesterday. What's with that?"

"Okay, I did. But I didn't ask Mrs. Vanderslice what kind of exercises she did. You were checking out her figure, weren't you?"

"That's what men do, Nephew. So what?"

I didn't want to discuss this any further or get Roscoe riled up. I needed his help to find Frank and, more importantly, to keep this bad guy, whoever he was, off my ass.

"So nothing. Forget it." I chomped down the last two bites of my sandwich and said, "I'm going to the club. Maybe Moldy knows this Gino Duratz guy."

I left the two canines—one a bulldog, the other a hound—to finish their meals.

I had mixed feelings driving to the club. On the upside, it had been years since I'd driven a sedan, having traded in an old Chevy for my van when I started Desperate Domestics. Driving the Lincoln MKZ was exhilarating, almost overwhelming. On the downside, Roscoe seemed to be taking a liking to Mrs. Vanderslice, and it really bothered me. She was attracted to him; maybe her charms were working. I might have to talk to

Milt Anderson

Paranoid Perry Sanders and have him mix up a potion for me to sprinkle on Aldine's cacciatore that would switch her romantic desire from Roscoe to me.

    I parked the driving machine near the right corner of the club, ten feet from Archie "Bunker" Brown's 2002 Buick Century. I sat alone for a few minutes, taking in the stillness and quiet of the night, wondering why anyone would be following me and trying to hurt me in this perfect and peaceful world. The sound of a dog barking brought me back to a nervous reality. I checked the area in all directions before exiting the Lincoln. I glanced over my shoulder as I made a hasty entrance into the club.

    Moldy was bent over a cooler, stocking it with bottled beer when I eased onto my favorite stool. Archie Brown and his wife, Doris Jean, sat directly across from me, playing a trivia game. Paranoid Perry and his wife, Grace, sat to their right a few stools away. As usual, Tommy "Two Shots" Tuttle and his gorgeous wife, Reba sat near the TV. Reba was engrossed in a rerun of *The Newlywed Game*, and Tommy sat upright with only one shot glass in front of him.

    "Looks like you've lost some weight, Mold," I said. Moldy turned around. "Scratch that, not from this angle."

    "Augie, how you doin', brother? And that's not funny. I lost three pounds."

    "Sorry, Mold. From this angle I can't see the difference."

    "Yeah, right. I figured you'd be coming in about this time."

    "Why's that? Did I hit the dollar pool?" In order to sustain business, most clubs and bars offer a type of lottery in the form of a "pool." Patrons have to be present at least one day each week and sign "the book." When the pool reaches 500 dollars, a numbered chip is drawn from a container and a winner is declared.

    "No, things have been too quiet lately. The Sanders and the Browns have been noticeably quiet this evening. Something's up, and you're usually around when things come to a boil."

Following Roscoe

Just as I was hoping the club would provide sanctuary for me for a few hours, Archie said to Perry, "How's it going in the covenant?"

Perry screwed up his face. "Covenant?"

"You mean *coven*," Doris Jean corrected. "Covenant is a type of agreement between two parties. It is also a religious term."

Archie pointed his finger at Perry. "A coven! You're a vampire. Vampires join covens."

Doris Jean interrupted. "A coven is not a place, it's a group."

"Grace heard it at the salon," Perry said. "Didn't you, Grace?"

"I sure did," Grace said. "Minister McCarthy's wife said it is a place where witches and vampires meet. She used to live in Salem, Massachusetts. And who would know better than someone from Salem?"

Minister McCarthy? Reverend Rashad? What was this world coming to? A reverend who speaks in a profane manner and a minister who is living in the superstitious past. What next?

"You're all full of shit." Archie pointed to Perry. "Look at your gum wrapper. What's the name on it? Trident, right? That's the devil's weapon."

Grace threw the first ashtray. Archie shoved a jar of pickled pig's feet toward Perry. "Devil's hooves," he said. "Dump them in your caldron at your next coven."

Perry and Doris joined the fracas. Objects of all shapes and sizes flew through the air. Reba continued to stare at the TV. Moldy ducked for cover, and I left thinking it might be best to take my chances with the guy who's been stalking me.

Chapter 22

I sat in the Lincoln for a while looking over the creature comforts that I didn't have in the van, not wanting to think about the fracas in the club or the man who was following me. I could still see his face: square with a two-inch scar above his right eye. He had salt and pepper hair.

Maybe I'll go to Murph's Bar and have a beer with Roscoe, I thought. No, he'll take my presence as being in his space, spying on him. And besides, I couldn't keep up with his drinking. If I tried to match Roscoe beer for beer, I'd be on the floor in no time, and being his relative would be a disgrace to him.

I slid the gearshift into drive and glided out of the parking lot. I decided to go home and spend a quiet evening with Pissmore and watch a rerun of *Two and a Half Men*. I took the scenic route.

Dutch Run snaked its way up a gradual incline of suburban, tree-lined residential areas to a forested spot near the top of Wood's Run Hill. The sun was low in the sky, peeking through the locust trees on Beyer's Ridge. It was a peaceful and serene sight, nothing like the atmosphere at the club. Crestview Cemetery sat ensconced at the top of the hill on a plateau of approximately one hundred acres of well-manicured grounds dotted with trees and shrubbery. A stone wall and wrought iron fence lined the roadside boundary.

I let the Lincoln coast leisurely past the city of the dead, taking in the magnificent view. As I started down the other side of the hill I touched the brakes. They felt spongy. I touched the pedal again and the resistance turned mushy. That damn Ron, I thought, he gave me a real rattletrap. This didn't look good.

I came upon a bend in the road and squashed the pedal to the floor. It went totally limp. I veered left, careening around the corner, but I knew the road ahead declined at a steeper grade.

I panicked. I pumped the brake rigorously, but to no avail. I stood on it, straining, but the Lincoln kept picking up speed.

What was that television program where people discuss situations like the one I'm in and then tell you how to get out of it? I had no idea how to get out of this situation. I couldn't even remember the name of the program.

Were you supposed to put the gear in neutral? No, that didn't make sense. Downshift? Yes that's it. Pput it in second gear and then into first. Whoops, there was no second gear. Why didn't a fancy vehicle like a Lincoln have a second gear?

Okay, I'll go for first then. Even though I was going too fast, I tried it anyway. I yanked the gearshift back into first with a resounding gnashing and clunking sound. Well, that didn't work—there goes the gear box.

What next? Of course, the emergency brake. Why hadn't I thought of that sooner? I pulled the brake handle back with less resistance than the brake pedal. Why would both brakes go bad at the same time?

It dawned on me then: somebody had fooled with my ride.

The Lincoln picked up more speed as the road continued to decline and the curves became more sharp and frequent. I had to stop before I flew off the road into a huge tree.

I noticed a level patch off to the left about fifty yards ahead, but I was going too fast into the curve, and the centrifugal force was pulling the vehicle away from it. I had to pick the right opportunity or else it was curtains for me.

An S curve was coming up, a left and then a right. At the far end of the right curve was a stand of saplings. That would be a perfect place, I thought, to go off road. The saplings would bend and break under the force of the Lincoln and eventually slow it down, avoiding a sudden, and deadly, stop by something bigger.

The speedometer read fifty-five miles an hour when I burst into the stand of saplings. I hit the opening square in the middle, a perfect entrance and a perfect plan—except for the pin oak that jumped out in front of me.

My father stood and watched as Billy Brogan pummeled me. It wasn't fair; he was bigger than me and I hadn't done anything wrong. Well, not really. I had told Mrs. Hathaway, our fifth grade English teacher, that Billy had cheated on his test. Somehow he found out about it and was pounding his dissatisfaction into me. I turned my head and noticed the disappointment on my father's face. That's when Billy's final blow connected with my brow.

I reached up to the pain and felt a large lump. I looked at my fingers to see if there was any blood, but it was pitch black, the darkness filled with splotches of purples and reds and a flock of minuscule bits of light twinkling in their midst. I reached out in desperation for my father's help and hit something. What... a steering wheel? And then I remembered what happened.

I pushed aside the deflated airbag and pulled the keys from the ignition. A miniature penlight attached to the key ring illuminated white dust, like talcum powder or cornstarch, all over me and the car's black interior. My watch read 3:00 am. My chest and face hurt like hell, and my head was throbbing. I guess airbags worked better with seatbelts. I looked around but only saw obscure shades of black. I reached into my pocket and pulled out my cell. I had to shine the light on the keypad to punch in Roscoe's number.

"What the hell time is it?" Roscoe said.

"It's three o'clock."

"In the morning?"

"Yes. I need—"

"What's so important that you have to call at this ungodly hour?"

"The brakes failed on the Lincoln. I hit a tree."

"Where are you?"

"Somewhere in the woods between Crestview Cemetery and Flaggart's bottom."

"Are you hurt?"

"Kinda. Nothing serious, I think."

"That's a long stretch of woods. Can you make it to the road?"

"I'll try."

"Okay, I'll be there as soon as I can."

All I had to do was flag Roscoe down and I could get the hell out of here.

I pulled the handle on the door but it wouldn't budge because the car was resting against the pin oak's younger brother. As I slid over the armrest storage compartment I felt a severe pain in my left ankle. I guess I was too worried about the crash and the pain in my head to notice anything else. I yanked the handle on the passenger door. It was jammed. I started to panic. What if a fire broke out? What if there was an explosion? I braced my backside against the storage compartment and kicked the door with my right leg. It didn't budge. I tried again with the same result. Nothing.

I wish I could remember what they did on that television show. I remember someone being trapped in a car underwater, but that wouldn't apply here. Or would it? They still had to get out of the car. What did they do? They rolled the window down slowly. Shit—I've got electric windows. I tried them anyway. Nothing. Of course, I didn't have the car turned on. I reached over and slid the key into the ignition and turned it to accessory. I pushed the button for the window again. I heard a grinding noise but the window wouldn't budge. Double shit!

I reached over to pull the key out and noticed smoke filtering from under the dashboard. Now my panic alert shot up to DEFCON 3. Windows were made of glass. Why hadn't I thought of that sooner? I kicked the window three times with my right foot. It felt like kicking a brick wall. They made these Lincolns sturdy, that's for sure. I kicked with both feet, my left ankle shooting with pain. I stopped for a moment because of the pain, but the increasing smoke kicked in my adrenalin.

I went wild, like a kung-fu master and finally smashed the window. The only thing between me and safety was the jagged glass that remained. I opened the glove compartment, broke off its door and used it to swipe off the protruding glass. Then I draped the opening with a rubber floor mat and slid out the window.

I crawled away from the smoking vehicle, thinking an explosion was imminent. Looking for protection, I collapsed behind a thick tree trunk. I could see nothing but dark, muted colors. I waited awhile for the hissing of the car and the sound in my head to diminish before heading toward the road. I was disoriented and had lost the penlight when exiting the Lincoln.

I crawled around on my hands and knees, trying to find an indication of a slope. That would lead me to the top of the hill and safety. But the area was level. I had to land in probably the only level area in the forest. Stumbling ahead, I bumped into the Lincoln with my head, sending shockwaves of pain through my body. I almost passed out, but survival kept me conscious. I felt the car and determined that it was the trunk. Since I had traveled downhill, the rear of the car would be pointing uphill.

Now that I knew the direction to safety, I felt a little better. That feeling soon waned after crawling into the crowns of downed saplings. As I encountered one, I moved around it and then proceeded uphill. My knees ached and I tried to stand. That didn't work out, so I continued crawling, using my elbows as much as possible.

I don't know how long I continued in this manner, but it seemed like an hour. I was getting exhausted and felt faint when I saw the beam of headlights sweep over the tops of the saplings. I had to be thirty or forty yards from the road. I wondered if the lights were from Roscoe's MKZ. I struggled harder and faster until I thought I was going to lose consciousness, but I finally made it to the top of the hill and Dutch Run. I grasped a sapling and used it to pull myself upright, then leaned my back against its trunk.

I must have nodded off briefly as I dreamed that Alan and Jake from *Two and a Half Men* were talking to me.

Chapter 23

A beautiful brunette with full sensuous lips leaned over me. When I grabbed her breasts she jerked backward and stood up.

"Mr. Gustafson," she said. "What are you doing?"

"Who's Mr. Gustafson? And I must say, your two friends are spectacular."

"You're Mr. Gustafson, and keep your hands to yourself."

"Oh, I get it. At the bar. That's when I told you my name was... what? And I've got this terrific hangover. How much did I drink last night?"

"You're August Gustafson and I wasn't with you last night."

"I've had as many women as there are corrupt politicians. And any woman that's been with Charlie Harper doesn't forget it. But *I* do on occasion. How was it, by the way?"

She smiled wide, her pearly white teeth and lips lowered to my mouth.

"It was spectacular," she said, and kissed me. "Now get some rest. I'll be back later."

I heard a voice in the distance, a familiar one. It got closer and louder.

"Wake up, nephew, I haven't got all day."

I opened my eyes to a smiling Roscoe Kronek wearing a Pittsburgh Steelers gray shirt and blue jeans. A Pirates baseball cap topped off his attire.

"Roscoe? Where am I?"

"You're in Monview General. Good to see you're doing better. The nurse said you've been in la-la land."

"Really?"

"You hit your head when you crashed into a tree in the woods. Do you remember that?"

"Sort of... maybe."

"Didn't have your seatbelt on, did you?"

"What's this, an *I told you so* lesson? I'm in enough pain. I don't need another pain in my ass."

"Sorry. The doctor said you had a concussion." Roscoe straightened, pressing his hands against his lower back.

"What's the matter, too many pelvic thrusts last night?"

"I think I have caudia equine syndrome."

"What, you had sex with a horse?"

Roscoe narrowed his eyes. "It's a neurological problem affecting the lower back and legs."

"How can you be sure that's what you have?"

"I have the symptoms. My lower back and legs ache like hell... plus the loss of bowel control. I shit my pants this morning."

"Let me guess. Last night you partook of Murph's cuisine consisting of Slim Jims, pizza with pepperoni and anchovies, pigs feet, and a couple of hard-boiled eggs topped off with a few quarts of beer."

A knowing look dawned on Roscoe's face. "But what about the lower back and leg pain?"

"So she wasn't a horse."

"Oh," Roscoe said. "No, but I don't think that's it."

"Getting back to my predicament, what's the chance of having both brakes go out at the same time?"

"Next to zero. And they didn't just go out. The main brake line was cut, and the emergency brake was disconnected."

"You checked the car?"

"Yes, while you were checking your eyelids for holes. When you left home you said you were going to the club. I checked your parking space at home and at the club. I didn't find anything at home, but I did find brake fluid in the club's parking lot. Did you park near the right side of the building?"

"I'll be damned. That prick followed me to the club... my sanctuary."

Roscoe's head turned toward a gorgeous nurse who had walked in. She was a brunette with a round pixie-like face. Roscoe hiked up his pants and smiled at her.

"I guess that horse disease miraculously disappeared," I said. "Your back and legs seem to have healed."

"Excuse me, Nurse Good Body—"

"How are you doing Mister Gustafson," she said, ignoring Roscoe. "Or should I call you Charlie?" She walked over and grabbed my hand with both of hers. "Do you feel better now? I've been taking good care of you." She placed her second and third fingers on my wrist and took my pulse.

I remembered the kiss. She was the one; it wasn't a dream. While she was looking at her watch, I noticed the puzzled look on Roscoe's face. I thought it would be a good time to... what's the phrase... twist the knife a little?

"That's nice, I appreciate your expertise," I said. "And when I get out of here I'd like to return the service." Did I just say that? "I mean take good care of you too."

She blushed. "I'd like that," she said.

I looked at Roscoe to see the jealousy dripping from his face, and also from Lieutenant Fahey, who had silently walked in and stood in back of Roscoe.

"Lieutenant, what are you doing here?"

Roscoe turned. "Well, hello, Lieutenant. Are you here because of the accident? I have certain evidence—"

Following Roscoe

"Yes," the lieutenant said, "and to check on Mister Gustafson. I see you're busy. I'll come back later."

Mister Gustafson? What the hell was this about? A chilly visit for sure.

"Can I walk you to your car?" Roscoe asked as the lieutenant turned and started to leave. "There's a nut running loose." He dashed out the door after her.

I had to agree with Roscoe. There was a psycho out there—after me—and it was probably that Duratz guy.

I asked Miss Good Body, "By the way, when am I going to be discharged?"

"Maybe tomorrow morning if the doctor says it's okay."

"Tomorrow morning!"

"You have to stay overnight for observation. You have a pretty nasty bump on your head."

The scene from *The Godfather* popped into my mind where Don Vito Corleone had been shot and was lying unconscious in a hospital bed. The people who had shot him were on their way to finish the job. If it wasn't for Michael, Vito's son, who rushed Vito from room to room and floor to floor on a gurney, the killers would have succeeded. Being trapped in the hospital, I was a sitting duck for whoever was after me.

"I can't wait. I've got to leave."

Nurse Good Body patted my shoulder. "Relax, I'll take good care of you." She started to take my blood pressure.

"No, really. I have to go."

"One twenty over eighty," the nurse said. Pulse seventy-two. Perfect."

"He's perfect, all right," Emma said, walking into the room. "A perfect example of one lucky white man."

"Emma, I'm glad you came."

Emma would be my ticket out of here. I couldn't rely on Roscoe, he was off chasing women again, and besides, I wanted to get a look at this Duratz guy that Roscoe wanted me to stay away from. Maybe he was the one who has been following me.

"Of course you are, Mister G." Emma looked at the nurse. "I seen the lieutenant running down the hall and Roscoe in hot pursuit. You chase her out?" Emma pointed a finger at her. "You not chasin' me out."

The nurse turned on her heel and left.

"You okay, Mister G?"

"I'm fine, just a little headache and a sprained ankle."

"That sumnabitch tried to kill you this time. We gotta stop this muthafucka, pronto. You asked about this Duratz dude at the funeral home. Is he the one?"

"I don't know. Maybe. I could use your help in finding out."

"Bouya! That's slammin'. I'll go get my mace, handcuffs, and stun gun. I lent my Glock to my sister."

"You have a Glock?"

"Affirmative. Forty-caliber."

I wondered what Emma did in her spare time, but was afraid to ask. "We don't need any of those items, not yet anyway."

"Ok then, what we gonna do, Mister G?"

"They won't release me until tomorrow morning. I've got to break out of here. I need your help."

"Goody, like a prison break. What's the plan?"

"Go to the office and call Stella. Have her pick you up and drive you to Wince's Garage. He said my van would be ready this morning. Pick it up and come back here at eleven forty-five."

"Why at that time?"

"Because they serve lunch at eleven and they won't be checking on me after that. And besides, most of the staff will be eating their lunch at the cafeteria. It'll be easy to sneak out."

Emma pointed to the hospital gown I was wearing. "You can't sneak out like that."

"Go to the Army-Navy Store on Grant Street and pick up some clothes for me. I'll pay you later."

"Then what?"

"Then we go see Gino Duratz."

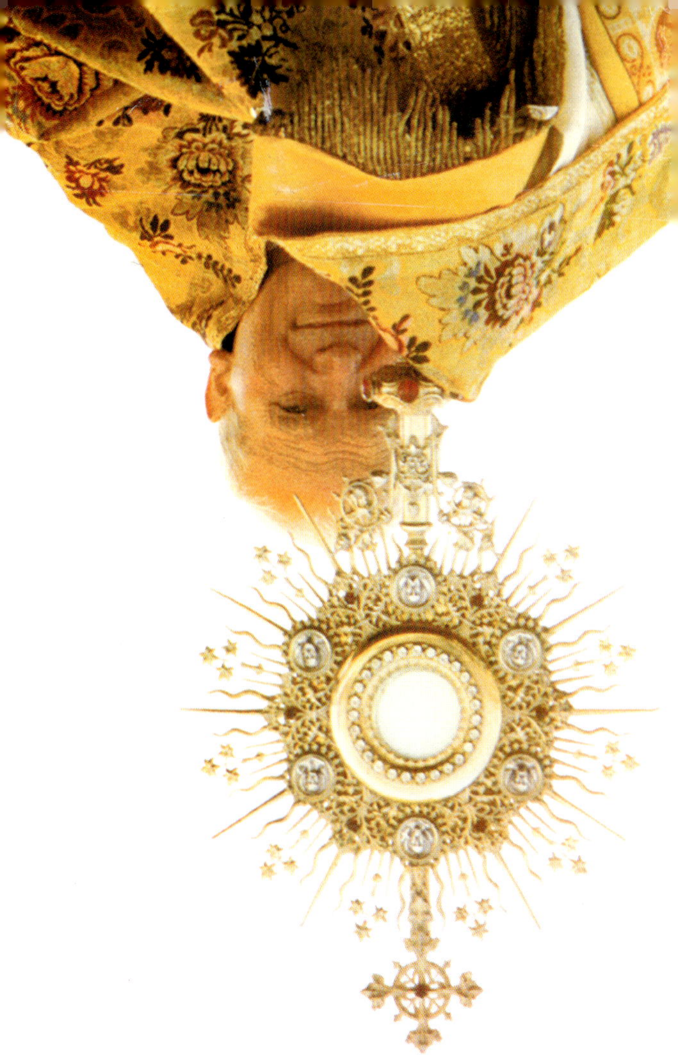

POPE JOHN PAUL II: GREAT APOSTLE OF THE EUCHARIST

E - Eat His Body, Drink His Blood (Jn 6:53): *"Participate fully in the Eucharist by receiving the body and blood of Christ"* (36). *"Mass [is] fundamental for the life of the Church and of individual believers"* (41).*

U - Union with Jesus: *"It is pleasant to spend time with him, to lie close to his breast like the Beloved Disciple (cf. Jn 13:25) and to feel the infinite love present in his heart. . . have I experienced this and drawn from it strength, consolation and support!"* (25).*

C - Communion with God (Jn 17:11): *"In the Eucharist we have Jesus, we have his redemptive sacrifice, we have his resurrection, we have the gift of the Holy Spirit, we have adoration, obedience and love of the Father"* (60).*

H - Heart of The Church (Mt 28:20): *The Holy Eucharist is "the heart of the mystery of the Church. . . . Lo, I am with you always"* (1).*

A - Adore Jesus: *"I wish once more to recall this truth and to join you, my dear brothers and sisters, in adoration before this mystery; a great mystery, a mystery of mercy. What more could Jesus have done for us? Truly, in the Eucharist, he shows us a love which goes 'to the end,' (cf. Jn 13:1), a love which knows no measure"* (11).*

R - Receive Jesus (Jn 20:2): *"From. . . the sacrifice of the Cross and her communion with the body and blood of Christ in the Eucharist, the Church draws the spiritual power needed to carry out her mission"* (22).*

I - Intercede (Ps 6:56): *"Christians must be distinguished above all by the 'art of prayer,'. . . spend time in spiritual converse, in silent adoration, in heartfelt love before Christ present in the Most Holy Sacrament"* (25).*

S - Sacrifice (Mt 26:28, Mk 14:24, Lk 22:20): *"The Eucharistic Sacrifice is the source and summit of the whole Christian life"* (13).*

T - Thanksgiving (Lk 24:33): *"Once we have truly met the Risen One by partaking of his body and blood, we cannot keep to ourselves the joy we have experienced"* (24). *"Christians ought to be committed to bearing more forceful witness to God's presence in the world. We should not be afraid to speak about God and to bear proud witness to our faith"* (26).**

Pope John Paul II. * *Ecclesia de Eucharistia.* ** *Mane Nobiscum Domine.*

Pope John Paul the Great, pray for us . . . to believe, receive, love, adore, venerate and encounter Jesus in the Most Holy Eucharist!

MBS, POB1701, Plattsburgh, NY 12901 Ph:(518)561-8193 Fax:(518)566-7103 www.ACFP2000.com **D-18**

Chapter 24

"Hey, handsome." A voice accustomed to talking to octogenarians awakened me. "Time for your pills."

I opened my eyes to a chubby, smiling face. She was very cute, about thirty years old and had the prettiest hazel eyes. She shook a small paper cup at me.

"What pills? I don't take pills."

"You have a concussion and a swollen ankle. These pills will make you feel better."

"I feel just fine. I don't need any pills."

"Is there a problem here?" Another nurse walked into the room. She looked to be about fifty-five, walked and talked in an authoritative manner, maybe a nurse sergeant.

"Mister Gustafson doesn't want to take his meds," the chubby nurse said.

"Is that right, sir?" Sergeant nurse grabbed the paper cup from her subordinate's hand.

My eyes wandered over her curvaceous figure, stopping on her nametag, which read: CANDICE.

"That's right, Candy. And you can call me anytime."

"Mister Billings has been calling for ten minutes," Candy said to the chubby nurse. "See what he wants." The chubby nurse left the room.

Candy sashayed up to me. Her blue eyes shone with a scintillating brightness and her full lips betrayed the hint of a smile.

"Do you want to do this the easy way or the hard way?" she asked.

"That depends."

"On what?"

"On how you like it."

She ran her fingers through my hair, the hint of a smile growing larger. "You're a naughty little boy, aren't you?"

Well hello! Candy the Cougar.

"Maybe we can come to an arrangement about these pills," I said. "I don't want to take anything that would suppress sensations."

"I wouldn't want that either." Candy squeezed the paper cup into a ball and dropped it into the trash can.

"Okay, I'm back," Emma said, barging into the room. She had a duffel bag slung over her shoulder and was dressed in a camouflage shirt and cargo pants. A camo fatigue cap with a major's insignia sewn on the front was stuffed onto her "high hair do."

"Excuse me," Candice said.

Emma brushed past her. "You're excused." She greeted me with a *Benny Hill* salute. "Colonel Emma Lou Rawlins reporting for duty, Mister G."

Candy's jaw dropped as she watched Emma heave the duffel bag onto the bottom of the bed. She looked stunned, frozen in time for a minute and then left with a bewildered look on her face.

"I got what you want, plus some extra special stuff."

"Extra special stuff? I'm afraid to ask, but did you get me clothes?"

"Oh yeah. I got you a slammin' outfit."

Emma pulled out an army dress blue uniform from the duffel bag. She held up the jacket in admiration. It had a spray of medals pinned above the left breast pocket.

"Check out the bling," she said. "And look at this." She pointed to shoulder straps that had two stars on each of them. "The man at the store say you're a general. A major one."

Oh shit. Why did I ask Emma to go to the Army Navy Store? For used and cheap clothes, I thought. Not army stuff. What could I say, she looked happy. That's what happens when you send a woman to shop for a man. You should expect anything.

"And check out this lid." Emma held up an officer's hat with golden scrambled eggs on the beak. "This is obese." She put the hat down and said, "One more surprise."

Oh my God, what next?

"I got you a pair of eighty-two jump kicks."

Emma held up a pair of Corcoran jump boots. She probably heard the clerk say they were worn by the Eighty-second Airborne Division.

"Thank you, Emma. I'm sure no one will notice me leaving the hospital in this outfit."

"Army peoples are always walkin' in and out of hospitals, aren't they?"

Not major generals in dress blues wearing jump boots.

"But I can hardly walk, Emma. They'll notice me right away."

Emma rubbed her chin. "I didn't think of that." She looked disappointed.

"That's okay. Once we get out of here, nobody will recognize me."

"Okay, I'll come up with a plan," she said, and started to leave.

"Where are you going?"

"To get a candy bar. I think better with a Milky Way and a Pepsi under my belt." She saluted and left.

My head was starting to hurt again, probably from thinking that I wouldn't be getting out of this Lysol-smelling place tonight.

An orderly wearing camouflage fatigues entered the room, pushing a gurney. I squinted at the clock. It was

11:45. I must have dozed off after I ate. I focused on the orderly.

"Emma, is that you?"

"Shhhh, it's me. It's time to make our bustout." Emma slid the gurney next to the bed. "Hop on, I'm your chauffer to the getaway van."

"What's the plan? Are you going to push me out the door and think nobody is going to notice?"

"They'll notice, all right," she said, pulling a sheet from underneath the gurney and unfolding it. "They'll see a stiff goin' to the morgue in the cellar."

That might work, I thought. I quickly dressed in the uniform Emma brought and laced the jump boots. I put the hat on and climbed onto the gurney.

Emma covered me with the sheet and said, "You be quiet now, Mister G. We're outta here in a skosh."

I felt the gurney move, its wheels magnifying the small irregularities on the floor.

"Out my way," I heard Emma say. "I got a dead body here."

Nothing like free advertising.

I felt we were picking up speed. When Emma rounded a corner I slid to the left, almost rolling off the gurney.

"Whoooeee," she yelped. "It's Emma Lou comin' down the stretch, Chewin' Gum stickin' to the rail, Toilet Paper coming up the rear, now it's Turtle By a Neck—"

"Cut the shit, Emma," I whispered.

"Sorry, Mister G. I got carried away. Uh oh."

"What's the matter?"

"Shhhh.

There's a group at the elevator. I'll wait for the next one."

"You can use this one," I heard a voice say. "You don't want to use a regular elevator."

"Ok," Emma answered. "That's nice."

"I see you're going down," a woman's voice said. "Can my boy and I go with you, lieutenant? We're really in a hurry."

Following Roscoe

"Yeah, sure. Jump on in. What floor you want?"
No, Emma! Aw shit.
"First floor," the woman said.
Double shit. Anything could happen in the time it took the elevator to go from the eighth floor to the first.
"Bobby, stay away from that," the woman said. "Come over here. Thank you so much for letting us on. It would have taken us forever to get another elevator. Oh, what a lovely necklace. What is that stone?"
"It's alexandrite," Emma said.
"I love the green color. Bobby! I said to stay away."
"Yep, and I have matching earrings and bracelet."
That's just terrific. Two women engaged in a jewelry discourse and a curious little boy were within a few feet of me. The first floor couldn't come fast enough. A little hand slipped under the sheet and found my hand. The little bastard pulled my finger. I remember my uncle had me pull his finger and then he would fart. I didn't know whether to laugh, fart or scare the shit out of the little son of a bitch.
"Bobby! Don't do that."
Of course he did. He pulled the sheet off me.
"Mom look, it's another soldier."
"Gimme' that, little boy," Emma said, and covered me again. "Keep your little mitts to yourself."
"Excuse me," the woman said. "That's no way to talk to my son."
"You didn't, so I did. And I can do worse than talk, lady."
"And what's a soldier in full uniform doing in this hospital?"
I heard the elevator door open.
"He done have Legionnaires disease. Now take your little brat and leave."
"Well, I never," the woman said.
"You did at least once. That inquisitive little mutt's the result."
After the doors closed Emma said, "Coast is clear."
"Where the hell are we?"

"Goin' down. Ladies undergarments, kitchen utensils, bath—"
"Down where?"
"To the basement. That woman think we goin' to the dead room. Soon as we get there we're goin' back to the first floor."
"And then we leave?"
"Affirmative."
"Make it fast to the van," I said. "I can't stand being under this sheet."
"Okay, we're almost there. Hush up."
I heard the elevator door open and the sound of people milling about in the hall. I could tell Emma was moving as fast as she could.
"Git out the way," she said. "This here's a hero. I be takin' the general to Arlington. A helicopter is waitin' at the airport. Watch out."
Talk about embellishment. Where did that story come from? After an agonizing couple of minutes, the gurney came to a stop.
"We're here, Mister G."
"Roll this buggy to the back of the van and open the rear doors."
I heard the doors open. Emma said, "Okay."
"Is anyone looking?"
After a few seconds, she said, "No."
I threw off the sheet, rolled off the gurney and dove into the back of the van. "Take off. Hurry."

Chapter 25

Either I had fallen asleep again or I had been in concussion la-la land. I didn't remember the fifteen-minute drive to the office or climbing into the passenger seat, so the head injury must have had something to do with it.

"Damn, I forgot." Emma pointed to a Chevy Nova in front of the office.

"What?"

"Gertrude scheduled an interview for a new maid."

"Rosie's old job?"

"That's it."

Emma pulled next to the Chevy and turned the engine off. Gertrude and a red-haired woman were sitting in the Nova talking. Gertrude slowly slid out of the car with a look on her face that read: *Where have you been?* The passenger sat frozen, looking as if she had made a terrible mistake.

Emma swung the door open and jumped out. She approached the other car. "Come on yous two. We ain't got all day."

Gertrude had moved around to the passenger's door and implored the redhead to come with her. "It's okay," Gertrude said, "I think she's in the National Guard."

The applicant reluctantly agreed. She had green eyes in a movie star face. She slowly opened the door, swung out her legs, and stood up.

What a marvelous set of boobs, I thought, and those legs have that perfect taper I love. What the hell does she want to be a maid for?

Emma and the two ladies had walked halfway to the office by the time I stepped out of the van. I was a bit groggy and stumbled a little.

"Are you in the National Guard, too?" the redhead asked me.

"No, I'm the supreme commander of this company."

She looked frightened. She turned to Gertrude and said, "I've been thinking that it would be better for me to go back to Uncle Fred's place."

"But you said the farm wasn't for you," Gertrude said. "You didn't like milking the cows, the goats spit on you, and shoveling the manure was—"

"I've reconsidered. Aunt Berta needs me there. I'm going back to the farm." She started for the Nova.

Emma placed her hands on her hips and told me, "That was a short interview."

Gertrude waited until the redhead got in the car and said, "She would have been a good maid."

"No, she wouldn't," I said. "She'd turn out to be a housewrecker. She's way too gorgeous for this job."

"Harumph," Emma mumbled. "What we maids be, hideous?"

"Certainly not, Emma. You know I love you. It's just that she—"

"I know, Mister G. I just wanted to hear you say you love me."

Emma said to Gertrude, "Find another girl and set up an interview. Our army career will be over by then."

Gertrude drove off. Emma headed for the office.

"Where are you going?"

Emma turned around grinning. "I have a few things to pick up."

"Bring a couple cushions from the couch."

The windows on the back doors of the van were darkly tinted, as was the window next to the right side door. I didn't want to alert Duratz that I was on to him, so instead of occupying the passenger seat where I was visible, I opened the side door and crawled into the back of the van where I could surveil his house in relative secrecy.

A few minutes later, I heard, "Where you at, Mister G?"

"In the back."

"That's a good idea," Emma said, and opened the back doors. She threw two cushions in and slid a large red Igloo cooler across the floor.

"What's in the cooler?"

Emma winked at me. "We might be awhile. I got some goodies." She jumped into the van and started the engine. "Here we go, Steelers, here we go," she chanted.

"Did you get Duratz's address from Maria?" I asked.

"Yep, fourteen twenty Prospect Drive over in the Brentwood area."

I moved the cushions behind the driver's seat and made myself comfortable. "I'm glad you decided to come along. I'm still groggy, and I'm sure I can't drive yet."

"This will be an adventure for sure. I got my army costume, my bling, and I'm a colonel, to boot."

"That funny little thing on your hat says you're a major."

"Is that better than a colonel?"

I didn't want to tell her that a major is one step *lower* than a colonel; she would want to go back to the Army-Navy Store and get another hat. "Major is good. It means you're a major officer."

"Booya. Major officer sound slammin'. Did I tell you my uncle Booker was in the army?"

"No, I don't remember you mentioning it."

"He also was a major... a major disaster. He got out on section eight."

"That's funny, Emma."

The view gradually changed from urban to suburban to substantially sitting pretty. Tudor homes, expansive stone mansions, and high-end condos sat comfortably ensconced in the affluent, old money area of Brentwood.

"This place is off the hinges, not like the hood I grew up in. This Duratz guy, what's he about?"

"He's bad news. He just got out of prison two months ago."

"What did he do?"

"He tried to kill Walter 'Nuggets' DeFiglio. They tried him for attempted murder, but a high-priced ambulance chaser got him off on a lesser charge."

"What this have to do with Frank Pallone?"

"Frank provided the information that got Gino arrested in the first place."

Emma pulled to the curb and stopped. "Fourteen twenty not too far away."

The right side of the street had even house numbers and at 1410, we were very close.

"Drive slowly down the street. I want to see which house is Duratz's."

Emma slowly pulled away and continued down the street.

"That's it, Emma. The Tudor with the evergreens in front."

"Okay, now what?"

"Pull up about fifty yards and park on the left side of the street."

Emma pulled to a stop and turned the engine off. It was 1:15.

"Terrific. I have a perfect view of the house."

"Awesome, now pass me the cooler."

Instead of bending forward to grab the cooler, I tried to move it toward me with my foot. I only moved it a few inches, and with great effort.

"What's in this thing, bread sticks or lead sticks?" I shifted my weight, maneuvering toward the cooler. In a seated position, it was too heavy to pick up. I had to slide it. I positioned it between the seats where Emma could reach it. She flung open the lid and pulled out a liter of Diet Pepsi and a ham sandwich at least two inches thick.

At least eight bottles of pop, five or six sandwiches wrapped in aluminum foil, a small bucket of Colonel Sanders, and a number of potato chip and other snack food bags remained in the cooler.

"Where are all the others?" I asked.

"What others?"

"You've got enough food here for the company picnic."

"This is *our* picnic, Mister G. This is the surveillance picnic. Don't need nobody else. Well, maybe Deener's oriental chicken. I loved that meal, and you know what? I liked her too."

Good idea, I thought. I like Mrs. Vanderslice myself, more than I could tell Emma.

"Why don't you come over for dinner tonight? I'll invite Aldine."

"Ah, shoot! I can't. I'm waitin' for Darnell White. He's takin' me out on a date tonight."

"The undertaker?"

"That's him. Five thirty, he said."

That blew that idea. "Well, another time Emma."

Emma finished her first course and reached for another Dagwood before I found a root beer. She unwrapped the second sandwich and took a bite. It smelled really good.

"What kind of sandwich is that, Emma?"

"This is a hot sausage patty."

I really wasn't hungry, but thought I'd have something to eat before Emma devoured the entire contents of the cooler. I peeled away aluminum foil to a thick roast beef sandwich with a thin spread of horseradish. I ate it slowly, savoring every tasty bite. I continued the surveillance through a series of lip smacks, yummy yums, slurps, and burps. I checked my watch; it was 1:45. Enough time had elapsed for Emma to digest the concoction of food she had devoured, creating gas and the possible evacuation of the van.

Motion caught my attention directly across from the van in the governor's driveway of a mammoth stone mansion. It looked like a woman going to a party or an evening event. She was wearing a retro stylish hat and evening gown. She was pushing a baby carriage, totally out of the ordinary considering the hot August afternoon. As she neared the street I determined she was at least in her seventies. Scratch that, late seventies. She marched across the street directly toward the van.

"Emma, there's an old woman walking up."

"I see her. She's too old to have a baby."

The carriage was a fancy one with a convertible canopy and air-filled tires. Four pockets were sewn-in the fabric that wrapped around the body. One pocket held a water bottle. It even had a cup holder on the handle.

The woman approached the passenger door. She said, "What are you doing here, young lady?"

"I'm a major with the National Guard. I'm on terrorist alert. You live here?"

"Yes I do," she said, pointing to the mansion.

"That's a slammin' crib, ma'am. Wow, that dress is beautiful. What kind is it?"

Good work, Emma, taking the woman's mind off a strange vehicle in the neighborhood.

"It's an Oleg Cassini," she said, smoothing the green silk satin and velvet fabric. "I wore it the night I graduated from Yale in 1965."

"Nice hat too," Emma said. "What! Is that a dog or what?"

I stretched toward the window to get a look at what Emma was talking about. Sure enough, there was a white dog with large, dark eyes and droopy ears sitting peacefully in the stroller.

"That's my Sylvia. She's a Chacy Ranior. Pure-bred, of course."

"Uh-huh, of course. Well, you best be gittin' back home, those terrorists like little dogs, you know."

The woman took off without saying good-bye.

"Good work, Emma. We don't need more exposure in this neighborhood."

"And just in time, too," Emma said, pointing through the window.

I turned to see a black Mercedes S500 pulling out of Duratz's driveway. I couldn't tell who was driving because the windows were tinted.

"Do a U-turn and follow it," I said.

The tires chirped when Emma floored the accelerator. Two hundred and twenty-five horsepower pulled the van into the turn and down the street.

"Keep a safe distance, Emma. We don't want Gino to know we're following him."

"I know how to tail someone, Mister G. I'm an expert. I watched every rerun of *Remington Steele*. Don't you worry. I'm your partner, Laura Holt. And besides, I followed Rodney Beecham for four months until I started going with Malcolm Payne."

"After spending four months of watching Rodney, why did you start going with Malcolm?"

"Malcolm is a friend of Rodney's, and I was watching him, too. In fact, I found that I liked to watch Malcolm much better than Rodney. Get it?"

Emma must have paid attention to the detective reruns. She drove for twenty minutes through four boroughs to a coffee shop on Braddock Avenue in Hazelwood with no indication that we were following the Mercedes.

Emma said, "He's getting out. He's short, fat and baldheaded."

"It's not the guy from the funeral home. He was tall with salt-and-pepper hair and a scar above his right eye. Damn, I was so sure." Had we wasted half the afternoon on a wild goose chase? For some reason, that phrase brought to mind chicken and Mrs. Vanderslice. I pulled out my cell and punched in her number.

Chapter 26

The wall clock above the stove registered 3:00 when I walked into the kitchen. Pissmore greeted me by wagging his stubby tail. Roscoe greeted me by wagging his lips.

"What the hell were you thinking?" he said. "You have a concussion. You could have blacked out and run into a pole."

I opened my mouth to explain, but he continued. "The hospital is concerned— they've called two times. You just can't walk out of a hospital."

"I had some help." I explained how Emma busted me out.

Roscoe chuckled. "You're kidding, on a gurney? Wearing dress blues? And a general's uniform, to boot?"

"Emma's a pip, isn't she?"

"She certainly is, but the hospital said you disappeared right after lunch. Where have you been?"

Uh-oh, shit was going to hit the fan. "Well, it's a… you know…"

"Spit it out, Nephew."

"Did you ever see *The Godfather*?"

"What the hell are you talking about?"

I went over the scenario how Michael saved his father, Don Vito Corleone, from enemies who had come

154

to the hospital to murder him. "I had to get out of there. I had to go on the offensive."

Roscoe seemed to understand. "That's good, I guess. Good military tactic," he said, and then his face sobered. "You didn't go to Duratz's, did you?"

"Just to surveil his house. I wanted to see if Duratz was the man at the funeral home."

"You could have walked into serious trouble. He's not a nice man. What's the name of that maid that works for him?"

"Maria Pallini. Why?"

"You could have called her for Duratz's description."

I smacked myself on the forehead. "Shit, I wasn't thinking. Everything's happening so fast."

"That's your concussion, Nephew. I understand, I had one once."

"I guess I wasted time with the surveillance, but I followed the black Mercedes to a coffee shop. The passenger got out, and it wasn't Duratz."

"What about the driver?" Roscoe asked.

"The butler? Didn't see him."

"Maybe Duratz was driving and was having his butler do errands for him."

"I didn't think of that."

"Better get a description of Duratz and his butler from the maid." Roscoe got up from the table. He groaned and grabbed his back.

"Is that your ulcer again?"

"No, I think I have spinal stenosis. That happens to people my age."

"Sorry. By the way, I invited Mrs. Vanderslice for dinner."

Roscoe's face brightened. "Really? That's good, because I invited Lieutenant Fahey." Roscoe started to walk away. "I'm going to get out of these basketball duds and jump into something more respectable."

I went to my apartment and lay on the bed thinking about both Aldine and Colleen being at the same dinner table and the chemistry that might develop.

The alarm rang at 4:45. I took a quick shower and jumped into pleated khaki Dockers and a French blue fitted dress shirt. A black pair of loafers completed my ensemble. When I walked into the kitchen, I thought a burglar had broken in. It turned out to be Roscoe, and he was dressed to the nines.

"Whoa, you startled me."

"Why? You walk into the kitchen every day and I'm usually here."

Roscoe wore a lavender dress shirt and a pair of gray slacks. He had traded his sneakers for a pair of black Rockport Ellingwoods. A fragrance unfamiliar to me hung over him.

"You're all dressed up. I never saw you dressed to kill before."

"It's nice to put on some cool threads once in a while, especially when we have guests. I see you got rid of the military duds and went civilian."

A tap on the door and a face in the window caught our attention.

"It's Mrs. Vanderslice." I rushed to open the door for her.

She scampered in, carrying a large casserole dish. She was dressed in her usual sports attire, a Steelers long-sleeved shirt over blue jeans. Sneakers carried her in.

"Mmm, something smells good," I said.

"Cajun shrimp. You like shrimp, Roscoe?"

Wait a minute, *I* was talking to you.

"I like shrimp. Especially Cajun," I said.

"I can take it or leave it," Roscoe said.

I felt invisible, like someone had sprinkled pixie dust on me. I slogged over to Pissmore, who was looking at his empty dish.

"Speak," I ordered. Pissmore retorted with a yap. He listened and he actually talked back, unlike Mrs. Vanderslice.

I heard another knock as Roscoe and Aldine were continuing their conversation. I opened the door for Colleen Fahey. She looked completely different. A stylish hairdo, not like the business type she usually wears but softer and longer, framed her pretty face. She wore a tailored black-belted pant suit. She carried a small insulated picnic cooler and handed it to me.

Colleen smiled and said, "Here, handsome, I brought some home-cooked food." She reached into her pocket and pulled out some doggie treats for Pissmore, who danced around her feet.

"This is for you, pretty boy." She dropped the food into his bowl and patted him on his broad head.

"Oh," Aldine said in a somewhat disappointed tone. "You brought an entrée."

Colleen pointed to the cooler. "Sauerbraten."

Mrs. Vanderslice's jaw dropped. "What?"

"Sauerbraten. Also known as German pot roast. I'm sure you like pot roast, don't you, Augie?"

"Uh, actually I do."

"But I already have an entrée for the evening," Aldine said. "Why would you bring another one?"

"I thought it the polite thing to do, to show my gratitude for being invited to dinner."

"You weren't invited to *bring* dinner, were you?"

It looked like a food fight might break out, so I thought I'd try my mediation skills.

"Why can't we eat both? I could eat Aldine's shrimp and Roscoe could have the pot roast."

Roscoe said, "I don't like pot roast."

Colleen punched me in the shoulder. "Why do you want her shrimp? I thought you liked pot roast?"

Apparently, my mediation skills could use a little work.

Aldine slammed her spoon on the table and started to get up. "See what happens when you bring an entrée to another person's dinner."

"Who made you chef number one?" Colleen said, making a move toward Aldine.

A loud knock on the door interrupted a potential beatdown. I didn't recognize the woman at first, but when she smiled I remembered her full lips and bright blue eyes.

"It's the nurse from the hospital." I opened the door to one of the most gorgeous cougars I've ever met. She wore white linen slacks that hugged every curve and a ruby-red, low V-necked front top. The kitchen fell silent. Roscoe's jaw dropped.

"You're a very bad boy," she said. "You left the hospital without authorization and you didn't say goodbye. You have to sign insurance papers, or they will send out investigators, and that could get very messy."

"Okay, I'll sign them, then." I waited for her to produce the papers. She didn't. "Where are they?"

Candice looked around the kitchen, taking in everyone's face. "Oh, I didn't bring them with me. I have them in my apartment." She extended her arm. "Come with me. Let's take care of business."

I took her hand. Why not? Make love, not war.

"I'll see you guys later," I said, and started to walk out with Candy. Colleen stood frozen.

"Why are you leaving with her?" Mrs. Vanderslice asked. "You can't leave. You invited me for dinner."

I turned and said, "I thought I invited you to dinner, not a debate." And then I left.

I didn't know Candy was ambidextrous. She steered the Mustang with her left hand, fondled me with her right hand and, at a stop sign, leaned over the console and nibbled on my ear. I didn't want her to stop, but the threat of crashing into another tree was a boner killer.

"Watch what you're doing." I pushed her away. "I'd like to end up in one piece."

She took her hand off my now flaccid penis and returned to a proper driving position. She said, "Be nice, and you'll get more than one piece."

Following Roscoe

I would describe Candy as an aggressive cougar, and I was beginning to feel a little apprehensive.

"Are we there yet?" I asked as we turned off Sycamore Street onto Marne Avenue in the Egglewood section of town.

"In a few minutes, mister horny. Relax." She reached over and grabbed my penis again.

Who's the horny one? She was still holding onto me when she pulled the pony to a halt and stopped in the middle of the street.

"We're here," she said, pointing to a raised ranch style house. The upper level was sheathed in white aluminum siding, the lower level stucco-covered block. A red door sat in the middle of the house and separated the levels.

She pulled into the driveway and punched the garage door opener that was clipped to the visor. The door started to close as we glided to a stop. She hopped out of the Mustang like an eager preschooler. Of course she was the teacher, and I wondered what lessons I was in store for. She motioned for me to follow her.

I walked through a doorway at the far left of the garage into a game room, up six steps to the entrance landing, and five more steps to the living room. Candy was standing in the hallway that led to the left side of the house. She crooked her finger at me. I scampered across the living room, eager to see the cougar's beaver. She ducked into the second room on the right.

At first I thought the room was made into some sort of home gym. There were cables that worked through a system of pulleys that were mounted to the walls and ceiling. Leather straps of all sizes and shapes were attached to the cables, as was a large wicker basket that hung suspended over the bed. The basket had a four-inch diameter hole in the bottom. A bench near the right wall had a motorized contraption on it with a rubber penis on the end of a Plexiglas shaft.

The feeling of apprehension I had earlier turned to extreme anxiety when Candy pulled a set of chrome-plated handcuffs from a dresser drawer. The scene from *The Godfather* flashed into my consciousness again. What if she worked for Duratz? She could handcuff me to the bed and call for the bad guys to come and dismember me. I was trying to think of a way to get out of this predicament when my cell rang.

"Don't answer that!" Candy urged, "We've got all evening—"

The phone's LCD screen told me it was Emma. "Sorry, it's business." I opened the phone. Candy dropped the cuffs on the bed.

"Emma, what's up?"

"I called Maria Pallini and got her home phone number."

"That's terrific. I'll call her right now." I figured I'd make the call sound serious as an excuse to get the hell out of this torture chamber.

"She won't be home. That's why I called."

Shit! Double shit. "When will she be home?"

"Don't know. She's at her sister's place in Webster. But I got some information for you. When I axed her what Duratz look like, she said he's baldheaded and fat, just like the guy that got out of that Mercedes."

Shit! Triple shit. "That's not the guy then. Did she say who was driving?"

"His butler Russell was driving. He's with Duratz all the time."

"She didn't say what he looked like by any chance, did she?"

"As a matter of fact she did. She said he's a big man. He has salt and pepper hair and has a big scar above his right eye."

"That's the guy! That's the guy, Emma. You're beautiful."

"I know that. What else?"

"I have to go now, and I need to call Roscoe. Thanks a million."

"Who's beautiful?" Candy asked.

"That was my manager at work," I said while punching in Roscoe's number. "Something important came up. I have to go."

Candy picked up the handcuffs from the bed and stalked toward me. Fear propelled me from the house as Roscoe answered the phone.

Chapter 27

I didn't know the length of Marne Avenue, but it had to be longer than the eight blocks I had run, walked, and jogged fleeing from Candice the nutty nurse. When I heard a car coming, I'd hide behind a car or a tree, thinking the degenerate damsel might be in hot pursuit.

I decided to take a much needed break and sat on a pair of concrete steps. I didn't know the steps led to a large yard with a huge Great Dane in it. Rats. Double rats. Why did I have to pick the only steps that led to the only yard with the only giant dog in it? Of course, the mutt trotted up and stopped a few inches behind me. I felt his hot breath on my neck and slobber dripping on my back. I learned from watching Cesar Milan on *The Dog Whisperer* that I should avoid making eye contact with the humongous hound and keep my back turned to him. It worked. Cesar knows what he's talking about. The friendly Fido licked the side of my face with what felt like a foot-long piece of raw liver, turning my horror to relief.

In dealing with the not so terrible tail-wagger, I hadn't noticed the black Lincoln MKZ stopped in the middle of the street.

Roscoe lowered the window and said, "She must have been really bad for you to go to the dogs." His laughing waned as he raised the window.

Following Roscoe

I sheepishly sauntered across the street, around the back of the car and sidled up to the passenger door. When I reached for the door handle, Lieutenant Colleen Fahey's questioning face looked back at me.

Oh, great! What could be more embarrassing?

I slithered into the back seat. "Thanks for coming," are the only words I could muster.

"You okay?" Roscoe asked. "Your voice sounded desperate. Was she into something kinky?"

"The words licentious and menacing come to mind."

"Really?" Roscoe said. "Do you have her phone number?"

Colleen threw Roscoe a scowl; he must have been rude on the drive over.

"This isn't funny. I think she works for Duratz."

"What makes you think that?" Roscoe asked.

"Remember I mentioned the hospital scene in *The Godfather*?"

"That was really tense," Colleen said. "Michael had to move Don Corleon from room to room."

"My nephew thinks... no, scratch that. His concussion thinks the bad guys were coming for him in the hospital."

"No, they sent a nurse to entice me to her place where the nasty deed would be done by professionals."

"You mentioned Duratz," Colleen said. "Is that Gino Duratz you're talking about?"

"Yes, and I'm hungry. I didn't get to eat earlier. How about stopping at that pizza shop?"

Roscoe agreed and pulled to the curb. When we walked in, Colleen asked the cashier to call a cab for her. I guess Roscoe's charm didn't work on women cops.

"Do you have to leave?" I asked her. "You just got here."

"I have to get back to headquarters. A sexual harassment case came up." She gave Roscoe a dirty look.

So Roscoe was being more than his lecherous self on the way over.

Roscoe motioned us to a table in the far right corner of the room, away from the windows. He always sat with his back to the wall and kept from being seen from outside. Something out of a Special Operations Training manual, I guess. I ordered a large pizza with pepperoni and anchovies. I grew up poor and got accustomed to the salty little critters because I never had to share my pizza; no one would eat them.

"So tell me about your nurse," Roscoe said. "Did she inflict any techniques on you that hurt?" Then he looked at Colleen. "You might learn something here, honey."

Colleen looked out the window.

"No, I'm okay. She didn't have time to get started. By the way, how's your spinal stenosis? Giving you any trouble?"

I knew he wasn't in any pain. He looked like the cat that swallowed the canary—in this case the panther ready to pounce on unwilling prey.

"Tell me about Duratz," Colleen said. "How does he fit into this?"

"He's a very bad guy," Roscoe said. "He's involved in bookmaking, prostitution, loan-sharking and other activities too gruesome to mention. But you already knew that, didn't you, sweetie?"

Colleen nodded.

I spoke up. "Frank was responsible for Duratz's trip up the river. Duratz got out two months ago."

A pimply-faced waiter arrived and slid the pizza pan onto the table. I was surprised to see Colleen grab a piece and take a bite.

"Good pizza," she said. "But that doesn't mean Duratz had anything to do with Frank Pallone's disappearance."

I explained that the person who had threatened me and tried to hurt me physically had to be following me. And that was Duratz's driver, Russell.

"Did you see him following you?"

"I was at Darnell White's Funeral Home yesterday."

"Over on Lenawee?"

"I think so. And this white guy is standing back in the doorway all by himself. You know it's a black mortuary?"

Colleen said, "I've been there a few times. Have you ever heard Reverend Rashad give a eulogy?"

I burst out laughing. Colleen laughed with me.

"What are you two laughing about?" Roscoe asked.

Colleen waited for me to answer. When I didn't, she said, "Reverend Rashad has this neurological problem... ah, he—"

"Grunts, swears, flaps his arms, barks, contorts his face, but mostly cusses up a storm. Augie already told me about the peculiar pastor."

Colleen said, "So you know that this man was Duratz's driver and that he was following you."

"I didn't know then. I just found out today."

"What, that he was following you or that he was Duratz's driver?"

"Duratz's driver, Russell, and he had to be following me."

"Why? Because he was paying his respects to a friend?"

"If he was paying his respects, why didn't he come into the room?"

"Some people are averse to funeral homes and can only manage to stay for a brief period of time."

Roscoe said to Colleen, "It sounds like you don't think Duratz had anything to do with Frank Pallone's disappearance."

"I'm a law enforcement officer. I have to work with the facts. Where is the evidence that Duratz *is* responsible?" Colleen looked at both of us. "Where is the evidence?"

Roscoe and I looked at each other. I waited for Roscoe to spill the beans about our ill-gotten evidence from Frank's office and home. He didn't. Instead, he said, "You could check out if Duratz's driver was a friend of the guy taking the dirt bath at White's Mortuary."

"I can't officially go snooping around on a non-existent case—it could by my ass."

"And what a nice ass it is," Roscoe said. "Could I be your supervisor for a day?"

I heard a horn blow outside and Colleen stood up. I didn't know if she was going to smack Roscoe or walk toward the door.

She chose the latter, turned around and said, "I'll talk to you later, Augie."

As soon as I heard the door close, I asked Roscoe why he didn't divulge the evidence we had.

"I don't think it would help right now."

"I understand she has to follow police rules and regulations, but she could find other ways to help us."

"I think she'll check under the radar to see if Duratz's driver was a friend of the deceased at the funeral home. In the meantime, we have to find more evidence. That will get the police involved immediately."

"Where do we obtain this evidence? We can't divulge the blood samples we illegally stole from Frank's office and home."

"Let's start with the person responsible for Duratz's incarceration."

"That's Frank," I said. "Who are you talking about?"

"The guy he almost beat to death, Walter 'Nuggets' DeFiglio."

Chapter 28

The door to Nuzzacci's Pizza Shop opened to a familiar voice. A black couple entered. I immediately knew who the woman was by the way she strutted to the counter.

"Emma, is that you?" The couple turned around and I was right, it was Emma. She was with Darnell White, the owner of White's Mortuary.

"Mister G. What chu doin' here?" Emma smiled at me. And then her gaze fell on Roscoe. "Why you bring him? He belongs somewhere under a doctor's supervision."

"Now, now, Emma. Try to be civil." Darnell looked at me as if trying to place my face. He turned to Roscoe, looking him up and down, as if measuring him for a casket.

"Call the civil authorities," Emma said, pointing to Roscoe. "That man is a sexual prevert."

"That's no way to talk to your soul-mate, sweet cheeks." Roscoe blew her a kiss.

"Soul-mate? You need to call the devil to git your twisted, heathen soul back."

"Emma, I thought we were friends, actually more than friends, something on a cosmic level."

"Cosmic level? That is where you are all right, out of this world if you keep messin' wit me."

Darnell stepped forward. "Excuse me, sir, this discussion has gone a little too far. I'd appreciate it if—"

"If what?" Roscoe asked, staring into Darnell's face, a face that displayed distress.

I nudged Roscoe's leg with my knee. When I got his attention, I gave him the *What the hell are you doing* look.

Roscoe's threatening facial expression eased. "I guess we should leave."

"I haven't finished eating," I said. "I'm starved."

"We're takin' you home," Emma said, looking to Darnell for approval. He nodded. "I have to talk to you anyway."

I gave Roscoe a sympathetic *Thanks, but it's all right* look.

"Okay, Nephew, I'll see you later." Roscoe pushed himself away from the table. He pointed at Emma. "And I'll see you Monday morning. Maybe sooner if you come to your senses."

Emma jammed her hands onto her hips. "Are you drinking something stronger than beer? You betta' watch that liver of yours, it's probably hard as a rock—just like your head."

Roscoe said, "I knew it all along. She loves me."

Emma reached for a container of hot pepper flakes as Roscoe disappeared into the night.

"Somethin's seriously wrong with your uncle. He's a depraved degenerate. Maybe you should git him some help."

"I've thought about that, but right now he's helping me, and I need all the help I can get."

"That's what I wanted to talk to you about," Emma said. "But first I have to order some grub. What chu want, Darnell?"

Darnell rubbed his chin. "I'll have a piece of pepperoni pizza and a soft drink."

"Comin' right up," Emma said, and scampered off.

An undertaker would go unnoticed in a crowd, just another average person with an elevated desire for preserving cadavers. But Darnell wasn't exactly average. He looked exactly like Erkel, from the nineties TV show *Family Matters*. He was thin, had close-cropped hair, wore huge dark-rimmed glasses, and his voice squeaked.

I felt a chuckle coming on, so I started a conversation with Darnell, hopefully to squelch any embarrassment. "How'd your date go?"

"Very well," Darnell said in Erkel's voice. "We had dinner at Redd Dawg's All-Star Clubhouse over on Maritz Boulevard."

"That's a sports bar, isn't it?"

"I guess so. They had a lot of televisions hanging around the room."

"What'd you have to eat?"

"I had the shrimp and scallop pasta. Emma started with the stuffed jalapeños appetizer. She picked the Dawg's BBQ platter for her entrée and polished it off with a mug of Iron City."

Emma walked back to the table with a Mountain Dew for Darnell and a Diet Pepsi for herself. Darnell grabbed a straw and pushed it through the slit in the plastic lid. Emma drank from the cup. She burped when she finished and said, "I have some news about Duratz's butler, Russell."

I dropped the half-eaten slice on my plate and leaned forward. "Terrific. What is it?"

"I told Darnell about what happened with this Duratz guy, and I described what Gertrude told me about what his driver look like. He's no friend of Roland's, that for sure."

"How do you know?"

Before she could answer, the waiter slid a tray of Buffalo Burnin' Hot Wings and a piece of pizza between Emma and Darnell.

Emma devoured two wings, and then she said, "Me and Darnell called my step-brother Booker Jefferson, Monkey George, and Otis, and nobody know anyone remotely similar to what that driver look like."

Darnell spoke. "Looks like this man was at the funeral home to see you."

"He certainly didn't come to pay his respects to Roland, that's for sure," I said, wishing Colleen had heard what Emma and Darnell told me.

Emma said, "Looks like the big man is getting nervous sending his driver to spy for him. You must be gettin' close to sumpin'."

Emma, Darnell and I mulled over a variety of scenarios involving Duratz while Emma finished her wings and dusted off half an Italian hoagie. The conversation continued on the drive to the club where they dropped me off.

———

"Your eyes look funny," Moldy said. "Like Mexican jumping beans on ecstasy."

"Must be the concussion," I said. Moldy's expression told me he hadn't heard. "I had an accident after I left here last night."

"No shit! You weren't drunk. What happened?"

"No brakes. I did a header into a pin oak off Dutch Run between Crestview Cemetery and Flaggart's Bottom."

"That's the way they design cars," "Paranoid" Perry Sanders said. "They want them to fail."

"What are you talking about?" "Professor" Doris Jean Brown asked. "Who wants them to fail?"

"For being a teacher, you don't know shit," Perry said. "The car companies want the cars and, in this case, the brakes to fail because they want to make more cars. More cars, more money. Doctors, hospitals and pharmaceutical corporations want equipment to fail because they get to suck the blood money out of injured people."

Grace Sanders nodded her head in affirmation and I was beginning to think "Paranoid" Perry was starting to make sense. He continued. "And then there's the lawyers, the bottom feeders that pick up all the miserable scraps and manipulate facts into huge personal gains."

"Is that all?" Doris Jean asked.

"Everything is run by the cartel. They have absolute control."

Doris Jean rolled her eyes. "The cartel being?"

"The Bilderberger Group, the Trilateral Commission, for beginners."

I had to interrupt. "That certainly makes sense, Perry, but the brakes didn't fail, the brake lines were cut."

"Paranoid" Perry looked disappointed. Grace threw down a shot of Captain Morgan. Archie "Bunker" Brown said, "What about your efficiency brake?" Another Bunkerism. Doris Jean shook her head. Tommy "Two Shots" Tuttle's head was doing a Vulcan mind-meld on the bar. His wife Reba was engrossed in an episode of *Blue Bloods* on TV.

Moldy looked stunned. "Who would do such a terrible thing? Is it someone who's involved in Frank's disappearance?"

"Gino Duratz spent some time up the river courtesy of Frank's detective work. I heard Gino was very pissed."

"Frank's work sent a lot of people to the Grey-bar Saloon. Why single out Duratz?"

"Because his driver, Russell, has been following me."

Moldy said, "You're saying Duratz's driver cut your brake lines."

"That's what it looks like. He probably pushed me off the road in Sleepy Hollow also."

"What about the threatening note shot to your door with an arrow?" Moldy asked.

"That too, and I aim to prove it."

"You be careful, brother," Moldy said. "This guy sounds dangerous."

"I'm not too worried. Roscoe's helping me. That reminds me, I've got to get home. I have some information for him."

Chapter 29

I usually sleep in on Saturday mornings. But after yesterday's events I felt I should get an early start today, to see what direction Roscoe was going to take. Last night I had told him about Emma and Darnell questioning Emma's stepbrother, Booker Jefferson, and Roland's friends, Monkey George and Otis. They had seen no one resembling my description of Russell at the funeral home, or anywhere else for that matter. Roscoe said we were going to have a busy day today.

After showering and shaving, I dressed and headed into the kitchen. Pissmore was waiting for me at his food bowl. Roscoe sat at the table, sipping coffee.

"I see you got the mutt a new Steelers doggy dish?"

"Yep," Roscoe answered. "Stainless steel. It'll last a lifetime."

Roscoe wore a black and gold Pittsburgh Steelers #58 Jack Lambert throwback football jersey over blue jeans.

Over pancakes and sausage I reminded him of the information we talked about last night.

"I knew it all along. The driver, what's his name, Russell? He's the strong-arm for Duratz."

"Okay, but we have to prove it."

Following Roscoe

"That's what I said last night, but we need to get more information. We'll start by talking to Walter "Nuggets" DeFiglio. He has a hair salon on Fourteenth Street."

"What kind of name is DeFiglio?" I asked, pulling into a lot across the street from a row of upscale businesses. Roscoe didn't answer.

Cheerful Curl and Cut Hair Salon sat between a floral shop that displayed flowers in its expansive front window and a dress shop that featured youthful, colorful clothes. The salon, however, was filled with women hoping to look younger while sitting under hairdryer canopies and wearing restorative, muddy masks on their faces.

Roscoe and I entered the salon and asked the receptionist for Walter DeFiglio. The aromatic shampoo was instantly overcome by the pungent permanent solution and nail polish remover.

"Mister Walter will be with you shortly. Please have a seat," she said, pointing to a row of four chairs across from her against the wall. She walked to the rear of the shop. Displays of beauty, hair and nail products decorated chrome shelves in the waiting area.

A few minutes later she marched back to her station. A very thin man who followed her was dressed in a short-sleeved black shirt and skin-tight black slacks that displayed his cojones in a lumpy package. His narrow face was pointed and animal-like, as were his beady eyes peering through small round glassless frames. His orange and blue hair rose in a five-inch punk rocker Mohawk. He walked strangely graceful, some might say light in the loafers.

Roscoe said, "You asked me what kind of name DeFiglio was. DeFiglio is a homosexual name. Now you know."

Walter approached us. He looked suspiciously at Roscoe. "What can I do for you gentlemen?"

Roscoe spoke. "Is there somewhere private we can talk?"

"I'm really busy."

"Your office, perhaps?" Roscoe grabbed Walter's elbow and started to usher him toward the back of the salon. "It will only take a few minutes. I need information about a person you know."

"What person? What's this about?" Walter asked.

Roscoe led him unwillingly past the curious gazes of patrons under hairdryers.

"The information I need might help put a certain someone behind bars where he belongs. Someone who roughed you up about eight months ago."

Walter's eyes widened in recognition. "Oh, I know who you mean." He tried to pull his arm away from Roscoe, but that proved futile. "I can't help you. I don't know the man. I don't know anything about him."

Roscoe pushed Walter through the door to his office, a small room at the rear of the salon. Walter shook himself free of Roscoe's grip and sank into a chair behind a small walnut desk. We sat in the only two remaining chairs that faced the desk. Walter leaned back in his chair, and clasped his hands across his stomach.

"I take it you want to know about Mister Duratz, is that right?"

"That's right," Roscoe said. "I want to know why he beat the shit out of you and why you didn't tell the police."

"But I did tell the police. It was a road rage thing. I cut him off and he lost it."

"You didn't tell the police until you were forced to," I said. "It took Frank Pallone's investigation to jar your memory."

Walter hung his head.

Roscoe pulled out a small note pad from his blue jeans and flipped a page. "The police report said this supposed incident took place on Route 201 between Fairchance and Dunningsville. Is that correct?"

"Yeah, that's right."

"How did you cut him off? It's a winding, two-lane road."

"Well I... just pulled in front of him and he—"

"That stretch of road is not only curvy, but very hilly. I drove that road this morning. A person would have to be out of his mind to pass on that road."

"Well, that's what I did."

"No, you didn't. You did something other than cut Duratz off to deserve the beating you took."

Walter's face sobered.

"What was it? Financial? Personal? Business?"

I noticed the phone on Walter's desk. From my viewpoint I could see five buttons for outside lines. I wondered why he needed so many lines in here when the receptionist handled appointments at her desk.

Roscoe said. "You work for Duratz, don't you?"

"No, no, I don't have any connection with Gino—" Walter cringed. "—I mean Duratz."

Roscoe smiled. "So, you did work for him. What does a hairdresser do for Gino Dutatz? Let's see, prostitution comes to mind." Walter made a verbal noise that sounded like prostitution was the last thing he would be into. "Drugs, maybe?"

Walter sat up and leaned on the desk. "I would never sell drugs. Never."

"Prostitution then," Roscoe persisted. "You meet a lot of women here."

"No way. And I didn't have any business dealings with Mister Duratz."

Roscoe said. "Now it's *Mister* Duratz."

I looked at Walter's phone again and then it made sense. "You're a bookie. That's how you're connected to Duratz."

In a few short minutes, Walter's facial expression had changed from concern to fear.

"Ah-ha," Roscoe said. "So that's it, bookmaking. What'd you do to piss him off?"

"I didn't—"

Roscoe sprang to his feet and pounded his fist on the walnut desk. "Yes, you did," he shouted. "You pissed off Duratz. What did you do?"

Walter lowered his head and closed his eyes.

"Were you light on your bag? Did you fail to make a payoff?"

"What?" Walter started to weep.

I looked at Roscoe and shrugged.

"I'm going to find out," Roscoe said. "But I'll be very mad if it takes me more than an hour, so you better tell me right now. Don't worry about Duratz. He won't bother you, we'll see to that."

Walter's head hit the desk. He was now in full sob mode.

"I did a very dumb thing," he said through saliva and snot. "I tried to start my own book."

"Ouch," I said. "Why'd you do it? You knew he'd find out."

"Business is bad and..."

"And what?"

"My brother Bob is a woman trapped in a man's body and it's adversely affecting him. Do you know how much a sex change costs? He's out of work and can't afford the operation. I have to raise a ton of money and this business is so slow." He started sobbing again.

"Okay, take it easy," Roscoe said. "Take your time. You can save enough money for your brother's operation. You've got a good business here. Cut your overhead, buy your supplies in bulk and use good businesses practices. You can do it."

Walter stopped sobbing and raised his head. "You think so?"

"Absolutely," Roscoe said. "And we won't bother you anymore." Roscoe motioned to me and we started to leave when Roscoe turned around. "Oh, by the way, where is Gino's place of business?"

Without hesitation, Walter said, "On Braddock Avenue in Hazelwood."

Chapter 30

Being a passenger in a car driven by Roscoe Kronek can stimulate emotions that range from tranquility to absolute terror. Right now I was in a state somewhere between the two. I had forgotten that school was out for the summer when Roscoe made a U-turn in a school zone. I occasionally think school is out for Roscoe as well.

I asked Roscoe, "If Russell is the muscle for Duratz, why did Gino savagely beat DiFigio?"

"Probably because he could." Roscoe looked at me as if I didn't comprehend what he said. "You have to understand that these so-called big shots like Duratz are cowards. They have men like Russell hanging around for the money, the prestige, and the power, and in return they do their master's bidding. Guys like Russell are the muscle, the strong-arm for their gutless benefactors. But when given the opportunity, they'll pick on someone completely helpless like Walter DeFiglio to make them feel like a man."

"I can see it wouldn't take much to whip Walter's ass," I said. "The women who work for him probably could beat him senseless."

"It takes a bully to pick on someone like Walter. I'm glad Gino got caught. People will now see him for the oppressor he really is."

I was going to respond to Roscoe's statement when my cell chimed. The readout indicated it was Emma.

"Emma, what's up? Any trouble?"

"Naw, no trouble. Everything's smooth as a baby's ass. Gertrude called. She has another recruit for bein' a maid."

"That's good. Did she set up an appointment?"

"She said she'll be here at ten-thirty. That work for you?"

Roscoe said, "Is that Emma? Tell her I love her."

"Who is that? Is that that degenerate, Roscoe?"

"Ah... yes, ten-thirty is fine."

Roscoe reached over. "Hand me the phone, I want to talk to Emma Lou."

I closed my cell. "No, you're driving. Drop me off at home. I need the van."

When I walked into the office/garage, Gertrude and the applicant were already waiting for me. Gertrude looked apologetic. The applicant wore U.S. Army olive-drab fatigues and black low quarters. Her curly close-cropped hair looked like she was wearing a football helmet.

"Sorry I'm late, ladies. There was an accident on the Elizabeth Bridge, had both lanes tied up."

Gertrude said, "Mister Gustafson, this is Hilda Weiner. She's applying for the vacant maid's position. Hilda, this is Mister August Gustafson, owner of Desperate Domestics Maid Service."

Hilda reached out to shake my hand. "Very nice to meet you." Her voice was deep and masculine. We shook hands... well, I shook her hand; she vise-gripped mine. Her rough hands were larger than mine and her knuckles were huge and callused as if she monkey-walked on her fists.

"Nice grip you have there, Hilda," I said.

Hilda was a big-boned, husky woman who looked like a prehistoric food gatherer. Her eyes were wide-set and sunken beneath an overlapping brow and sloping forehead. She had very hairy arms and her face revealed a four o'clock shadow. Her nose was wide and bulbous and she spoke through thick lips. The term "Neanderthal" came to mind when describing her.

"Have a seat," I told her, motioning toward the couch. "Do you have any references?" I hoped she didn't, but she pulled three papers out of her saddlebag-looking purse.

Hilda handed them to me. "I think you'll find these satisfactory and in order."

I quickly scanned the references. They all were from men of authority: a retired United States Marine Corps major, a superintendent of a public school system, and the warden of a county jail.

I pretended to read through the references, but the vision of the bipedal hominid in front of me consumed my thoughts. What would customers think of her? Would her presense affect business? I had never seen anyone like Hilda before, and didn't want to see anyone remotely similar to her in the future. Hilda and Walter DeFiglio were too much for me in one day.

"Okay," I said. "They seem to be in order. I have your number. I'll let you know."

Hilda stood up and extended her mitt. *Not this time, Brutus.* I placed my hand on her shoulder and guided her toward the door.

"Have a nice day," I said to Hilda. I cut my eyes to Gertrude and said. "Be careful, it's mating season. There are a lot of animals running around out there." Gertrude stifled a grin.

Emma and I watched Mutt and Jeff walk to Gertrude's Chevy Nova. Hilda snugged into the car. Gertrude turned around and waved before folding herself into the driver's seat.

"Did you bring lunch, Emma?"

"No, didn't have time to pack a lunch. I'm not very hungry."
"How about Blockheads?"
"Hmmm, my appetite just came back."

Parking always seemed to be a problem at Blockheads Restaurant. The popular eatery has a distinctive curb appeal with its designer multicolor striped awnings and glass window-walls.

The waitress skipped away after taking our orders.

Emma leaned back against the oak booth. "I'm scared of that woman, and I don't frighten easy. She's one ugly, spooky bitch."

"She's different, all right." I told Emma about the meeting Roscoe and I had with Walter DeFiglio this morning.

"Oh my God, you're really havin' a bad day. You say this dude savin' up for his brother's sex change?"

"DeFiglio needs a bunch of money quick for the operation. That's what got him in trouble with Duratz in the first place."

Our waitress arrived with a tray. She wore a version of the cheese-head hat, only square and blocky. She served Emma a southwest firehouse burger, spicy cheese balls and potato skins. She slid a chicken fajita in front of me.

Emma took care of the spicy cheese first, probably warming up for the super hot burger. I guess the potato skins were to cleanse the palate.

Emma took a forkful of the skins and said, "Maybe when Walter's brother gets his sex change, Hilda might want his leftover parts."

I almost choked on my fajita and had to take a slug of Dr Pepper to wash it down.

"You okay, Mister G?"

"That was quite a visual, Emma."

"I think that's what Hilda is needin' to complete her inner child. I watched all of Oprah's shows."

I noticed a large man with a huge square head chewing out a waitress a few tables away. "Take a look at that guy." I nodded in the direction of the angry man.

"Whooeee," Emma said through a mouthful of a firehouse burger. "I never see a head like that in my life. That's slammin.'"

"By the way, how'd your date go after you dropped me off last night?"

"Redd Dawg's had really good food and the pizza shop was nice, but after… well, that be somewhere between amazing and chanky."

"Could you interpret 'between amazing and chanky'?"

"Darnell is different. He do things spur of the moment. You know… what he feel like right then."

"Okay, like what?"

"Well, we went to his place."

"The funeral home?"

"Yeah and I wanted to see the caskets again and…"

"You didn't!"

"Yep. We did it in a twenty-gauge steel casket, two-tone blue with light blue crepe interior."

I was trying to extinguish the visual in my mind when my cell chirped. The display indicated it was Roscoe.

"What's up?"

"Pick me up in half an hour. We're going to have a cup of coffee."

Chapter 31

Roscoe stood on the sidewalk staring at me as I pulled into the garage. I turned off the engine, got out, and closed the garage door behind me. As I approached Roscoe, Pissmore peered through the slats of the fence.

"Why'd you park?" Roscoe asked. "Saving up on your gas money?"

"I figured your car wouldn't be recognized, but the van would."

A contemplative moment passed. "Good thinking, Nephew. Let's go." Roscoe folded himself into the Lincoln. I sat shotgun.

The drive to Hazelwood usually takes about fifteen minutes if traffic is light—but it wasn't. We were stopped at a red light when a husky woman with close-cropped hair walked across the street in front of us.

"I interviewed an applicant for a maid today and she was a doozy."

"Oh, yeah?" Roscoe said excitedly. "When can I meet her?"

"You know my position on my maids. Hands off. And besides, you wouldn't want to meet her anyway."

I described Hilda to Roscoe and Emma's suggestion of giving Walter's brother Bob's leftover sex change parts to her.

"She's a gem, Emma is. She has spunk."

The community of Hazelwood sat on the fringe of a former industrial area that had provided jobs, produced taxes, and given birth to satellite businesses for the community. Now the area is depressed: residents shop elsewhere in malls, young people leave for better jobs, and remaining mom-and-pop stores serve the indigent, landlocked people of the community.

Rose's Coffee Shop not only provided nourishment for the poor but dreams as well. For only five cents, a lucky person could pick a three-digit number and win thirty dollars, and for ten cents they could win sixty dollars. Local bookies provided small businesses with a side income from the numbers game and a chance for their customers to win some dream money.

Roscoe parked at the curb half a block away. We got out and passed a shoe repair shop, a small appliance store and a fruit market. As I entered Rose's, the door rang a tiny bell attached to the door frame above. Five square tables sat in the room, two against each wall and one in front of the window. Six revolving stools lined the counter at the rear of the room. A waitress stood behind a nineteenth-century cash register.

Roscoe and I took seats at a table against the right wall. Four men playing euchre sat at a table directly across the room from us. They looked old enough to have mastered the technical skills of the game and old enough to have acquired the wisdom to be in another place, but here they sat, bickering over who should have played what card, or trumped what trick. One man wore a fedora, two wore Steelers caps, one wore a faded Pirates cap. All wore different logo t-shirts and shiny polyester slacks.

The man in the fedora said, "Nellie, where's my hamburger? Light a fire under Metro's ass."

A baldheaded man rang a bell and shoved a plate with a hamburger and fries on it through a two-foot square opening in the wall that separated the kitchen from the dining room.

Nellie carried the hamburger to the euchre table and served the man wearing the fedora. "'Bout time," he said.

"Go home and have your wife cook your burgers," she said, and headed in our direction.

Nellie walked slowly with a slight limp, her shoulders slumped forward and her head hung. She looked as if she was ready to surrender to an unseen enemy. She looked ten years older than she was. Premature gray hair, wrinkled and saggy skin, and sad, baggy eyes seemed to say life was futile.

"Whaddya gents have?"

"Coffee," Roscoe said.

She looked at me.

"Same."

Nellie retreated behind the counter. She returned a few minutes later with two cups of java and served them with a check.

Roscoe picked up the bill and handed it back to her. "Here, Nellie, just run a tab for us. We'll probably want something else."

Nellie cut her eyes at Roscoe, grabbed the check and limped away.

"How long do you think we'll be here?" I asked.

"Don't know. Depends."

"On what?"

"On how well I can rustle Duratz's feathers."

I looked at Roscoe, prompting him for further explanation.

"I want to force his hand, to let him know we're on the offensive. We can't continue to sit back and wait for him to keep attacking you."

Uh-oh. "So you're going to piss him off, and then we're going to get shot or something worse."

"Do you remember what I told you this morning? This guy's a coward. He doesn't have the balls to start anything with us."

"I also remember that he has his driver, Russell, do his dirty work for him. What do you say about that?"

"I say we talk to Russell and convince him to change jobs."

Oh shit! "What if he doesn't want to?"

"Then we'll convince him to give up his wicked ways. We'll make him an offer he can't refuse."

The door chimed. A woman in a flowered housecoat came in and scurried to the register. I heard change hit the counter, but she left without buying anything.

"She must have played a number," I said.

Roscoe nodded. "There will be a lot of customers coming in to play, but we want the big fish—the carp and the bigmouth bass—to see us in their place of business."

"And that'll rustle their feathers... or worse."

"I'm getting hungry. I noticed pastries on the counter." Roscoe motioned to Nellie. "I'll have a maple roll."

Nellie trudged over with Roscoe's order and set the plate on the table. "Anything else?"

I shook my head. Roscoe waved her off.

How could I eat at a stressful time like this? It certainly didn't bother Roscoe, munching on the roll and licking maple icing from his fingers. From my point of view this scene looked like the Last Supper.

"This is really good," he said, smacking his lips. "Reminds me of old lady Vanderslice's meal the other day. She's a good cook."

"Old lady? She's only five months older than you."

"But an older woman doesn't do it for me."

"Why not? You two have a lot in common: healthy food, exercise, sports, skydiving. And she really likes you." Why was I promoting Aldine to Roscoe?

Roscoe rubbed his chin. "And for some strange reason that I can't comprehend, you like her."

Roscoe didn't know the half of it. "Well, I—" I felt a flush spread over my face and I couldn't answer.

"You should be chasing after the lieutenant. She's young, beautiful, intelligent... well, not so intelligent." Roscoe looked as if his testosterone level dropped. "She likes you, Nephew, can't you tell?"

It took a while for Roscoe's statement to sink in. *The lieutenant has the hots for me?* What was going on here? Where was Colleen Fahey when Genie DeFlorio's blabber-mouthing newscast about my liaison with her mother spread throughout southwestern Pennsylvania? But that didn't change anything. I still dug the cougars and wanted Mrs. Vanderslice to join the feline pack. The problem was, she had the hots for Roscoe.

While we were talking, two women, a man and a boy came in, approached the counter, and played a number. Another man followed them, carrying a small fabric bag. He continued into the back room. He left a few minutes later, and the bag looked a little fatter.

Nellie was limping toward us with a coffee pot when a police officer walked in. They passed each other in the middle of the room. Nellie stopped at our table, and the cop disappeared into the back room.

"One more cup," Roscoe said, "and we'll take our check." I waved off the coffee. Nellie smiled and shuffled away.

"Are we finished? What did we get out of this visit?"

Nellie returned with the check and the officer left. Roscoe handed her a five-spot and said, "Keep the change." After he watched her walk away, he said, "Who said we were finished?"

Roscoe waited until Nellie moved behind the counter then, in a loud voice said, "What's the payoff for a dollar?"

"Excuse me?" Nellie said.

"For a hit on a three-digit number."

Nellie hurried to our table, her limp seemingly gone. In a low voice she said, "Six hundred dollars. And keep it down."

"Why can't I get six hundred and fifty dollars? If you can afford to pay off the cops, you can afford to pay a little more on a hit."

Nellie scurried off and dashed into the back room.

Metro's face appeared in the service window, his eyes squinted into a menacing glare. He mouthed what seemed to be profanities.

Nellie limped back to the table. "It doesn't work that way. I have to ask you to leave."

"We're not ready to leave," Roscoe said. "I think I'll stay and tell your customers that I'm willing to pay six hundred and fifty dollars for a dollar hit. I don't have to pay off the cops."

Nellie lost her limp again as she scampered into the back room. Metro's face appeared in the hole in the wall, this time talking on a cell phone.

Triple rats. Roscoe had stirred the pot to the boiling point.

Chapter 32

It didn't take long for Russell to show up. He burst through the door and tramped into the back room like a man on a mission, and I'm assuming Roscoe and I were the objects of that pursuit. Three of the four men playing euchre got up and left. Only the man wearing the fedora stayed—but not for long. When he heard the heated words between Metro and Russell he left as well, leaving only Nellie as a possible witness to our impending assault.

Russell sauntered out of the back room and stood in the middle of the coffee shop. He wore a black short-sleeved t-shirt that looked as if it was painted on his body, his wide V-shaped torso tapered to a slim waist. His arms seemed as thick as his neck. His arrogant smirk evaporated and changed to curiosity when he recognized me.

"What are you doing here?"

Russell's size and musculature astounded me, leaving me temporarily speechless.

Before I could answer, Roscoe said, "We're checking on you for a change."

Russell's face morphed into a harsh, granite glare. "Who the hell are you, old man?"

Uh-oh, not the age card.

"I'm Augie's uncle, but you already knew that, didn't you? You've been following my nephew around for almost a week now, watching where he goes, when he arrives, when he leaves."

"I don't know what you're talking about," Russell said, lowering his voice. "Nellie, you can leave now. I'll lock up."

Nellie quickly grabbed her purse and left without a word. A few seconds later I heard the door close in the back room. Metro had left also.

Oh shit. Russell was clearing the place out for a beatdown. I should've left with Nellie.

"You know what I'm talking about," Roscoe continued. "Your boss is afraid of the information Augie will dig up to put his ass back in jail."

"I think you'd better leave."

Roscoe took a slow sip of coffee. "I've been thinking about starting my own business in the neighborhood. Maybe you can help me get started."

Russell made a move toward Roscoe but stopped when the doorbell tinkled. The old man wearing the fedora came in, rushed to the table where he had been sitting, and picked up a pair of sunglasses. He managed a frightful glance at Russell as he scurried back through the door to the safety of the street.

"I've got to hand it to you, old man, you've got chutzpah," Russell said. "But if you don't leave now, the paramedics will be carrying you and your nephew out on a stretcher."

"You should get another job," Roscoe said. "You're going to end up in prison where there's tougher guys than me."

"You've got more than a set of balls, old man. You're crazy."

Double shit! Roscoe had stirred the pot a little too hard this time. Russell was so incensed with Roscoe's disrespect that he was paying no attention to me. That must be Roscoe's plan—to beat this humongous humanoid into submission. I guess I was to hit Russell over the head with a chair, table, fire plug or something while he was busy pounding Roscoe into the ground.

"I'm not crazy," Roscoe said. "You lift weights and take steroids to look good and put on a show for the girlies, but I can tell by looking at you that you don't have what it takes. You're not tough, you're a sissy boy."

Triple shit! Roscoe had pushed the envelope right out of the mail box.

Russell was ten feet away when he started his charge. Roscoe didn't move until Russell closed in on him and tried to pull him out of his chair by his shirt. Roscoe grabbed Russell's right hand, twisting it so that Russell's wrist locked. Roscoe intensified the pressure, turning Russell to the side. He kicked Russell in the stomach, sending him flying over the next table. Russell sprawled on the floor.

It happened so fast I didn't have time to grab a weapon. The episode was quite a feat for Roscoe, considering he hadn't gotten up from his chair. Embarrassment showed on Russell's face as he scrambled to his feet.

Roscoe stood up and stepped to the center of the room. Russell looked like an animal stalking its prey as he slowly closed the distance between Roscoe and himself.

I resumed my search for a weapon and spotted a baseball trophy in the window. It was a six-inch gold-plated baseball player swinging a bat on a twelve-inch walnut base. A plated insignia read: Rose's First Place Monview Pony League. I grabbed it while the two combatants circled each another in the center of the room.

Russell lunged at Roscoe like a bull wanting to gore him, but Roscoe sidestepped like a matador while delivering a karate chop to the base of Russell's neck, sending him facedown to the floor.

I couldn't believe my eyes. Roscoe had decked this hulk of a brute twice with only one kick and one chop. I felt relieved and started to put the trophy back in the window when Russell jumped to his feet and growled like a vengeful animal. He didn't charge this time but slowly circled Roscoe, looking for an opportunity. He threw a couple of jabs to test Roscoe's defense, followed by an overhand right haymaker.

Roscoe leaned back far enough to escape the blow and countered with a left hook that sent Russell to the floor.

Again, Russell jumped to his feet, an embarrassing flush flooding his face. He looked determined yet cautious, and hadn't lost his patience in trying to find a way to outsmart Roscoe.

I put the trophy back in the window and took a ringside seat to this awe-inspiring battle between David and Goliath.

Russell feinted with a left hook then tried to deliver a kick to Roscoe's midsection. Roscoe moved to the right just far enough to evade the kick and caught Russell's leg and held it. He delivered a powerful kick to Russell's *cojones,* dropping him again to the floor. Russell lay in a fetal position, writhing in pain, and coughed up his lunch.

Roscoe stood over the defeated bully. "Tell your boss he's going to pay for what he did." Roscoe winked at me and said, "Let's blow this pop stand."

Roscoe hadn't said a word as he drove sedately through Hazelwood, his face reflecting the satisfaction he must have felt by bringing down a huge hulk like Russell.

"That was quite a spectacle, Roscoe. Where did you learn to fight like that, the army?"

Roscoe smiled one of those smiles that told me I wouldn't get a straight answer and said, "Yeah, the army."

When Roscoe turned off Inglewood onto Twenty-third Street, I asked, "Where are we going?"

"To police headquarters. We have to file a report."

Roscoe must have noticed the question mark on my forehead. "Russell committed assault, and the police have to be notified."

"What assault? You kicked the shit out of him."

"And what do you think Duratz will do when Russell tells him what happened?"

"Press charges against you?"

"Good guess, Nephew. That's why we have to beat him to the punch."

The desk sergeant was preoccupied with his favorite activity—ogling a girly magazine.

Roscoe stopped behind the sergeant and looked over his shoulder. "Isn't that the girl on *CSI Miami*?"

Disturbed by the interruption, the sergeant wheeled around. "No, that's not her, but there is an uncanny resemblance."

"Is that the August issue?" Roscoe asked.

"No, September. I'm on the preferred mailing list."

Roscoe was writing down information on how to get on the preferred list when I headed for Lieutenant Fahey's office.

A generous smile lit Colleen's face when I walked in. "Augie, I didn't expect a visit."

"Well... it's not exactly a visit. How does one file an assault charge?"

Her smile changed to disappointment. "Assault charge? Get mixed up with another nurse?"

"No, I don't mean me. Roscoe wants to file a report."

"Did he get mixed up with a nurse?"

"No, it's—"

"By the way, I was checking up on Gino Duratz for you and found that your Nurse Candice is related to Duratz's driver, Russell. She's his second cousin. I thought you would want to know."

"Holy mackerel, just like the scene from *The Godfather,* except I was being duped into being led to the wolf by a sheep. It's a good thing Emma broke me out of the hospital before Nurse Candy injected me with a terminal shot of some untraceable drug."

"You're so dramatic. We really don't know what she was going to do or if Russell would have been involved at all."

"I'm sure Russell's involved. That's why Roscoe wants to file an assault charge against him."

"Did I hear my name?" Roscoe sauntered into the office. "My, my, you look gorgeous in your uniform, lieutenant."

Chapter 33

"What's the matter, Roscoe?" I asked. "Are you feeling okay?"

"I feel great, why?" Roscoe pushed a button on the radio, changing the channel.

"You breezed through filing the assault charge against Russell without making a play for Lieutenant Fahey. That's not like you."

"I don't make a play for every woman I see."

"You don't?"

"No. And besides, you're family, and she has the hots for you."

That settles it, he wasn't feeling well. "That wouldn't have stopped you last week. Why the sudden change?"

"No change. You're my nephew and you deserve a relationship with a fine, good looking woman like Colleen Fahey."

"Uh-huh."

"Believe this, Nephew, if you don't jump at the chance for the lieutenant, all I have to do is snap my finger."

From what I'd seen earlier today at Rose's Coffee Shop, I believed Roscoe could do anything he wanted to, including date Colleen Fahey. I suddenly became nervous and a shiver shot up my spine.

"I'll think about it," I said as Roscoe parked in front of the house.

I followed Roscoe into the yard. The gate closed with a clap. Pissmore bounded through the doggy door and lumbered up to us.

"That dog's got good hearing when he's hungry," Roscoe said. "Doesn't listen to me at all. Chewed up my slippers. Ate one, I think."

We all went into the kitchen where I filled Pissmore's dish with his favorite recipe. Roscoe went into his apartment and I into mine where I noticed the blinking light on my answering machine.

I pressed play. Emma's voice greeted me.

"Hey, Mister G, I got a great idea for you. I don't like that guy that answers your phone. I think Lily Tomlin's voice doin' that 'one ringy-dingy, two ringy-dingy' thing she did on that Roman and Martin laugh show would be much better. Oh, yeah, I forgot. Gertrude called. She's feeling bad 'bout that Amazon woman she drive over this morning. She's bringin' another maid applicant over at four o'clock. She knows you need someone for Monday. And besides, if no one is hired, I'll have to chip in and take up the slack. That means no maid service for you. I'll be seeing you at four."

I guess she was telling me in her own special way that I needed to interview this girl today—and hire her.

I dashed into the bathroom and took a quick shower. Khaki slacks and a black short-sleeved sport shirt felt like the right uniform of the day—or in this case the evening as well—if my plan came to fruition.

On the drive to the office I called Lieutenant Fahey and asked her to meet me at Ruggerio's for dinner and talk about Frank's disappearance. I was surprised to hear her say yes so quickly.

I walked into the office/garage at 3:55, demonstrating that punctuality is essential for a business to run properly—for the employees of course, not the employer. Gertrude and the applicant were looking over the collection of cleaning supplies and equipment on the other side of the garage. The applicant followed Gertrude to Emma's desk where I joined them.

Gertrude spoke first. "Mister Gustafson, this is Lorin Scott. Lorin, this is August Gustafson, owner of Desperate Domestics."

Lorin stood approximately five foot eight and had a rosy-cheeked cherubic face. She came dressed for work—a blue short-sleeve housekeeping smock over khaki work pants. Her sinewy arms and wide shoulders were evidence that she was no stranger to manual labor.

I motioned for Gertrude and Lorin to take a seat on the couch. I sat on the edge of Emma's desk.

I said to them, "I see you've already met Emma Lou Rawlins, my office manager and director of operations. Emma, do you have Lorin's application?"

"Harumph," Emma muttered and shook a paper at me.

I got it. She was pissed off that I sat on the edge of her desk. I took the application and moved to a chair in front of her desk. I caught a glimpse of a roguish smile on Emma's face.

Before I could finish reading her application, Lorin said, "I could start today if you wish. I came prepared to work."

Wow, someone eager to work! That was a new twist around here. She didn't look desperate—although that would fit in with Desperate Domestics—no needle marks on her arms, no ankle bracelet. Probably no parole officer, either.

I didn't answer her, but finished going over her application. She was born in Reading, Pennsylvania, moved to Connellsville when she was thirteen and lived with her grandmother, delivered papers until she was fourteen and was hired at a grocery store as a stock person until she was eighteen and old enough to work on an assembly line at a fabricating plant for four years until the plant closed.

"Why did you move to Connellsville to live with your grandmother?"

"My parents were killed in an automobile accident. I didn't have anywhere to go."

Following Roscoe

Oh my God. I hated to hear stories like that. I managed to say, "I'm sorry."

I continued to read her application. She worked as a maid in Layton, Pennsylvania, for two years, followed by a three-month stint at the Sheets Hotel across the river in Dawson.

"You didn't list why you quit your job in Layton... let's see... working for a Mrs. Quigley."

"Oh, I'm sorry. She passed on. Was that question on the application?"

"No, but most people give a reason for leaving their employment. What about your job at the Sheets Hotel in Dawson?"

"That place was terrible. The things that went on there shouldn't be allowed." Lorin pointed her finger in the direction of where she thought Dawson would be. "I needed the money, but I couldn't take the debauchery, cheating husbands and carrying on by young people. I had to leave."

"Do you have any references?"

"Mrs. Quigley died, so I couldn't get a reference from her, but I did get one from the Sheets Hotel." She pulled out a folded paper from her purse and handed it to me.

The reference was written on a sheet of hotel stationery. At the top of the page was a photo of the hotel, a large white Victorian building, with an expansive sign on its porch roof that read: Sheets Hotel. A short description of the hotel and its accommodations were listed under the photo as well as address and telephone number. In scribbled handwriting, the reference read: *Lorin Scott worked here for three months as a maid. She did an okay job.*

Nice people she worked for, I thought. She's worked hard all her life only to be met with bad breaks. I'll have Emma start her on Monday.

"Okay, everything seems to be in order," I said. "You mentioned you needed money. Is it something that—"

"My little brother. When my parents were killed, my grandmother could take me, but not Steven. He went to

Social Services and foster care, and I haven't been able to find him. I've been saving up to hire an investigator."

Double wow! "Emma, start Lorin Monday and assign her to Gertrude's crew.

"Yes suh," Emma said through a wide smile.

Lorin sprang to her feet, rushed over and hugged me as I was trying to stand up. I looked over Lorin's shoulder to see a smiling Gertrude.

"Thank you. Thank you so much," Lorin said. "You won't regret hiring me."

"I'm sure you'll be fine," I said, feeling a little embarrassed. "Emma has some paperwork for you to fill out and Gertrude will tell you where to report on Monday."

Emma grabbed a clipboard and a pencil and handed them to Lorin. "Fill this out. I'll be right back." Emma motioned for me to follow her outside.

"You're one big softie," she said when we were safely outside and out of earshot from the maids. "That what make you the real Mister G. I'm proud to work for you. And to show my appreciation, I'm buying you dinner tonight."

What was this? Show a little empathy for someone, and Emma turns into a bleeding heart office manager.

"That's really nice of you, but I've got a dinner engagement tonight."

"Oh yeah, where?"

"Ruggerio's Restaurant."

"That's a nice place. Wit who?"

"I can't answer that."

"Why not?"

If I told Emma who I was having dinner with, she would turn into a card-carrying, bow-and-arrow cupid.

"About that dinner invitation, can I get a rain check?"

"I can't answer that," Emma said, planting her hands on her hips.

"Okay then, I'll see you on Monday."

"I changed my mind about you," Emma said. I got into the van and left.

Chapter 34

The Dunsworth Hotel sat on the corner of Fourteenth Street and Blytheway Avenue in the Shady Hill section of town. The early twentieth century four-story building couldn't be more square; the only projections from the vertical walls were canvas canopies that covered the entrances from both streets to Ruggerio's, the restaurant where I would be having dinner with Lieutenant Colleen Fahey.

    I parked in the lot on Blytheway and casually sauntered across the street as if I hadn't a care in the world, although I did have mixed feelings about the evidence Roscoe and I illegally obtained from Frank's home and office. I was glad we had a list of suspects and had eliminated all but Gino Duratz, but the police needed this evidence to legally proceed with their investigation. And the sooner the better. Frank could still be alive, held by Duratz in some dark place where he was being tortured at this very moment, and the thought haunted me. I had to figure a way to get the police involved without getting Roscoe or myself arrested for breaking and entering and withholding evidence. That's why I had called Lieutenant Fahey and arranged the dinner meeting. The Fourteenth Street entrance led to the bar, where the tang of alcohol and cigar smoke greeted me.

Colleen sat at a small table against the far wall, sipping one of those fancy girly drinks. She looked gorgeous in civilian clothes. She wore a black and blue printed blouse over slimming high-waisted pants. Short auburn hair topped off her facial palette of emerald green eyes, red pouty lips, and alabaster skin.

I squeezed through the crush of patrons with their alcohol-induced gibberish and hilarity, and slid into the chair opposite Colleen.

"Been waiting long?" I asked.

"Just a few minutes. I'm glad you asked me out. It's about time we got to know each other a little better."

Uh-oh. I was only here to talk business. But I'd forgotten to mention this to her when I'd called. Shit. A waitress appeared and interrupted my dilemma. I ordered an I.C. Light and asked her to check on my reservation.

"Ah, yeah... get to know each other." This was going to get messy. "So... you're a cop. I mean policeman, policewoman." It was getting messy faster than I thought. "What prompted you to stick your face into the jaws of evil?"

"My grandfather, father, uncle, were all cops. It's in my blood. Why did you get into the maid business?"

"I hate housework."

"I don't understand."

"Let me put it this way. If you don't want to buy cars or fix them, what do you do? You buy a car dealership. If you don't want to buy or shop for food, you buy a supermarket. If you don't want to shop for clothes—"

"I get it, you buy a men's store."

"You're learning. And one more thing. I don't have to perform any manual labor."

"So you can spend time golfing, playing the nags and working part time for a private investigator."

Colleen's last statement was the perfect segue to shift the conversation to Frank's disappearance and possibly finding a way to involve the police. But the maître d' caught my attention and nodded. Shit! What bad timing.

Only five minutes had passed. I usually wait longer than fifteen minutes to be seated, and I wanted to continue our conversation.

"Our table is ready," I said. We grabbed our drinks and headed into the dining room, where we were escorted to a table for four at the far left corner of the room.

I offered Colleen a chair and sat opposite her. A greeter suddenly appeared and labored through today's specials. As soon as he finished he turned on his heel and scampered off to welcome guests at another table.

"What do you suggest?" Colleen asked.

"The pasta Scolgio is absolutely delicious. Veal saltimbocca or shrimp scampi come in second."

Colleen studied the menu. "What are you getting?"

"The Scolgio. It's my favorite."

Colleen scanned the menu again. "That looks good. I'll order that also." She sat back and took in the room. "This is a nice place. Do you come here often?"

"After a new client signs a service agreement, I bring them here for a good meal. It's good business. And when Roscoe cooks pork chops for dinner, I beat a path here."

"Do you bring your dates here also?"

Here we go again, I thought, this is not a date. I was only here to find a way to convince her to get the police involved in Frank's case. That's all. Nothing more.

A young waiter stepped to the table before I could respond. That was fine, because I didn't want to admit to being here with more than a few cougars.

Since I already knew what Colleen wanted, I did the gentlemanly thing and ordered for both of us. I watched the flirtatious waiter write the order as he continued to ogle Colleen. She was a gorgeous woman, but he was much younger than her. When he trotted off, Colleen's gaze didn't follow him.

"They have some good looking waiters here," I said.

"Yes, but they all are so young."

Hmmm, she'll never make cougar first class.

"Hello there," a sexy female voice said. I felt a finger glide across my shoulder. Audrey Perkins, a perky cougar

I dated a few years ago smiled as she walked past. Her short, gray hair contrasted with a snug blue dress that covered every curve of her lovely body. I believe she had turned fifty-eight in June, but she looked only 40.

I opened my mouth to say hello, but she was already out of earshot.

"Someone you know?" Colleen watched the feline sashay through the tangle of tables to where she took a seat.

"Uh... she's a former client."

"I think it's nice for a woman to have dinner with her son, don't you?"

Her son! I followed Colleen's gaze to where Audrey and the man, or should I say boy, were seated. That bitch! She should be arrested for statutory rape. He was a mere child.

"Yes, good parenting."

"Ever been married?" she asked.

I felt as if I'd been struck by a lightning bolt. Talk about getting right to the point.

"No."

"Why not?"

A young man in a gray pin-striped suit swooped in from the knot of people that had entered the room, walked up behind Colleen, put his hand on her shoulder and said, "Colleen, I thought that was you. Nice to see you out and about."

When Colleen turned and saw who it was, she recoiled. "Captain DeNardo. What are you—"

"I'm with a few council members. Sort of a business meeting." Disfavor crept over his face when he looked at me. "Don't forget about the retirement party for Sergeant McManus tomorrow. Come a little early. I want to go over some procedural changes I've made."

He sounded like he was giving orders to her. He stalked off.

"Your boss?"

"Councilman Martinet's nephew. A real suck-up. He doesn't have the experience or training I have."

"Politics, huh?"

"Absolutely." With a frown, she watched the captain take his seat. "And that twenty-eight-year-old thinks politics can get me in bed with him."

Why, that son of a bitch! "Isn't there anything you can do about it? Sex discrimination? Sexual harassment?"

"He's too connected. And wearing blue is just like being in the army. Have to follow orders. No complaining."

Sounds like the guy needed an attitude adjustment. "Politics has a way of turning around and biting you on the ass. Sooner or later he'll dig himself into a hole that he can't slither out of."

"I hope it's sooner. He turns my stomach."

Just then a disturbance broke out near the doorway. *Oh my God, it's Emma.* She was in a heated hassle with the maître d'. Darnell White stood stoically behind her. I couldn't hear what they were saying over the dining room's din, but Emma's expression and gestures seemed highly solicitous. Emma and the maître d' looked at me over Emma's outstretched arm.

"Is that the woman from the pizza shop? Emma, the woman who works for you?"

"Couldn't be anyone else. Looks like she has a problem. I'd better go over and see what's going on."

Heat flooded my face as I walked across the room. They waited for me in temporary abeyance.

"What's going on, Emma?"

"Dis here major pain in d'ass say there's no seats. I say there's plenty of seats. Empty seats at every table."

"I tried to explain to—" The maître d' started to say.

"You're jumpin' on my conversate again, you—"

I stepped between the two potential combatants, holding up my hands in a surrender motion. "Excuse me. There is a logical solution to this problem. Emma, why don't you and Darnell join us at our table?" Had those words just come out of my mouth? I looked at the maître d' for approval. He reluctantly nodded. I followed Emma and Darnell to the table, not wanting them to see the disappointment on my face, but I could see it on Colleen's.

Emma dropped anchor in the chair across from Colleen. Darnell gracefully slid into the seat next to Emma. Shit! That left me sitting next to Colleen. Any hope of convincing her to get the police involved in Frank's case disappeared.

The astute young waiter with the ogle problem appeared. "Will you be having dinner?" he asked, looking alternately at Darnell and Emma.

"Dinner?" Emma asked. "I thought we were at the Consol Energy Center for a Penguin's game. Of course we want dinner. Darnell, you order for us." Emma focused her attention on me.

"I'm glad to see you two together. I knew it at the pizza shop. I saw sparklers going off."

"That was the bad fluorescent lighting," I said.

Colleen managed a chuckle.

Emma studied Colleen's face. "Mister G always makes light of his emotions."

Darnell finished ordering their dinner and then asked me, "Where did you two first meet?"

Was that the kind of question he asked widows and widowers when they came to make funeral arrangements?

"Okay, let me see," I said, looking to Colleen for help.

"How could you have forgotten?" Colleen said.

I hadn't forgotton. It was when Roscoe and I had broken into Frank's office and she almost caught us. "Ah… it was at police headquarters."

"Yes," Colleen said. "Go on."

"Police headquarters when I invited you to dinner."

Colleen slumped in her chair. "No, that's not the first time." Apparently, she remembered the day in Frank's office. "It was when you came in to report Frank Pallone missing."

Holy hell, she was right! I was so concerned about keeping information from her that I forgot the most

Following Roscoe

important thing. Frank. "How could I forget? I got my days mixed up."

Colleen smiled and started to giggle. "You came into my office with a strawberry on your forehead. You said you were attacked by a woman who packed a mean broom."

I started to laugh. "It wasn't funny at the time. She had all the moves. Chased me out of town."

"Who's that witch?" Emma asked. "I'll kick her behind for her."

"Nellie Niznanski," Colleen said. "She's the neighborhood watch sergeant. She calls in frequently and does a good job preventing crime in her neighborhood. We take her calls seriously."

That was it! The she-devil that had pigs trapped in her moo-moo. This was perfect. I had to call Roscoe. Just as I started to get up, the waiter arrived with our meals. As he served us, I formulated a plan that would not only get the police involved, but get me out of the restaurant as well.

After a few bites of the pasta Scolgio, I excused myself to make a phone call. I stepped out the Blytheway entrance to a vacant sidewalk. I punched in Roscoe's cell number.

"Charlie Sheen. Winning."

"Roscoe, I need your help."

"I was just about to call you. I got a call from Duratz. He wants to meet."

"Okay, good, I think. But first call Nellie Niznanski, the neighborhood watch person on Balazia Avenue."

"Is that the chubby woman that lives next to Frank?"

"Yes. Call her on one of your super-duper clandestine electronic call devices that won't leave your identification or number. You have one, don't you?"

"Yes, and it's called a disposable cell phone."

I slapped myself on the forehead. "Whatever. Call her and give her some cockamamie story that will make her feel compelled to call the police."

205

"Good thinking, Nephew. That will get the cops involved. I should have thought of it sooner."

"One more thing. In exactly six minutes, call me on my cell. I need an excuse to leave. Where will I meet you?"

"I'll tell you when I call."

I rejoined the dinner party. Emma had Colleen in stitches over one of her e-mail jokes. Darnell was watching an elderly couple sitting in a booth next to our table. They seemed to be celebrating some kind of special occasion. Darnell had that look in his eye, like he was estimating their size for a casket.

Colleen's laughter subsided enough to ask me, "Anything wrong?"

"Just setting up a golf match." Shit, I shouldn't have said that. Emma knows I have a standing arrangement on Mondays.

Emma asked Darnell, "Why don't you take up golf, sweetie?"

"I can't find people to play with. The last guy didn't even show up."

I couldn't pass this up. "So you're saying it's *hard to dig someone up* and when you do, they *stiff* you."

Emma and Colleen broke out in laughter. Darnell looked confused.

I dug into the Scolgio, savoring every tasty bite. Colleen had almost finished her portion when her cell rang.

Colleen checked the caller ID. "It's headquarters," she said. She got up and crossed into the hallway near the bar. A minute later, she came back to the table smiling. She said to me, "Looks like your prayers have been answered."

I tried to look surprised. "What's up?"

"I left standing orders to be called if anything came up about Frank."

"What is it?"

"I'll let you know," she said, and left.

"Oh, too bad she had to leave," Emma said. "I think she's good for you."

My cell rang saving me from an awkward answer. It was Roscoe. I took the call and told them, "Sorry, but I have to leave." I dragged a fifty from my wallet, dropped it on the table and left.

Chapter 35

I drove to Ed's Electronics Store at the intersection of twenty-first and Columbia where Roscoe had asked me to meet him. As I pulled into the lot, Roscoe walked out of the building and motioned for me to park next to his MKZ. When I got out of the van, I saw he was carrying a small paper bag. He opened the Lincoln's door and jumped behind the steering wheel. I slid into the passenger side.

"Did the lieutenant take the bait?" Roscoe asked. He put the bag in the storage console.

"She practically ran out of the restaurant. What did you tell Nellie, the she-devil?"

Roscoe pulled a business card from his shirt pocket. He looked at it and said: "Nellie Niznanski, neighborhood watch sergeant. Her address is on the front. On the back"—he flipped the card over—"Robert Jefferies." He held the card so I could read it. "I wrote the name I gave her on the back of the card, just in case."

"In case what?"

"In case it would come in handy—like tonight when I called Nellie, the *she-devil* as you rudely called her, and told her about my concern for my brother, Robert Jefferies, who was deeply worried about Frank Pallone. I said he had a key to Frank's house and had gone there to

Following Roscoe

look for information that might shed light on what happened to him. I also told her that Robert asked me to park a block away and wait for him, but he hadn't come back and that was three hours ago. I said I was really scared and that something was terribly wrong."

"Good thing you wrote that pseudonym on the back of her card."

"I guess it lit a bonfire under her ass."

"Now the police are involved. Good. So what's up with Duratz?"

"I'm not sure. We stirred up a hornets nest at Rose's Coffee earlier. We'll find out soon enough."

Roscoe drove slowly through Brentwood, admiring the up-scale houses, condominiums, and mansions. I told him about the old woman driving her dog around in a baby carriage when Emma and I were surveilling Duratz's house.

"No shit, a dog in a baby carriage?"

"Yeah, cute little mutt."

"So... tell me about you and Emma in the back of the van. Is she nice and soft all over?"

"Roscoe, you're a pervert!"

"I like to think of myself as sexually amplified."

"Sexually amplified?"

"Yeah, I'm sort of like a radio. You tune a radio to a station and turn up the volume, which amplifies the sound so you can hear it better. In my case, I'm naturally amplified when I get tuned in."

"Well, that certainly explains it. Your resonant frequency is lecherous ninety-five point three on the FM dial."

"That's one way of putting it."

I also believed Roscoe was tuned in to something not of this world.

"We're getting close," I said. "It's a Tudor with evergreens in front."

"What's the number?"

"Fourteen twenty. There it is," I said, pointing through the window.

Roscoe drove through the open wrought iron gate and parked next to a Mercedes Benz S500. He flipped open the console's lid and pulled a small object from the paper bag and put it in his pocket. Roscoe didn't volunteer what it was and I knew not to ask—not now anyway.

We walked to the house on cobblestone pavers that probably came from the streets of nineteenth-century Pittsburgh. The evergreens were impressive. They had been placed strategically in front of the house, to frame the entrance as the center of attention. A magnificent Stuart Plank mahogany Tudor door sat encased in a coped perimeter stone surround. The large, heavy door was held together by three eighteen-inch fleur-de-lis iron-strap hinges. Roscoe pressed the doorbell. A small eye-level window in the door held sixteen stained glass panels except for one clear one that exposed a vengeful eye.

The door opened to a demure Russell. His face and body language said retaliate, his eyes whimpered no. He stood to the side and pointed his arm in the direction of a pocket door on the right side wall. Russell walked ahead and slid one door into the wall. We stepped into what might be described as a rich man's den. Walnut woodwork was the first thing to catch my eye. Cabinets and bookshelves covered the walls except for a large stone fireplace in the left wall. Decorative walnut cornice molding surrounded the perimeter of the ceiling; the center consisted of square walnut panels.

Gino Duratz sat leisurely behind a massive walnut desk. A glass-enclosed bookshelf with lighted shelves backlighted him. He motioned us to the two black leather club chairs in front of the desk. Russell stood near the door.

Duratz glared at Roscoe. "What's the problem here? You filed charges against Russell after beating the shit out of him."

Russell lowered his head.

"He attacked me," Roscoe said. "I had to defend myself."

Duratz pointed at Russell. "And from the looks of Russell, you certainly did. I don't see a scratch on you, so why file the charges?"

"For that very reason," Roscoe said. "If Russell had filed charges first, I would look like the aggressor. So I filed first."

"Good thinking, Mister Kronek, but now Russell has to file counter-charges to stay out of jail."

Roscoe shrugged. "You gotta do what you gotta do."

"What do you want?" Duratz's face looked tired. "You created this problem for a reason. What is it, a piece of the action? You're not going to start your own book. Not in my territory."

"Or what? Are you going to finish the job on me that you started with Walter 'Nuggets' DeFiglio?"

Duratz's face glowed red. "Did that little twerp hire you to start trouble?"

Roscoe shook his head. "Relax, I'm not interested in starting a book or any other business venture. I came for information. And if I get the answers I want, I'll drop the charges I filed and you won't have to get involved. How's that sound?"

Duratz leaned back in his chair. His facial color returned to normal. "What can I help you with?"

"I only have a few questions, but first, there's something that's been nagging me. You're a smart businessman. How the hell did you manage to put yourself in a situation that could have put you away for a long time?"

Duratz smiled at the compliment then sobered at the question. "I lost my cool. I took it personal that a little piece of shit like DeFiglio thought he could step on my business."

"So you tried to kill him?"

"I was giving it a good shot until I realized I could be jeopardizing everything I'd worked for and stopped. I let my emotions get to me. It was stupid. That's why I have Russell."

"So you realized it was your fault that caused the trouble you were in."

"That's right."

"What about the police and the judge? Were you angry at them?"

"No, why should I be?"

"They were the ones that put you in jail."

"They were only doing their jobs. I was stupid and it was entirely my fault. I learned from it." Duratz's voice rose in volume. "What's this got to do with anything? Get to the question you were going to ask me."

"What about Frank Pallone, the private investigator that provided evidence that helped convict you?"

Duratz looked puzzled. "What? I just told you—"

"That's my question," Roscoe said forcefully. "Were you angry at Frank Pallone?"

"That's his name? Frank Pallone? I really didn't pay any attention to what was going on at the trial. I let my lawyer do all the thinking and talking."

Roscoe slid up the front edge of his chair. "You don't know the name of the cop that arrested and handcuffed you or the name of the judge who sentenced you?"

"No. I told you I don't blame them. I made the mistake. I screwed up. Why are you interested in this Frank Stallone?"

"Pallone. His last name is Pallone, and he's a friend of mine."

"Someone threatening him? Phone calls? It's not me. I served my time for my mistake and am getting on with my life. That whole episode is forgotten history." Duratz leaned forward on the desk. "Now what about dropping those charges?"

"They're as good as dropped," Roscoe said. He stood up and offered his hand.

Duratz also stood and grabbed Roscoe's hand. He said, "I won't be seeing you anymore, right?"

Roscoe said, "Right. We know our way out."

We left without saying another word. We drove onto the street and stopped just around the corner from the gate.

"Why are we stopping?" I asked.

Roscoe pulled the paper bag from the compartment in the console. He unwrapped a small rectangular object about three inches long. "I'll be right back," he said, getting out of the car. He walked to the stone gate post. He stood there for a minute or two looking it over and jogged back to the car and jumped in.

As Roscoe sped down the street I asked him, "What was all that about? What was in the bag?"

"What do you think about what Duratz had to say?"

"It sounds like he doesn't hold any grudges against Frank. At least not to the point of doing anything stupid to him. But then again, he is a common criminal. What about you?"

"I think he went a little overboard about not having any bad feelings about Frank. I think he mispronounced his name on purpose. I don't believe him at all."

"So tell me, what did we learn from this visit?"

"Nothing. Not yet anyway."

Roscoe had something up his sleeve. His answer was cryptic, just like the paper bag he had. "What was that gizmo in the paper sack?"

"I bugged Duratz's den."

"How?"

"I planted a voice-activated transmitter under the chair I was sitting on. It transmits up to one-thousand feet. I placed the digital receiver recorder in the gate post. We'll swing by tomorrow morning and download their conversations."

"That's genius."

"I know."

Roscoe dropped me off at Ed's Electronic Store where I had left my van. I crawled into the comfortable seat and relaxed for a minute, thinking there was light at the end of the tunnel due to Roscoe's street smarts. The information we'd get from Russell and Duratz's recorded conversations would tell us what happened to Frank and where he was—and hopefully still alive.

I treasured good memories of Frank as I drove home, not wanting any negativity to enter my world. I was a block away from the house when I checked my watch. I had just enough time to change Pissmore's water and make it to the club for the ten o'clock drawing. I parked at the curb and dashed into the house to the sound of a snoring bulldog. I changed the water in his ceramic dish. When I put the dish down, Pissmore opened one eye for a split second and then returned to dreamland. Just what I needed, a fierce watch dog.

A full August moon hung over the club, illuminating the three cars in the parking lot. It was a warm, bright light that seemed to reaffirm that everything was going to turn out okay.

That feeling faded when I walked into the bar and found Archie "Bunker" Brown sitting next to the chair I normally sit in. "Paranoid" Perry Sanders and his wife, Grace sat across the bar from my favorite seat. Gorgeous Reba Tuttle and Tommy "Two Shots" were perched in their usual spot at the end of the bar near the television.

"What's up, Archie?" I said, taking possession of my seat. "You get lost?"

"Doris Jean went to visit her sister in Oakdale. She'll be back Monday morning. This is my bachelor's weekend out."

That's why they call him *Archie Bunker* Brown.

Moldy sauntered out of the storage room carrying a bottle of Captain Morgan. He looked at me and nodded toward Archie as if to say *what an asshole*. Moldy continued toward Grace with the rum. He filled her glass and reached in the cooler for a bottle of I.C. Light. He strode over to me, popped the lid, and dropped the brew in front of me.

"What's up, brother?"

Following Roscoe

"Everything. Been busy all day."

"Anything new on Frank?"

"Yes and no." Moldy waited for an explanation. "We're on the right trail. Roscoe is like an urban bloodhound. He narrowed the suspects down to—"

Impatient Tommy "Two Shots" tapped his shot glass on the bar, signaling for another round. Moldy grabbed a bottle and scampered off to give Tommy his second and final shot of Jack Daniels. Reba was watching an episode of *Repo Men*, probably thinking of repossessing any part of her life that really mattered.

Moldy rushed back and anxiously asked, "Who? Who's the guy?"

"Yeah, who's the guy?" Archie asked.

I leaned to my left, away from Archie, and lowered my voice so that Archie would get the hint that I wanted to talk to Moldy. I said, "Gino Duratz."

"Gino Duratz!" Archie yelped. "I know him. He's in the rackets."

There went another theory of mine down the toilet. "We found that out this morning." I told Moldy about the episode at Rose's Coffee Shop.

Archie chimed in again. "I heard about that guy Russell. He's supposed to be one of those mercerizes."

"Mercenaries," I said.

"Right. That's what I said."

I heard a thud. We all looked toward the end of the bar to see that Tommy Tuttle had succumbed to his two shots and was face down on the bar.

Chapter 36

Most men my age are with their wives and kids on Sunday mornings observing their religious beliefs at a solemn, dignified service in a church or synagogue. I, on the other hand, spend Sunday mornings watching Uncle Roscoe, usually dressed in baggy, wrinkled pajamas or two-day-old sports clothes, rustling up breakfast while burping up last night's consumption of beer and farting to the tune of pig's feet, hard-boiled eggs, and pepperoni and anchovy pizza.

Today was no exception. The smell of cabbage hung in the air as Roscoe played his usual gastrointestinal repertoire while traipsing around the kitchen getting breakfast together. He wore a wrinkled Monview High School basketball t-shirt over Steelers pajama bottoms. I had chosen a short-sleeved blue and gray golf shirt and dark blue slacks. Pissmore's outfit consisted of a two-inch-wide spiked dog collar. He planted himself next to his doggy dish, waiting for his daily diet of dull dog food.

Roscoe slid two plates onto the table, each containing a ham and cheese omelet. He took coffee. I preferred orange juice.

"Have a late night at Murph's?"

Roscoe answered through a mouthful of omelet. "Not real late, considering the place is shakin' on Saturday night."

"You got home after me. In fact, I didn't even hear you."

"You sleep too much. And you get up way too late. You'd never make it in the military. Come to think of it, that's why you have this girly maid service. You couldn't make it in the real world with a *real* job."

I let that comment slide because he was my uncle. He lived under my roof for free and he should be thanking me. But thirty plus years in the military or some secret organization with an acronym made him feel entitled, and that mindset wouldn't change any time soon.

"You got that right. And why would I want to get up *that* early?"

"How about serving your country, state, city? How about helping your friend?"

What the hell was he talking about? I think he'd been on one too many covert missions. "Translate."

Roscoe reached into his pocket and pulled out the receiver/recorder he had planted in Duratz's gate post. "I picked this up this morning while you were in la la land."

I wondered how he could drive in the condition he must have been in. "Really! What's on it? Did you play it?"

"I thought I'd wait for my narcoleptic nephew to wake up."

I sat there staring at him with my mouth hanging open.

"You want to hear it, don't you?" he asked.

"Absolutely."

After we finished eating breakfast, Roscoe went into his apartment and retrieved a black, blocky device that he placed on the counter next to the toaster and plugged it into the wall outlet. He slid the receiver/recorder into the unit and pressed a button. The first thing we heard was the sound of our footsteps retreating out of Duratz's den.

Milt Anderson

"Shit, he knows about Frank Pallone." It was Duratz's voice.

"I think he's guessing," Russell said. "What can he possibly know?"

"Did you screw up?" Duratz was shouting. "Anyone see you? Did you use gloves?"

Russell answered, "I was very careful. I stole a car and parked a block away when I dropped the pigeon on Pallone's doorstep. It was four in the morning."

"What about the message?" Duratz asked.

"I went to the slaughterhouse like you told me and got the blood. Again, I used a stolen car and went at four a.m. I wore gloves when I wrote the threat on his bedroom wall. No one saw me."

"I don't understand," Duratz said. "Where's the connection to me?"

"I even took the hard drive from his computer," Russell said. "I have it hidden in my bedroom closet. I thought it might come in handy later."

"Good thinking." There was a long pause before Duratz spoke again. "After you left the slaughterhouse, did you change shoes?"

"No, why?"

"If you didn't change shoes you probably brought in sawdust or cow shit with you. That links the blood to a slaughterhouse, and I'm part owner of Weiss Packing Company. They probably had the blood analyzed after finding crap from your shoes.

Russell said, "What do we do now?"

"Keep an eye on the old guy," Duratz said. "He makes me nervous. And keep your distance. I don't want him to know we're watching him."

Roscoe winced at the old guy remark.

We heard footsteps leave the room.

Duratz said, "Why'd I get a peckerhead on steroids to work for me?"

After two minutes of silence, Roscoe turned off the recorder.

Roscoe slipped the receiver/recorder from its base unit and dropped it into his pocket. "Looks like Duratz and his pet gorilla had nothing to do with Frank's disappearance."

I said, "You mean after all this time and work, we've come to a dead end?"

"Not yet. I'll find another place on his property for the recorder in case there's more information we can use. In the meantime, we have to come up with a plan to get into Russell's apartment and retrieve Frank's computer hard drive. There may be some very important information on it."

"I hadn't thought about that. Frank probably has personal files and e-mails on it that could shed some light. But I'd still prefer that the police get involved and use their resources."

My cell rang. It was Colleen Fahey. Had she heard what I'd just told Roscoe? She said, "Augie, I have some good news. Can you come to the station?"

The desk sergeant's bowed head suggested he was reading another girly magazine. When I passed his station, my suspicion was confirmed. I could have been an escaping prisoner, but he didn't look up. It must have been the *Massive Mammary* summer issue.

I backed up a few steps to check out the centerfold. "Oh my God!" I gasped.

The sergeant wheeled around, a menacing look on his face

"How can those girls stand upright?"

The sergeant's face melted into a wide grin. "Big, huh?" He quickly fell back into his trance.

I walked down the hall toward Lieutenant Fahey's office, wondering how the police managed to function with officers like the sexual sergeant. Colleen's office, however, appeared to be the epitome of efficiency. She looked warm and soft even in the military-style dark blue police uniform.

She turned from her computer when she heard me enter. Her ruby lips spread into a smile and her emerald green eyes glistened with welcome that caught me off guard.

"I'm glad you came. I have good news."

"Great, what is it? Can you search Frank's home and office?"

"Yes. We got the go ahead this morning to intervene in Frank's disappearance."

"Wow! That's terrific." Only six days overdue.

"Nellie Niznanski phoned last night and said a man called her. He said his brother went into Frank's house and didn't come out."

I pretended to be surprised. "What man? Who?" Roscoe of course. Kudos.

"The brother of a Robert Jefferies. Nellie said she talked to this Jefferies guy a few days ago before he went into Frank's house. He said Frank had given him a key. I guess he went back with his brother for something else."

"And he didn't come out?"

Colleen looked at me with a sly knowing look. "You didn't have anything to do with this call, did you?"

She was a smart cop. "What? Absolutely not."

"Okay. Anyway, I sent a couple techs to Frank's house this morning."

The phone rang. Colleen lifted the receiver to her ear. "Fahey. Yeah, Wilson, what do you have? What! What's it say? Okay, keep me posted." She slowly dropped the receiver on its base. Her face became ashen, her eyes apologetic.

"What's the matter? Who was that?"

"That was one of my techs at Frank's house. I have some bad news."

"What is it?"

"There was a threatening message written on Frank's bedroom wall. It looks like someone wanted to harm him."

"What did the message say?" Let me guess. *Get another job—or else.*

"It said, 'Get another job—or else.'"

I pretended to take it hard. I had taken a six-week dramatics course in high school. I used the *sorrow face* technique. "Oh my God! That doesn't sound good."

"Don't worry. We'll get to the bottom of this. The techs are going over the house and office with a fine-toothed comb.

Chapter 37

I left the station knowing the full resources of the police were hard at work on Frank Pallone's case. But from what I had heard on the secret taping earlier, I felt that Duratz and Russell weren't involved in Frank's disappearance. It would take the police too long to reach the same conclusions Roscoe and I had come to. I needed more information, and fast. That's why I had invited two of Frank's closest friends to lunch at the Rainbow Café.

I headed west on Birmingham to Stanton Avenue to the Brighton section of town. The Rainbow, as the locals call it, sits between Layman's Dress Shop, a fashion-over-fifties boutique, and Edgewood Park, where senior citizens lounged on benches that encircled a large white gazebo, all secluded from the public by large, bushy azaleas and rhododendrons. I drove into the rear parking lot where Mike Latchem's blue Volkswagen and Bernie Ostapowicz's black E-350 Mercedes sat, cooling in the shade of a willow tree.

I scampered up the flagstone walk that led to the rear entrance of the café, eagerly anticipating talking to Mike and Bernie about any input they might have about Frank. I opened the door to the smell of baking bread, garlic, salad dressings. My mouth watered. As I passed through the dining room, the sight of broccoli-cheese soup, pasta, entrees of meat and potato dishes covered in gravy, and a rainbow of desserts further stimulated my appetite.

Mike and Bernie were bent over their menus at a corner table near the front window.

Bernie "The Attorney" was a nickname we used for him in the burg. He looked up when I approached the table. "You're five minutes late."

"I was held up at the police station."

Mike's facial expression turned from studious to serious. "Something about Frank? What'd you hear?"

"The police have finally intervened in his disappearance," I said. "They have techs at Frank's house and his office, checking for evidence at this very moment."

"It's about time," Bernie said. "Police follow ancient dogmatic procedures instead of using common sense. Frank wouldn't just pick up and leave like that—especially when a round of golf is at stake."

"And a multitude of gorgeous women milling around the burg," Mike said.

Bernie said, "It's possible a jealous husband is responsible for Frank's disappearance." Mike nodded.

A tall, slinky waitress holding out a receipt pad approached the table. She rattled off the luncheon specials and waited for a response. After a minute, she said, "Are you ready to order or do you need a few minutes?"

Bernie said, "I'll have the charbroiled steak salad special."

I looked at Mike and he nodded. "Make that two more," I said.

Mike watched her walk away and said, "Have they found anything yet?"

I considered telling them about the threatening message written on Frank's bedroom wall, but held back because Duratz's threats didn't seem to be related to Frank's disappearance. "Not yet. Roscoe and I are trying to figure out who had motive."

"Could be a felon he helped put away," Bernie said. "There's got to be a slew of them."

I cupped my hand around my mouth. "What I tell you must stay in this room." They all nodded. I told them about Karl Himmelman, Fat Freddy Moldinado, Harry "The Hat" Briscoe, and Gino Duratz.

"How'd you get that information from Frank's office?" Mike asked.

I said, "The less you know, the better."

"I didn't hear a thing," Bernie said.

"Good," I said. "There's more. We also found two pictures." I told them about the photo of the copperhead in Frank's car and a picture of his car with four flat tires. I didn't tell them about the pigeon with its throat cut, as this was Duratz's doing.

"Sounds like someone wanted to stop an investigation," Bernie said. "Could you tell where the pictures were taken?"

"Not really. The picture of the snake was confined to the interior of Frank's car. The flat tires... there was a building in the background, but I couldn't make out what it was."

Bernie raised a finger. "Finding the location could be very helpful. You could canvass the area and maybe find someone who saw Frank or the person who flattened his tires."

"I thought of that, but Frank travels everywhere and the photo doesn't show any background, only a small part of a building, a sign with only three letters on a sign: S, H, and E."

"Bring it to the office," Bernie said. "I'd like to take a gander at it."

"Yeah, me too," Mike said. "I travel a lot to personal care homes. Maybe I could recognize something."

The tall waitress returned with our orders and placed them on the table. Mike started to dive in.

"Yoo-hoo! Yoo-hoo, Mister G!"

I turned around, as did everyone in the room, and yes, it was Emma.

Following Roscoe

She wore a blue floral tunic over denim cargo capris. She hoofed it to our table, her bosom and other soft parts of her anatomy swaying and heaving. Black Paloma sandals carried her and the shopping bag she clutched from Layman's Dress Shop.

Emma waved her hand around the table. "Hi, y'all," she said in a way that begged for her introduction, which I did. Mike and Bernie sat, staring at Emma, holding their forks in midair.

"Why don't you join us?" I pointed to the empty chair next to Bernie.

"Oh no, Mister G, I be with Trés P." Emma turned around and motioned for someone. A tall man moved through the crowd, his head covered with shiny black finger waves. He had small peaceful eyes, and a smile you couldn't take your eyes off of—the gold teeth were dazzling. As he broke through the crowd, I could see his skin-tight lime green t-shirt that read, "Gay Men Think Outside the Box." He also wore tailored Banana Republic blue jeans with leather thong sandals.

Emma wrapped her arm around his skinny neck. "This is Trés P. He's a famous hairdresser over on Tidsdale Street.

I introduced myself and then Bernie and Mike. Bernie and Mike nodded. I pointed to the bag Emma was carrying. "I didn't think you shopped at Layman's."

"Oh, I don't," Emma said. "That store is for ol' biddies, but I find good intimate personal wear there—and cheap." She pulled out a super-plus size pair of skivvies and proudly held them up as she stretched them—wide. "This is from the *Hanky Panky Collection.* Ain't they smokin'?"

Bernie dropped his fork. A strange smile developed on Mike's face. Trés P nodded in agreement.

Before I could interrupt Emma's display of her drawers, she pulled out a brassiere. It must have been a Wonder Bra. I wondered how a bra could be so large. It looked like a parachute harness with two five-quart Kevlar cups attached. Natives in underdeveloped countries could attach these bras to poles to carry water for their villages.

A waitress motioned for Emma and Trés P. He turned on his heel and headed for their table. Emma stuffed the bra into her shopping bag.

"Is Trés the new man in your life?" I asked.

"Hell no. He's gay as a politician against same-sex marriage. And besides, I'm seein' Damarcus. He's one real cool dude. You know what I mean? He so cool there's always three or four ho's traipsing after him."

Bernie and Mike stared at their salads.

"So, you'll be seeing him later?" I asked.

"No, I'll be seeing Reverend Rashad. We're going to the cinema."

Mike raised his head with wide eyes. "You know the Reverend?"

"We're close. Very close, if you know what I mean," Emma said. She started to follow Trés P's footfalls to their table when she stopped and turned around. "I'll see you tomorrow morning," she said, waving a cutesy bye-bye. All the customers in the room looked at me.

Bernie asked Mike, "Who is this Reverend Rashad? I can't remember what I heard about him."

"Does the word *Tourette's* ring a bell?" I asked.

Bernie aimlessly shoved his salad around with his fork. "Oh, now I remember. How do you know him, Mike?"

Bernie paused, waiting for an answer to the question that hung in the air, but no response came, nor did any answer about Frank's disappearance.

Chapter 38

"Guess who I saw at lunch today?" I asked Roscoe, who was sitting at the kitchen table bent over the morning newspaper. A half-eaten ham and cheese sandwich sat next to an almost empty glass of milk.

"Charlie Sheen. He rode in on a mercury surfboard and ordered a pint of tiger blood."

"Funny. What's with the milk? Another late night at Murph's?"

"Duh. Where do I usually go when the sun goes down? And, okay, who did you see at lunch?"

"Emma."

"Emma? Where?"

"At the Rainbow Café. She was with a gay fellow named Trés P."

"Tray what? And what's she doing with a gay guy?"

"Shopping. I understand gay men have an eye for fashion."

"They do dress kind of fancy."

"She said her real man is a dude named Damarcus. But get this, she said she was going to the movies later tonight with Reverend Rashad."

"A reverend? She's a loser."

"Oh, I see. She's a loser because she has nothing to do with you."

"That's not it, Nephew. I've changed my thinking a little bit lately."

When he exaggerates the word *nephew*, he's a little pissed off. "What, Emma's not good enough for you?"

"It's not that. I like her a lot, but she's a little… young maybe."

What was this, Roscoe changing? I didn't believe he was finally growing up. "Something to do with Mrs. Vanderslice?"

Roscoe straightened in his chair, outstretched his arms and planted his hands on the table. He looked directly into my eyes. He said, "I think so."

"Wow, this is monumental."

He shut me off. "What were you doing at the Rainbow Café?"

"I had lunch with Bernie and Mike. I thought they might shed some light on Frank's disappearance."

"Any luck?"

"Not really. They both wanted to look at the photo of Frank's car parked in front of the white building. That picture seems to be the only lead so far."

Roscoe grimaced and picked up the sports section.

"And, oh, the police are finally involved."

Roscoe dropped the paper. "Really? How'd you find out?"

"I stopped at headquarters this morning."

A sly, knowing grin spread on Roscoe's face. "Talk to Lieutenant Fahey, I suppose?"

"Yeah, I talked to her. So?"

"So you might be moving from the cougar team to the team I left behind. And it's about time."

"What are you talking about?"

"You know what I'm talking about, Nephew."

He exaggerated the word *nephew* again. I didn't respond.

After a minute that seemed a lot longer, I said, "It's good the police are involved. They can search Frank's office thoroughly. Maybe they'll find a secret compartment, maybe a—"

Following Roscoe

A knock on the door alerted Pissmore, who staggered to his paws and let out a feeble attempt of a guard dog howl. I turned to see Colleen's face in the window. "Lieutenant, what brings you out on a Sunday afternoon?" I asked, ushering her in.

Colleen smiled again, sort of in a shy way. "I received an initial report from the tech assigned to Frank's case and, since I was on duty, I thought I'd come and tell you about it person."

"What is it? Is it bad?"

"No, it's not bad. I told you earlier that there was a threatening message in Frank's bedroom. Well, it was written in blood."

"Oh my God," I said, pretending to look shocked.

"It was blood but not Frank's. It wasn't even human blood. It was cow's blood."

I pretended to be relieved. "Thank goodness it wasn't Frank's blood. Cow's blood? "

"I don't know why someone would write a threatening message in cow's blood. Could be—"

"Could be a rustler Frank sent up the river," Roscoe said.

Colleen's cell phone rang. She flipped the phone open and held it to her ear. "Fahey," she said. Concern crept over her face and deteriorated into distress. "Oh my God." She slumped into a chair across the table from Roscoe.

Both Roscoe and I said, "What's the matter?"

Colleen closed her cell and slid it into her purse. "They found Frank."

Chapter 39

Roscoe followed Fahey as close as possible as she sped through another red light.

"I didn't think it would end like this," I said. "We were into the investigation from day one. I just thought, maybe one more day."

"Nothing you could have done, August. Frank could have been dead since last Saturday for all we know. We'll see what the medical examiner has to say."

I looked out the window, watching the tall buildings turn to houses, the houses to trees, thinking when he died really didn't matter—Frank was dead. "We have to catch the son of a bitch that murdered him."

Roscoe nodded. "That will happen."

"But the only lead we have is the building in the photo. What if we can't identify it?"

"Then we'll use what we *do* know." Roscoe noticed the question mark on my face. "We know from the other picture that he can handle snakes, and we know he can pick locks because he put the snake in Frank's car."

I hadn't thought of that. "Okay, that's good. What else?"

"He has a crossbow or access to one."

Following Roscoe

    I had forgotten about this. "And he knows about cars: he cut my brake line and disconnected my emergency brake. He must have had tools."
    "See, we *do* know something about this guy."
    "But all those facts could apply to hundreds of men in the city."
    "Maybe, but once the police narrow down the suspects, these facts will be very useful in pointing to the murderer. That's why we have to retrieve Frank's hard drive from Russell to get further proof."
    Fahey turned right at Skillet Hill onto a blacktop, two-lane road. Another half-mile and we were at Dutch's Corner, the patch that had housed Black Diamond Coal Company's workers and their families in the early twentieth century. Remnants of cinderblock, stones, and wooden stumps marked the plots where houses once stood. These were overshadowed by a weed-covered slag dump the height of a ten-story building.
    Five minutes later, Fahey turned left into a group of scrub trees. We followed in a cloud of dust, the swooshing of overgrown weeds and the crunching of red dog on the narrow road continued for a minute or two until we reached an open, treeless area the size of a midget league baseball lot. We entered from what I would call center field. Fahey veered to the right and parked in back of a police cruiser. She jumped out of the Crown Victoria and jogged up to an officer talking to an EMT. The officer had his hat under his arm. He was bald. We parked behind Fahey.
    To our left, or left field, sat an old, rusty pickup truck with a confederate flag in the rear window. In front of it was an emergency vehicle basking in the sun. Next to the emergency truck was a police cruiser with a man in his fifties and a young man in his twenties handcuffed in the back seat. A railroad track ran from where third base would have been to home plate, where the mine portal burrowed into the hillside. Huge rectangular-cut stones made its outline resemble Napoleon's hat. The boarded-up opening sat at ground level under the peak of the hat.

Grass and weeds grew between the cracks and crevices of the stones. A few of the weathered boards lay on the ground in front of the portal where two of the EMTs had just exited, half pushing, half carrying a gurney. A feeling of despair overcame me when I saw the black body bag.

Colleen must have seen me watching the men haul Frank's body to the truck. She moved toward me, empathy showing in her features.

Roscoe spoke. "What's the story?"

Fahey turned to Roscoe and pointed to the old truck. "An officer on routine patrol noticed that truck and thought he should investigate. He left his vehicle on the road and walked into the area. He found the father and son team climbing out of the mine with armloads of copper and arrested them."

"What's this got to do with Frank?" I asked. "Did they find him?"

"They did," Fahey said. "But I didn't get all the details yet." She waved over the bald-headed officer and introduced us. "Officer Teska, you said the thieves gave you the location of the body and that you identified it. Do you have any further details for Augie and Roscoe?"

"Well, to start with," Teska said, "they didn't come right out and tell me about the body. I arrested them for trespassing and theft and read them their rights when the father wanted to exchange some information for immunity. I told him if his information was important, I would take it to the DA."

"Immunity?" I asked. "You're not going to give him immunity, are you?"

Teska answered. "Certainly not. I didn't make a deal, I don't have the authority. And besides, they obstructed justice by not coming forward with their information. I added that to the other charges."

"And that's when he told you about Frank?" Fahey asked.

"At that time I didn't know it was Frank Pallone. He said someone put the body in the mine last Saturday because it wasn't there Friday."

"What about the body?" Roscoe asked.

Teska put his hands on his hips and looked at the ground. "He was in pretty bad shape. I identified him from a card I found hidden in his wallet. The EMT told me he had been dead for at least a week. His face had been severely slashed with a sharp object and... his private parts were cut off."

"Holy shit," Roscoe said. "Somebody really had it in for Frank."

"Bernie and Mike were right," I said.

"About what?" Fahey asked.

"Had to be a jealous husband."

Chapter 40

The drive home seemed a lot longer than the trip to the Black Diamond Mine. Roscoe and I slogged into the house, dragging bad news behind us. Pissmore seemed to sense our angst. He didn't jump out of his bed, but only whined a soft whimper. We slumped into chairs at the kitchen table. Roscoe seemed to be contemplating recent events as he stared at the refrigerator. I wondered how something this terrible could happen; the overall scene suggested hopelessness.

A knock on the door interrupted our gloom. Aldine Vanderslice's large bright blue eyes shone through the window, invoking a primordial desire within me.

I jumped up and opened the door. "Aldine, nice to see you."

"Roscoe, I just heard about Frank." She rushed past me carrying a tray with two plates of spaghetti and placed it in front of Roscoe. "I'm so sorry."

What, she just rushed past me? Roscoe didn't even know Frank.

"How'd you find out?" Roscoe asked. "We just got home."

"I have a friend who works at 911."

"Won't you join us?" Roscoe asked.

"No, I can't. I'm late for my self-defense class. I have to leave." She kissed Roscoe on his forehead.

Although I stood in her path to the door, she sidestepped me and left.

Kissed him on the forehead? "Ain't that the shit?" I said.

"Yeah," Roscoe answered, "she's got spunk. Self-defense class. Ain't that something?"

I grabbed a plate of pasta and sat down at the table, surrendering to the fact that Aldine was obviously infatuated with Roscoe. But she was unaware that Roscoe couldn't be with an older woman, not even five months older.

The spaghetti was good. I had eaten most of mine when I noticed Roscoe slowly stirring his almost full dish with a fork. "You're not eating," I said. "What's the matter, Frank's murder on your mind?"

"Yeah, that's it."

Another knock on the door. This time it was Lieutenant Fahey. She let herself in. Pissmore got up and wagged his stubby tail. Colleen petted him and came to the table and sat down. She placed a brown file pocket in front of her.

She said to me, "I need your help. You were a good friend of Frank's and you worked for him."

"What can I do?"

"We opened Frank's safe and found a Taurus nine millimeter pistol and night vision goggles. Do you know what he used them for?"

"He's... he was a private eye. I guess he used them to snoop on people at night. And I guess all private eyes carry weapons." I was telling the truth; the only time I had seen them was when Roscoe had opened the safe.

"Do you know of anyone who had it in for Frank?"

"Plenty. Frank's investigations led to people being sent up the river, fines for faking disability, marriages that ended in divorce, and then the settlements."

"I get the picture. There were a lot of people that didn't like Frank. What about the few that would actually kill him?" Colleen pulled out the files on Karl Himmelman, Fat Freddy Moldonado, and Gino Duratz. "These were also in the safe. He must have kept them there for a reason."

Before I could answer, Roscoe said, "Maybe he was working on their cases and kept them handy."

"No, some are old. The thing they have in common is their recent release dates from prison." She asked me, "Did you know these files were in his safe?"

"No I didn't." And it wasn't a lie.

Lieutenant Fahey put the files back in the pocket and pulled out the photos Roscoe had made copies of. She spread them on the table, pulling the photo of the dead pigeon and the copperhead in Frank's car together. "These are very threatening pictures. Do you know anything about them?"

"No," I said softly. This was only half a lie; I knew about the dead pigeon.

Colleen looked at me sideways, out of the corner of her eye, the way Pissmore does sometimes. "I've got to go back to the station. I've got a lot of paperwork to do."

"I'll walk out with you," I said, regretting my deception.

I followed Fahey to her car, watching her delicate derriere sway with each step under her policewoman's skirt. She turned quickly, as if she felt my eyes on her.

"I know you're holding something back. If you have information that will help find Frank's murderer, please tell me now." Her emerald green eyes invoked an involuntary response from me.

"Yes...."

"Yes, what?"

"Look, we do have some information, but I can't tell you how we got some of it."

Colleen looked at me as if she had known all along. "I don't care. I figured you might start something on your own."

"We had to, remember? Police don't get involved when a responsible adult male disappears and there are no signs of trouble. Something had to be done."

"Okay, I won't ask you how you obtained the information. What do you have?"

"Forget about those three men in the files and the picture of the dead pigeon."

"Why? Don't they all have motive?"

"We checked them out thoroughly. We settled on Duratz for a while, but it didn't pan out. I'll tell you about him later, but for now concentrate on the picture of Frank's car with four flat tires. Find the building in the background. It's the only clue we have."

"You could be in danger," Colleen said, placing her hand on my arm. "Be careful. Someone's been trying to stop your investigation. He even shot an arrow into your door."

"Yeah, it had Frank's blood on it."

"And you knew that when?"

"Before you did. Roscoe is very resourceful."

"Roscoe is an enigma."

Chapter 41

"Did you sleep at all?" I asked Roscoe.

"Not really, it's not unusual for me to hit the sack at three or four in the morning."

"Nothing else keep you up?"

Roscoe turned toward me with a questioning look. His face was partially illuminated in green pastel light from the dashboard. "Like what?"

"Like one of your ailments, you know, members of the *itis* or *osis* family. Skin problems? Muscle aches? Stomach pain?"

"I don't know what you're talking about. What the hell's your problem?"

"I don't have a problem. And neither do you, you're horny. I noticed it when Aldine dropped in with the spaghetti. None of your symptoms appear when she's around."

Roscoe seemed to think about this for a few seconds. "Naw," he said. "You're full of shit. What's that address again?"

"Fourteen twenty Prospect Drive, it's around the bend on the right."

"Is that it, the Tudor with the evergreens in front?"

"Yes, don't you remember we were here Saturday evening?"

"Details, details. I had other things on my mind."

"Like Aldine Vanderslice? Come to think of it, you didn't have any of your usual ailments Saturday evening either."

"You're still full of shit." Roscoe parked a hundred yards from Duratz's house next to a new home construction site.

We got out of the Lincoln, almost invisible in the night's darkness, and headed for Duratz's house. Roscoe carried an overnight bag and I didn't ask what was in it. In the distance I saw the old woman I had seen Friday when on surveillance with Emma. She was still pushing the fancy baby carriage. As we got closer, I noticed she wore the same retro stylish hat and evening gown.

"Who's that?" she asked. "Oh, it's you. Are you still on terrorist alert?"

"Yes ma'am," I said. "You have to be careful. They come out at night also." Roscoe looked puzzled.

"Who's he?" she asked.

"He's my assistant in charge of night operations." I pointed to the carriage. "Oh! Is that Sylvia?" I turned to Roscoe. "She's a Chacy Ranior. Pure bred."

Roscoe peered through the darkness down the road. "Do tell."

"Oh no," the woman said. "This is Fredrick, my pet coon."

I squinted through the dimness and saw the pointed-faced bandit under a pink blanket. The rodent looked at me as if I had valuables in my pocket. "Very handsome," I said. "But we have to go now. Keep vigilant."

She turned and pushed the carriage up her driveway. Roscoe and I continued toward Duratz's house.

Quiet hung over the neighborhood. Mansions sat still as if abandoned by some giant, master model-maker, cracks of light slipping through the windows the only evidence of a living presence. Birds and animals must have known they were unwelcome on their roofs or manicured lawns, lawns that stretched far enough from the road to keep their owners anonymous.

We arrived at the edge of Duratz's property and found the gate closed. The extreme left and right side of frontage was lined with tall evergreens that tapered to low shrubs at the centered driveway, making the mansion the focal point. Behind the foliage ran a wrought iron fence connected by intermittent stone pillars, two feet square and nine feet high. Roscoe ducked behind a cone-shaped boxwood and motioned for me to follow. He pointed to a pillar. "This is where we go in." He clasped his hands together, fingers intertwined, as if holding a heavy stone. "Step up."

I stepped onto Roscoe's foothold and he hoisted me up into the air like a human missile. I had to bend my knees to keep from going over the wall. I knelt there for a second, looking for a way to get down.

"Jump," Roscoe said. And I did, landing in a heap.

I stood up and was brushing myself off when Roscoe softly hit the ground, tucking into a roll and landing on his feet.

"PLF," he said. "Parachute landing fall. I'll show you how to do it sometime."

We didn't really need the dark clothing and caps, as heavy cloud cover masked the sliver of new moon. Roscoe pulled himself to the top of the fence and retrieved the overnight bag he had hung there. He pulled out a set of night vision goggles and put them on. I knew they weren't Frank's; the police had them.

"What else do you have in there?" I asked.

Roscoe didn't answer but headed in the direction of the garage that was located to the rear and left of the house. I thought I heard something to my right, where the house was, so I watched to see if there was a potential threat as I followed Roscoe and—WHAM! I thought a bolt of lightning had struck my head. I fell to the ground, my head spawning a galaxy of stars.

"Roscoe!"

"Quiet, Nephew. You stepped on a rake, asshole. Watch where the hell you're walking."

"I can't see. You have the night vision gismo."

Following Roscoe

"Follow me closely."

We slowly and cautiously stuck to the fence line, past Duratz's house, and stopped next to the garage. Roscoe knelt down and unzipped the overnight bag. He withdrew a thick rod that turned out to be a telescoping pole. He pulled out a ball of wool the size of a softball and attached an "S" hook to the wool.

"Put this on," Roscoe said, handing me a protective mask. He then took out a rolled up towel that wrapped a wide-mouth jar filled with a colorless liquid. He hooked the ball of wool to the pole. Roscoe put his mask on and unscrewed the lid from the jar. He dipped the wool into the jar, saturating it with the liquid. He screwed the lid on the jar and carefully extended the telescoping pole to the second level of the garage and hooked the saturated wool onto the humming air conditioning unit that extended from a window. He left the extended pole on the ground, wrapped the jar with the towel and stuffed them back into the overnight bag.

"What was that stuff?" I sounded like Darth Vader through the mask as I pointed to the jar.

"Chloroform mostly, and a substance I can't pronounce that prevents chloroform from becoming deadly."

"So Russell will be peacefully sleeping when we go in."

Roscoe pressed a button on his wristwatch, illuminating it. "A few more minutes ought to do it."

We sat there quietly, listening and watching for any activity. Roscoe checked his watch. "Let's go," he said.

Roscoe moved swiftly, keeping a low profile, bent over as if looking for night crawlers. I didn't catch up with him until he stood at the door that led to the upstairs apartment. Roscoe used the same pistol-looking contraption that had opened Frank's office door Tuesday, the day after Frank went missing. With a twist of his wrist, the door opened. We slipped inside. Roscoe quickly closed the door and pulled a penlight from his jacket pocket, illuminating a railed staircase that led to the second floor and a door to the garage where Duratz's opulent Mercedes rested.

I followed Roscoe to the second floor, pulling on the oak railing to help my hesitant ass up the stairs. I was more than nervous. If we were caught, "breaking and entering" seemed minor in comparison to what might happen if Russell was awake and was waiting for us. Would someone get hurt? Would it be me?

It could have been the living room we dashed through, for all I know. I just followed Roscoe's narrow beam of light down a hall into another room where he halted. The beam of the penlight darted back and forth, up and down until it stopped on a mussed, single bed. Russell lay under the covers, curled in the fetal position, hugging a stuffed giraffe.

"What a wuss." Roscoe directed the light on the closet door, behind which Frank's computer hard drive and possible information that might identify his murderer.

Roscoe rummaged through the closet like a woman shopper at Macy's the day after Christmas. He opened a shoe box and I heard him say, "Ah-ha," through his protective mask.

I also heard something else behind me—a scratching sound. Then a screeching animal landed on my head, digging its talons into my scalp. The incident happened so fast, I didn't yelp, but dashed toward Roscoe. He grabbed it and held it up by its neck. It turned out to be a guard cat that had jumped off Russell's dresser. The feline finally succumbed to the chloroform in Roscoe's grasp. Russell continued sawing logs.

"Did you get it?" I asked.

"I have it. Now let's get out of here." Roscoe retraced our steps to the stairway and I quickly followed him down the steps. Roscoe cracked open the door and scanned the area. He opened the door and stepped out. He grabbed my arm and pointed to Duratz's house. A light was on in a second floor room.

Following Roscoe

Roscoe quickly retrieved the chloroform ball and stuffed it into a plastic baggy. He then collapsed the telescoping pole.

"Okay, let's go." Roscoe took off, jogging toward the area where we'd left the overnight bag. As I ran, I glanced back to see a first floor room light up.

"Roscoe!"

"I see it." Roscoe had reached the overnight bag and pulled out a round object. "Hurry up!" He waved me on.

We dumped our protective masks in the bag and started to jog along the fence line when I stepped on the rake again. "Son of a bitch!" I yelped, grabbing my forehead. We were in line with Duratz's front door when he came out, waving a pistol.

"Who's there?" He turned in every direction, peering through the darkness.

Roscoe threw the round object he was holding at Duratz. It landed ten yards from him and rolled to within five feet of Duratz' slippers, emitting a thick cloud of greenish smoke. We quickly made our way to the pillar we'd used to enter the yard and left the same way.

"What was in that ball you threw?" I asked.

"Pixie dust."

Chapter 42

I was lying on the deck of a small fishing boat that heaved to and fro, its engine knocking under the strain, fish jumping out of the water into the boat, sliding across my face with their slimy bodies—and then I woke up.

Pissmore was licking my face, alerting me that someone was rapping on the kitchen door. I staggered out of bed, pulling last night's events behind me, and jumped into my blue Izod pajamas and leather scuffs. I slid into a green flannel robe as I left the bedroom. Pissmore followed me, excited that he might be getting company. When I entered the kitchen, I saw Emma's round face in the window. Pissmore must have remembered it was Monday, Emma's day to come and clean my apartment.

I opened the door to a questioning look. "What you doin' in your PJ's at nine fifteen in the morning, Mister G? That prevert uncle of yours keep you out all night? And what are those knots on your noggin'? That ol' fart git you in trouble? Were you shootin' the five wit someone?"

"Actually, I stepped on a rake."

"Nuh-uh. You didn't step on the same rake twice." Emma's pretty observant. "The second bump is from Roscoe's car door."

"I know that ol' fool be involved somehow."

I motioned Emma into the kitchen. She wore green nurse's scrubs. White sneakers carried her in. Pissmore wagged his stubby tail, his eyes beaming gratitude as Emma patted his broad head.

"What's with the outfit?" I said.

"I seen them nurses dressed in these threads when I visited you in the hospital Friday, and I liked the look."

Emma started for my apartment when Roscoe walked in, his oversized black and gold Zubaz zebra pajama bottoms swaying. He wore a Pittsburgh Steelers t-shirt silkscreened with a helmeted man kicking a football off a steel beam.

Emma pointed a threatening finger at Roscoe. "You're teaching Mister G bad habits, old man. You stop, or I'll show you how to take care of business."

Roscoe walked to the counter and started the coffeemaker. "Really? You and who else? Maybe the hairdresser, what's his name? Three P's?"

"His name is Trés P and he got good style."

"Uh-huh," Roscoe said. "I guess the Hanky-Panky collection is upscale? And what's with you dating a reverend that cusses up a storm?"

"You stringy old man, I'll—"

I jumped between Emma and Roscoe to prevent a possible kitchen remodeling job.

Emma started for my apartment. She turned and again pointed a finger. "I'll be seeing you again, prevert man," she said, and strode through the doorway.

Aldine walked in, wearing a Steelers jersey and black slacks. Her outfit brought a smile to Roscoe's face. Together, they looked like they had a date to go to Kennywood, Pittsburgh's local amusement park.

"I came to cook breakfast," she said. "You two had a bad day yesterday." She headed for the fridge.

Roscoe poured a cup of coffee and sat at the table, pushing aside the photos that remained there from yesterday.

Aldine hummed a tune I was unfamiliar with while gathering utensils and ingredients.

I poured a cup of java and joined Roscoe at the table. He was studying the photo of Frank's car in front of the unknown building.

Aldine slid a napkin and utensils in front of me. She looked over Roscoe's shoulder at the photo. She went to the counter for a place setting for Roscoe. She placed it in front of him.

"How did those tires get flattened?" she asked.

"That's Frank's car," I said. "We're trying to figure out who did it. Could be the murderer."

"Any clues?"

"None," I said. "If we could figure out where this photo was taken—"

"That looks like the Sheets Hotel in Dawson," she said.

Roscoe said, "You know this place? How can you tell?"

Aldine pointed to the partial sign in the photo. "The letters S, H, and E. Looks like the sign on the Sheets Hotel."

"I've heard that name recently," I said. "I know! I interviewed a job applicant Saturday. She worked there—it was on her resume."

Roscoe stood up. "Did you hire her?"

I nodded.

Roscoe continued. "Is she working today? Find out where from Emma and call me on my cell." Roscoe ran into his apartment. A few minutes later he came out with a briefcase and dashed out the door. A few seconds later we heard the Lincoln's tires burn rubber on the road.

"Where'd he go?" Aldine asked.

"Who knows? He's kind of secretive about what he does."

Chapter 43

I had just eaten supper when the phone rang. The caller ID indicated it was Roscoe. I hadn't heard from him since I called him this morning and told him where Lorin Scott was working.

"Did you find her?" I asked. "What'd she say?"

"Easy, Nephew. I have a lot of information and, if used correctly, it will convict Frank's murderer."

"What information? Who's the murderer?"

"All in due time. Here's what I want you to do...."

―――――

At eight o'clock sharp, I met Roscoe in the club parking lot and we walked in together. The smell of alcohol and tobacco, the sound of disagreement overwhelming the local news, invaded our senses.

The first person I saw was Lieutenant Fahey. Moldy was bent over the bar talking to her as previously instructed. As we passed the room divider, the rest of the bar came into view under a wafting cloud of cigarette smoke.

Grace Sanders tapped a shot glass on the bar. "I'll have another please," she said, looking across the corner of the bar at Lieutenant Fahey. "Paranoid" Perry's gaze followed his wife's.

"Professor" Doris Jean Brown hovered over her husband, Archie "Bunker" Brown. By the look on her face and her body language, she was again involved in some discourse about minutiae. The couple separated the Sanders from the Tuttles. Reba sat perched at the far corner under the TV, watching with dead eyes. Cater-corner from her, Tommy "Two Shots" had full view of the bar—until his head went south after two shots of Jack Daniels. Roscoe took a seat five stools away from Tommy at the corner of the bar, diagonally across from me.

Moldy walked up and set an IC Light in front of me. "What's yours?" he said to Roscoe.

"I'll have what he's drinking," Roscoe said, pointing to Tommy, "and a draught chaser."

I sat directly across the bar from Reba. What a beauty. Her auburn hair, blue eyes, and sensual lips did a number on me. I wondered how old she was.

Roscoe checked his wrist-watch. "So, how's the maid service going?"

"Fine. Business is picking up. I hired a new maid Saturday. Today's her first work day. In fact she'll be here shortly. Sort of a celebration I planned for her."

Just as I finished my sentence, Lorin Scott and Aldine walked in. Aldine headed in our direction, her blue eyes and silver hair shining in the din. Lorin followed closely behind, her rosy cheeks, dark hair, and wide shoulders testifying to her youth.

Grace Sanders seemed to be studying Aldine. Perry stared at Lorin. Doris Jean continued her lecture. Reba dragged her gaze from the TV for a second and then her sleepy orbs drifted back to the screen as if they were magnetized.

Lorin sat next to me; Aldine took a stool next to Roscoe.

"How was your first day?" I asked Lorin.

"Really nice. Gertrude drove me around this morning, familiarizing me with the city, and gave me a

Following Roscoe

map. She showed me the two houses where I would be working this afternoon and everything went well. Both families I worked for were really nice."

"So you like this type of work better than what you were doing?"

"Absolutely. That Sheets Hotel in Dawson was really the pits."

Reba managed to take her eyes off the boob tube and turned in her seat to look at Lorin.

Lorin waved. "Hi, Mrs. Smith, remember me?"

"No. And my name's not Smith." Reba turned back to the flat-screen.

Tommy "Two Shots" tapped his shot glass. "I'll have another."

"I'll be right with you," Moldy told Tommy, and returned to his conversation with Lieutenant Fahey.

"I remember you," Lorin said. "You came on Fridays, remember? The Sheets Hotel?"

Reba turned to her left. "I don't know what you're talking about. I've never been to the Sheets Hotel."

Doris Jean stopped lecturing Archie, Grace Sanders threw back a shot of Captain Morgan, and silence hung in the air.

"I'll take that shot now, Moldy," Tommy said.

"Oh yes, I remember," Lorin said. "You would meet a handsome man on most Friday afternoons. He drove a red Chrysler three-hundred."

"Paranoid" Perry Sanders said, "That sounds like Frank Pallone's car."

Tommy Tuttle pounded his fist on the bar. "Damn it, Moldy, where's my Jack Daniels?"

Roscoe said to Tommy, "I hear your head gets heavy after drinking only two shots. Is that what you want... to go unconscious and not hear about your wife and Frank Pallone?"

Reba's mouth dropped open.

Tommy pointed a finger at Roscoe. "Who are you, mister, and what do you—"

"But you're really not passed out when your head is on the bar, are you?" Roscoe said. "You pretend to be out of it, but you're listening, watching through half-closed eyes what your beautiful wife might be doing behind your back."

"Now wait a minute, Reba said. "What are you accusing me of?"

"Not accusing," Roscoe said. "It's a fact. I have copies of e-mail messages between you and Frank Pallone. And you also made the mistake of not removing the magnetic Tuttle's Hardware sign from your black Lexus."

"You did what?" Tommy shouted at Reba. "You advertised your infidelity? You're nothing but a whore."

Grace Sanders tapped her empty shot glass on the bar. "Moldy! Another drink," she said over the quiet—even the TV seemed to be listening for what would happen next.

"Look at you," Reba said, tears welling up in her eyes. "You're a business whore. All the time you spend in those stores, all the money you have doesn't add up to shit. What do you do with it? What do *we* do with it? Where do *we* go? We come here and I watch your head hit the bar."

"You have everything," Tommy said. "A mansion, jewels, clothes—"

"You thought that would make me happy? Thanks for nothing."

"Moldy! Give me a fucking shot." Tommy turned to Reba. "What did Frank do to make you happy?"

"He made me feel wanted, alive. He cared about me. He gave me more than things. He gave me love."

Moldy stepped over and filled Tommy's glass. Tommy quickly threw it down. "He ain't giving you love anymore, is he?"

Reba lunged at Tommy, scratching, clawing at him until Roscoe pulled her off.

"You murdered him, didn't you?" Reba said, trying to escape from Roscoe.

"You betcha, bitch. I gave him a dirt bath in a coal mine."

Following Roscoe

Lieutenant Fahey entered the fracas, and handcuffed Tommy "Two Shots." She was reading him his rights when Emma came in.

"What, did I miss all the action?"

―――――

Roscoe held up a champagne flute. "Here's to the fine job you all did in putting a murderer behind bars."

Lieutenant Fahey, Aldine Vanderslice and I reached across the kitchen table and touched our flutes to Roscoe's. Emma sat across from Roscoe and drank red wine from a glass tumbler. Pissmore drank from his bowl.

"Why were you late, Emma?" I asked. "Were you held up in traffic?"

"No, the movie was longer than we thought. Had to see the endin', you know."

Aldine said, "You missed a pretty good ending at the club, Emma."

"I seen that Tuttle guy in po-po cuffs. Must have been some ass-kickin' done."

"It was awesome," Aldine said.

Emma rested her tumbler on the table. "How did the new girl, Lorin, fit in? Didn't you have evidence?"

I spoke up. "Lorin worked at the Sheets Hotel where Reba and Frank met on Friday afternoons."

"That's evidence?" Emma asked. "That's called nooners."

Roscoe said, "It wasn't really evidence. Lorin worked there, yes, but she doesn't remember seeing Frank or Reba there."

Emma said, "So you tricked Tuttle into thinking Lorin seen them together?" Roscoe nodded. "But how did you know they were meeting there, smart-ass?"

Roscoe bit his lip. "Because he sent e-mails to Reba from his computer."

"Now *that's* evidence."

"Well... we couldn't submit the e-mails because the hard drive is missing," Roscoe said, sheepishly looking at Lieutenant Fahey.

"What about the crossbow arrow?" Aldine asked. "You know, the one shot into your door."

"I checked Tuttle's stores this afternoon and found a Quad Four Hundred crossbow being sold with a quiver of ten arrows," Roscoe said. "One was missing."

Colleen said, "A missing arrow doesn't prove Tuttle shot it into Augie's door. It could have been stolen."

Roscoe continued. "He also had a key-duplicating machine that could have been used to copy Frank's office and car keys. But again, it couldn't be used as evidence."

"I get it," Emma said. "You put on a show to git Tuttle to put his feet in his mouth."

"In a manner of speaking," I said. "And everything Tuttle said tonight was captured on a hidden electronic recorder in Lieutenant Fahey's purse."

Aldine asked, "Couldn't he say he was mad at his wife and made up the story about killing Frank to hurt his wife?"

Lieutenant Fahey said, "He cooked his goose when he said he gave Frank a dirt bath in a coal mine. Only the murderer knew that fact. The information wasn't released to the media."

Emma finished her wine and set the tumbler on the table. "Roscoe, you're a cool dude. Our investigatin' team be obese, really slammin'. I can't wait for another case."

I groaned and Roscoe laughed, a laugh that seemed almost cheerful. It was accompanied by a twinkle in his eye that told me he wouldn't mind if another adventure came up.

CPSIA information can be obtained at www.ICGtesting.com
Printed in the USA
BVOW002249070513

320148BV00006B/20/P

9 781621 372615